THE
DARKNESS WITHIN

Wendy

Thank you so much !   _June 14 2018_

Kevin Weisbeck

Kevin Weisbeck

THE DARKNESS WITHIN
An Owlstone Book

Published as a Print-on-Demand book through CreateSpace, an Amazon Company, for the author Kevin Weisbeck.

Cover design by Dan Huckle, Okotoks, AB Canada
Danhuckle.com

Final Editing by Marius Oelschig and Sherry Kasper

Copyright © 2018 Kevin Weisbeck
ISBN 978-0-9917566-1-2

First printing, May 2018

Kevin Weisbeck

Dedication

Sherry and I have a cabin nestled in the Kootenays. We love the fact that, even in the middle of nowhere, we are never alone.

I dedicate this book to the three bats that always visit us at dusk, the crickets that sing like teenagers in their parent's basement, the bear who knocked over the bar-b-cue, and the squirrel that always throws pine cones at me. I'm just glad he's a lousy shot.

Kevin Weisbeck

Foreword

The blades of the helicopter cut through the warm afternoon sky with the same ease a bullet might cut through flesh. Their thunderous claps torment me, yet a voice rises above and pushes through them. I can hear her cry.

Voices, fraught with urgency, surround me. They call out for IV's and bandages to stop the bleeding. I'm guessing that I'm the one doing the bleeding. I've been doing that a lot over the last few days. The woman's sobbing continues, unwavering.

Why can't I feel my body? Am I dying?

I've heard that your life will flash through your mind when you're dying. I have no experience with this, but I've never been one to doubt the Internet. This leads me to believe that, if I still have a fate, it's only moments from reaching its final act. The paramedic's efforts, although appreciated, aren't going to save me. Her sobbing burrows deeper into my brain. I know who she is, and I blame myself for her tears.

Suddenly, I'm drowning in electricity as somebody yells 'clear!' My body dances in an impalpable world that I no longer control. And then, like a fading echo, the electricity wanes to a far away presence.

Days ago, I said I'd give anything not to tell Katie my horrible secret. My death seems a fitting solution. One should always be careful what one wishes for.

As I draw my final breath, I feel your presence. With that presence comes a strange enticement to open up and tell you my story. They say nothing eases the burden like an old-fashioned confession.

Just remember that none of us are perfect.

Kevin Weisbeck

Chapter one

Her scent, as lovely as spring and as toxic as cyanide, hinted its existence as the darkness of the storm enveloped my plane. The sunshine and the chickadees of days ago, along with my inescapable lust for this woman, had trapped me in this darkened obscurity, and it would surely get me killed.

I took a deep breath as I taxied my Cessna on the LA tarmac. The engine had fired with its usual cough and sputter, caught, and quickly revved to speed. But the engine's purr, a should-be sign of its full co-operation, was merely a ruse to get me to drop my guard. I swear this plane hates me.

As I looked down at the instrument panel, my stomach lurched. The gauges glared at me with an evil defiance. I'd initially called them 'mother's cold stare,' but only in a whisper. There was no doubt in my mind that those damn things hoped I'd overlook a warning. What a thrill they'd have, plummeting me thousands of feet to a gruesome death. I never doubted their game plan each time we went out. But hey, if I crashed, didn't they crash too? No one said they were smart.

Even the undersized fuel gauge, acting the part of the little brother, felt an obligation to join in. Rather than share an honest moment, it was showing an empty tank. They're all such sinister little bastards. I gave the gauge a light tap with a slightly bent finger. The needle flinched, as if caught in an embarrassing lie, and slowly swept across the face, contacting the second 'L' in the word 'FULL.' The tank was topped up minutes ago, so it would have to do better than that to get one past me.

This was the plane I'd purchased just over a month ago, something I'd wanted all my life. My 1980 Cessna Skyhawk was an exotic, but practical toy. Granted, it was a few years old, but so was I. Back when I was plane-shopping, I'd preferred the gauge-style dashboard versus the computerised one. The older style seemed more personal. Now, as my sanity swirled with doubt, I wasn't sure I felt the same way.

Regardless, this form of flying was much more calming than commercial flights. This was my solution to the aggravating commutes, the airport waits, and to the babies who would rather cry than sleep. You see, I'm an author of sorts, and my writing has brought me to California. During the week, I created a jumble of words for my editor, and on most weekends, I flew back to British Columbia to be with family. It was an understatement to say that all the travelling had worn me out.

Two weeks ago, a young girl, wearing a white Hello Kitty t-shirt and Mickey Mouse ears, had been kind enough to deliver, to my lap, a fine mess of scrambled eggs, pancakes, and jelly beans. The mother, mortified, apologised over and over. I get it that she felt bad, but it wasn't her going through customs smelling like the last car of a bumpy roller-coaster on a sweltering summer day.

Looking back, it was hard to believe that less than two years ago I was having brews with my co-workers at the truck factory in Kelowna. Bernie had opened one of my beers with his eye. I'd made the mistake of betting against him and lost ten bucks. That being said, I won the money back from him four days later in a poker game.

Now, as a successful author, I spent my days sipping champagne with my new-fangled Californian friends. Don't get me wrong, these LA folks were great people, but they weren't the beer-drinking types.

My last novel, my only novel, seemed to be what everyone was looking for as it climbed its way to the top of the bestseller list. The royalties from that book netted me more money than I could have earned in five lifetimes turning wrenches. Still, my publisher wanted another book. He scribbled a number on a piece of paper, my advance, and I almost choked on a shrimp puff. I never expected that much, and as hard as it was to write a book, it was harder to turn down that many zeros.

And then there was my mother. The woman had been my biggest critic, which became my inspiration. Although I made a fair living, had a lot of friends, a good wife and produced a couple of wonderful children, these weren't the head-turners she'd hoped for.

I couldn't blame her for being disappointed. I'd always been an underachiever in her eyes. She'd seen a kid that didn't have it in him to dream big. Little did she know I used to throw on my headphones and pretend I was a singer in a rock band. The crowds would gather just to say they caught a glimpse of me. Their love and admiration followed me everywhere. But soon the album on my parent's stereo would end, as would the daydreams of that kid with over-sized headphones.

When the book hit the shelves, my life changed. I was surprised with the reviews and the sudden fame, albeit local at first. Who knew? It launched me into that world of stardom I'd always dreamt of, and surprisingly, the reality was as foreign as the surface of Mars. Granted, it was easy enough to accept, but looking back, I should have known this world wouldn't favour an outsider, which is what I was. This fast-paced lifestyle would eventually produce a hefty price tag. There were the endless book signings, the gruelling brainstorming sessions for that next novel, and a new set of friends that played a dangerous game that I didn't fully understand. I was a mouse among cats.

So now, with most of my deadlines met and the skies clear, I found myself fresh out of excuses. I had stepped in something, and it was a problem that wasn't about to solve it self. Much like that mouse, I had found myself cornered.

I tried a couple calming breaths, even though they never worked for me. My nerves still danced through my body like lightning on a busy golf course. You see, this was my first long flight and it scared me a bit. Still, that wasn't the real reason I was worried. No, these nerves had more to do with why I was going home. This wouldn't be the usual trip home. It was the unheard of 'midweek' visit. Those ones often required some explaining. At least I wouldn't have to worry about anybody expelling a belly full of jellybeans all over me.

I took one last look over Daugherty Field as I released the brake. It was a smaller public airport in Long Beach. Lately, I'd spent most of my evenings here. I'd been logging as much 'seat time' as I could. Not only did buzzing around the evening sky help me bank hours, it also helped me focus on my next novel. The story was a killer thriller involving a pilot's romance with his stewardess, a gorgeous blonde heroin addict named Christina. Bottom line, if I wasn't at the office writing with Eric, at a busy mall signing books or at some radio-station yapping it up, you'd find me here, up in these clouds.

The Eric that I mentioned is my champagne-swilling agent. He's the one who just dropped the tire chocks on the ground beside the plane. He also gave the door a dutiful slap.

"Good luck with Katie!" His voice strained to compete with the engine's drone.

Normally, the tarmac was off limits, but the weekday folk around here were as relaxed as the gophers that sunned their fat little bodies on the edges of the runway.

"It'll work itself out, buddy!" he continued. These words came from the friend I'd found in Eric. "She's a good woman. Just remember that!"

"She is!" I shouted back, more out of obligation.

I had to wonder how he could give such accolades to a woman he'd never met. Heck, I'd seldom talked about her. It would be like me lecturing climbers on an Everest trek when I've never climbed. Heck, I seldom walked the two blocks to the corner store. It was difficult understanding these big-city people some days. Who was I kidding, it was most days. He meant well.

I revved the engine and let the plane slowly roll forward. It was still hard to comprehend how this lumbering mass of rivets and sheet metal could sail me through the sky with such ease. As the wing passed by Eric, it almost clipped him, causing me to chuckle.

"Hurry back when you're finished!" This was concern. It came from the agent in Eric. "You're still committed to nine book signings this month."

Red-faced, he continued to trot alongside the plane as he waited for a response. The man was a Californian, which wasn't a terrible thing if you were a fellow-Californian. They understood one another. It got harder if you were a Canadian from a small town in the Okanagan Valley. We were worlds apart on everything.

Eric struggled to keep up. He knew there was something wrong and he was worried. What if his hotshot author screwed this whole thing up? The fans could sour with a scandal. And wouldn't it suck if I lost my head and quit, ending this madness before writing the second book? I wanted to yell something back at him, push his fears over the edge, but lately I'd been trying my damnedest to be a better person. Maybe it was selfish, but if I could get God to notice my efforts, I'd kindly accept his pity, and his help.

Beads of sweat trickled over Eric's wrinkled forehead. How far was he planning on chasing me? "Don't forget about us John!" He was starting to fall back fast. Definitely too much of the good life.

In the rear-view mirror, I watched as Eric fell. The tail of the plane had grazed his hip, spinning him to the ground. He quickly got up and clapped the dust from his hands. He wasn't hurt, and that was a good thing. I was certain that, deep down inside, he appreciated the end to his tarmac workout, albeit an abrupt one. With an apprehensive wave he motioned that he was okay.

The image was straight out of a comic book and it took everything in me not to laugh out loud. See God, I really was trying.

Chapter two

E ric's words echoed through my mind as if they were determined to bring down a mountain of snow. *'Don't forget them?'* Had he actually yelled that? These last few months had been hard enough to understand, let alone forget. One minute I was earning a modest living installing Freon hoses on class eight trucks, and the next I was signing autographs for fans, *my* fans. That wasn't so easy to forget.

As if it were yesterday, I remembered the guys at the truck plant throwing a party. It was for my send off. I knew I'd miss them. The practical jokes, the doughnut eating contests, and that feeling of a good day's work were just a few of the things I wouldn't experience in California. In Los Angeles it was more about style, composure and status. I once saw a man having a twenty-five-dollar cup of coffee. It was made from beans excreted by some exotic feline that lived in some remote area like the Himalayan Mountains. I could only shake my head and ask why.

In LA I'd found that it was smart not to trust anyone, nor to let your guard down. I'd recently learned that everyone had an agenda, and although you might not know what it was, you just

6

needed to accept that it didn't have your best interests in mind. My being an overnight success didn't help, making me an easy mark. I imagined it was the same adventure in every big city.

My literary adventure had begun three years ago when a dream woke me from a solid sleep. The damn thing kept me awake, embedding itself deeply into my brain, much like a tick. Eventually I accepted it, nurtured it, and turned it into quite an elaborate story. Not long afterward, I laboured it on to paper. That first draft was terrible at best, but perseverance kept it alive as I struggled to read books on style and grammar.

Soon the finished novel resembled what one might find on the shelf of an actual bookstore. At that point I handed it off to Katie for a sincere, but kind, review. My wife found it to be well-written, and in her words, fascinating. Well, she had a friend who did some editing and that friend knew someone who knew an agent. After eight months of endless queries I was ready to walk away, but this agent was tenacious. He wouldn't give up, and thankfully he was right.

I cashed a tidy advance and the truck plant became a memory. After a Facebook launch and a few radio shows, my book started to get noticed. As sales increased, so did the amount of public appearances. I knew I'd arrived when Eric got me a spot on a local TV talk show. Although I was shy at first, I soon took to the general public like a bat in a night sky. The designer clothes, along with the new hairdo and veneered teeth, didn't hurt my confidence either. My walk became a swagger as doors opened.

With Eric shrinking in the rear-view mirror, I continued to drive my plane forward, taking my position on the taxi lane. Would you call it driving or flying when you were still on the ground? A better question, why were these thoughts rattling around in my head? I should be thinking about my kids, my wife and what I'd be telling them when I got home. Usually, whenever I screwed things up, it was Katie who came up with these answers.

Case in point, my daughter, Brook, turned nine last weekend. She liked Ben, a boy who helped her with her math homework. He wanted to take her to a school dance and I almost freaked. I say almost, because Katie was smart enough to intercept me. She reminded me that we were that age the first time I took her out for ice-cream. Her father was out-of-his-mind angry, but her mother recognised the innocence and vetoed his decision to turn the garden hose on me. Pay it forward.

I wiped my hands on my pants while I sat waiting for clearance. The sweat reminded me how green I was at flying. I really hoped the removal of this liquid fear would loosen its grip on my nerves. It didn't.

My pants, designer low-waist boot-cut jeans, not only absorbed my perspiration, but they allowed me to look like a man who spun literary gold. Because of that, I'd bought several pairs. I needed to look my best at all times. Vanessa, my publisher's secretary, had set me up with an odd-talking young person named Devon. According to her, he was stylish and had impeccable taste.

Devon had taken me shopping and taught me all the dos and don'ts of dressing for success. The comfort-fit jeans that I'd become accustomed to, that I got for Christmas every year, made me look like a frumpy old married guy. Even though that definition summed me up perfectly, that image didn't sell books. No, the guy who sold these novels had to look young, buff, and confident. With these pants, I was all that and a bag of chips. This young lad worked his magic, peeling away the established layers of age, marriage, and dowdy acceptance.

Along with the pants had come shirts with alligators on them, glasses from Dior, and boots made from eel skin. I didn't even know they had this kind of stuff. He even talked me into buying a watch that cost twice as much as my first car. It was old-school and sleek, had a built-in compass and I could see the golden gears and springs busy at work. It was the kind of watch you'd expect some elitist author to be wearing.

Because of the book's success, and my handsome new image, the money started pouring in like water from a failing dyke. Katie and the kids were pampered with gifts and, although they acted like these things weren't important, I knew they were. Who wouldn't want to be spoiled? The house was paid off with the first few royalty payments and the savings account grew like a baby puppy. I had hoped that my wife might free up a little time for the new and improved me, but I was wrong. The PTA, her knitting club and the children kept her busy.

And now, I was never home. I missed my wife. I guess she was part of the payment on that price tag.

Almost as important as the money and the occasional glance from a pretty girl, was the fact that my mother was finally seeing a son she could be proud of. One night she called me, bragging over the phone about the women she referred to as friends. She may have had a few drinks in her. I'd bought some high-end jewellery for her to wear on bridge night and these pretentious old crows were beyond jealous. She flaunted my success, making them hate her like she had once hated them. She'd been waiting a long time for this moment and I'd delivered in spades…and perhaps a few diamonds.

The radio squawked, giving me the clearance to take off. I pulled back on the throttle and in seconds the wheels lifted from the runway. Getting off the ground produced the very same rush as my whirlwind success. Soon I was high up in the clouds with nowhere to look but down. When I did, I found Mother's cold stare.

Every rush has its tang.

Chapter three

The choking brown haze of Los Angeles soon gave way to majestic blues accented with clouds so crisp and white that they reminded me of the fresh bedding back home. Below, the eventual thinning of urban structures gave way to dense cedar forests, lakes, and long winding rivers.

As awe-struck as I was with Los Angeles when I first arrived, the pretzel-like freeways and towers of glass quickly lost their lustre. And then there were the streets that swarmed with cars and people. I'd had several arguments with my in-car GPS. Turning left didn't work when there was a pizzeria in the way. But to be honest, I didn't exactly know how to use the damn thing. You didn't need those contraptions to find places back home.

Katie, my wife, recently bought a hand-held GPS. She had taken to a game called Geocaching since I'd been away. She was cute that way, and the kids loved it. I wasn't sure what Geocaching meant, but she'd explained that it was like treasure hunting. Every time we talked about it, her voice raced through their last few adventures of finding these caches full of trinkets. I think the treasures were called swag. I just worried about her driving into a pizzeria some day.

Now that I was a success, there was no time for anything other than work, commuting, and the odd family weekend. Even my days back home were filled with chores, clingy children, and friends that wanted to hear my stories about California. I was beginning to think that getting away was more tiring.

Katie looked at me differently since my success. I didn't like it. It was like I'd become purposed, like an old piece of furniture. Life was a whole lot easier when I was home all the time. We could walk to the Dairy Queen for peanut buster parfaits. She used to tease me when I'd suggest we share one. The damn things cost seven dollars each. I considered it frugal. It was even tougher once the kids came. Brook and Danny ate like garburators. At least life was honest, and we were having fun.

Below me the trees and mountains hid the line that divided California from Oregon. Until recently, these places were just colours on a map divided by dots or dashes. Sadly, I was almost surprised when I didn't see those lines on the earth dividing the states and countries. It's funny how the brain works. Another oddity was that there were no road markers up here. All I had, to let me know when I was getting close, were these instruments. Oh, and I had that dreaded GPS. I understood the basics of it, but I'd still be keeping an eye out for my house when I got closer.

At the halfway point, I stopped in Eugene, Oregon. The plan was to land safely, stretch my legs, and grab enough fuel to ensure I could complete the trip. Two five-hour legs seemed less daunting than one ten-hour flight. I grabbed a pop and some snacks while I waited.

Back in the air, the once-soothing skies soon gave way to rain and some of the darkest shades of grey I'd ever seen. These clouds boiled in pots of black and refused to let me climb above them. Since flying through them wasn't an option, I dropped below them. The plane's wings shaved the underbellies of the charcoal beasts and as they did, my darkened mood returned to the reason for my rare mid-week visit.

Katie had already asked why I was coming home and I'd mentioned it was the stresses of being away. This wasn't necessarily a lie, but it wasn't the truth either. Regardless, she wasn't convinced. We'd been married a long time and I was a lousy liar.

I blamed everything on the money and the fame. I'd become a schoolboy spinning in a field of wildflowers with my arms outstretched. Life was weaving me through the land of crazy and I should have stopped to get my bearings. I didn't. So, for the first time in nineteen years, I crawled into bed with someone other than my wife. Granted, it was only the one time, a thing that guys do, but none of these guys were married to my wife.

Shit, I'm sure most would agree that this didn't make me an axe-murderer. All I did was allow a girl, damn near half my age, the opportunity to seduce me. I'd be a bad person had I gone back for a return engagement, but I didn't. I wouldn't! At least I was pretty sure I wouldn't. Did I tell you she was half my age? God, what was I thinking?

It was terrible what I did, and I'd give anything not to tell my wife. Katie deserved better. I never did this to hurt her and although this girl was incredible, the feeling wasn't love. It was naughty, exciting, and it curled my toes. God, it had been years since I'd felt toe twists.

And while Katie's lovemaking had become safe, respectable and tender, Vanessa's was animalistic. I was begging to be ripped apart and left for dead. My heart raced beyond its limits and I felt her passion roll through me like a rhinoceros charging through fields of daffodils and buttercups. When it was over, I was covered in sweat and couldn't produce a coherent thought to save my life.

If sex were ice-cream, Katie would be the ever-rewarding vanilla. It was silky, smooth, and perfect on apple pie, in a sundae or with sprinkles. Who didn't like a vanilla cone dipped in chocolate? Vanessa, on the other hand, was a dangerously addictive double-chocolate salted-caramel-pecan with rum and perhaps a few swirls of fudge. It was delicious, but not something you could have every day, or with apple pie. It demanded your undivided attention and should have come with a damn warning label.

Now, as I sat here flying through this storm, all I can do is wonder what I was going to tell my wife, if I told her at all. Should

I say anything? A part of me thinks I should just stick with the story of being stressed. What I did was wrong, but wouldn't it be better if Katie didn't have to deal with it? I doubt I'd want to know if she'd cheated on me.

What am I saying? She'd never do that to me. Besides, I could say with ninety-nine percent certainty that this would never happen again. This mental lapse in judgement was a lonely mistake and it would already be forgotten if Vanessa wasn't blackmailing me.

And if it were a few thousand dollars, I'd quietly pay her, but she wants some serious coin. My bank account has some serious coin, but I can't see handing it all over to her for a one-night stand. That would be one expensive hayride. Besides, how would I explain the expense to Katie? Fifty thousand for the plane was hard enough.

Looking back, I wasn't sure why Vanessa's greed caught me off guard. I should have seen the signs. She was a part-time receptionist at my publishing company. I doubt she made more than thirty thousand a year and yet she wore expensive dresses and toted Gucci purses. I had no idea what they cost, but I was sure they didn't sell them at Kmart. At first, I figured she had rich parents. Wake up Johnny.

What fooled me the most was her kindness. When I first met her, she was a single slice of sunshine in this murky land of vipers and viper wannabe's. Her smile was so welcoming, and talk about being resourceful. This girl had connections. She set me up in a decent apartment and seemed to be one step ahead of my every need. As good as any concierge, she took me under her wing and saw to it that I had everything to make my stay comfortable… perhaps a little too comfortable.

So, should I tell my wife about this? Every functioning brain cell I owned was telling me to say nothing. I thought about my golf clubs that were behind me on the floor of the plane. What if I went home, hung out with my family, and said nothing? After a few rounds of golf, I could go back to California. Katie would be none the wiser. She'd be happy to have me home spending quality time with the kids.

Once back in California, I'd tell Vanessa that I'd spilled my guts, told my wife everything. At that point I could reassume control. In the final phase of my plan, I'd ask for a week or two off to deal with a personal matter. They'd have to give it to me. Vanessa would have to conclude that I was salvaging a damaged marriage. Hell, if I played my cards right I could come home, tell Katie there was a stall on this end, and then work on my putting game.

Eric knew some of the story, so he'd unknowingly back me. The idea was perfect. Perfect, except I should have known better. I never should have fallen into Vanessa's trap. Did I mention the sun-kissed skin, the long loosely-curled blonde locks, or the fact that she was half my age?

There was no saying no to this woman, but you still think I should have. For that reason, we should go back a couple days.

Anybody who met her would understand.

Chapter four

In LA there's a unique little shopping district called 'The Grove.' It's a quaint little street, no cars allowed. Lined with historical speciality shops, this hidden gem sold everything from fashion to fine cooking. Weekend shoppers often crowded the aged sidewalks, each person searching for that must-have treasure.

My eyes were panning the signs above the shops when my foot caught one of the raised edges of the maintenance-deprived sidewalk. I tumbled to the ground. The concrete caught me in its arms and woke me from my trance. When I looked up, there was Vanessa, her hand stretched out to take mine.

Her eyes were warm, the smile flirtatious. "Are you alright Mr. Pettinger?"

I took her hand and let her help me to my feet. "I'm fine thanks." The hand was a lot softer than I'd imagined. "And it's Johnny."

My mouth dried up as a whiff of Channel #5 stirred my thoughts. Had this gal cast a spell on my senses? I was beginning to wonder if it was her perfume that had weakened my knees and not the uneven sidewalk.

"You look deep in thought Mr. Pettinger, I mean Johnny. Are you sure you're okay?"

There was a brief struggle to wipe away the bruising of my pride. I usually wasn't such a klutz. "Honestly, I'm fine. I was just looking for some tea-house place. My wife wanted some."

"Mmm, the Oolong." Vanessa's eyes widened as she licked her lips. "She'll love their collection of exotic South African brews."

"Yes, the Oolong. I'm sure that's the place."

"It's this way." She took my hand, running a fog through my senses. Hand in hand, we headed north.

Her playfulness was contagious, thickening the haze in my head to the consistency of cotton candy. All we needed now was a cartoon bird on my shoulder and a rainbow dropping skittles from the sky.

I allowed the hand-holding only because her light flirting oozed with playful innocence. Well, that and the fact that I'd have lost her in the crowd. We made our way down the busy street, weaving through the other shoppers. I was floating, close to giddy, as our hand-holding made us one. Suddenly I didn't feel forty-four. Heck, I didn't feel thirty-four.

She turned and gave me a suggestive wink. "Isn't it a beautiful day for a walk?"

"Um, yes?" At this point I didn't even feel twenty-four. I felt more like a pimply-faced teenager with his first crush.

I'd been too busy to notice how nice the day was earlier. Suddenly the sun felt warmer, the ocean breeze was fresher, and the twittering chickadees more vocal. What was happening to me?

Vanessa stopped dead in her tracks and turned to me. I bumped into her, but managed to stop before bowling her over. Our eyes met and in my world of adolescent haze, she wanted to kiss me. I wanted to kiss her. The stare lasted forever and that was fine with me. Did she want the kiss? Should I oblige her? Wow, she was awfully radiant today…oh, but she was radiant every day. I wanted to taste her kiss and feel those velvet lips pressed against mine. Surely, she wanted that too.

"Are you okay Mr. Pettinger? You look a little odd." She corrected herself. "I mean Johnny."

I scrambled to find the world that held reality. "I'm good. Why'd we stop?"

She pointed to the sign above a weathered old door. It read 'The Oolong.' "We're here."

I opened the door and held it for her. She stepped inside and started up the narrow stairway. I stole a mischievous glance at the rear pockets on her jeans and was instantly hypnotised by their rhythmic dance. It was a taught youthfulness that took my breath away. Quickly, I dropped my head in shame. What was happening to me? Wanting to make a moral effort, I tried to keep my eyes pointed at the stairs as she led the way. By the sixth step the heels on her stilettos pulled me in and I found myself studying the stitching that ran the length of those long slender legs.

At the top of the stairs I stopped and took a deep breath to clear my head. The place smelled amazing, exotic. Shadows from the aged windows cast a world of mystery about the room. I let my thoughts drift to eighteenth century boats loaded with crates of illegal tea. Each passage up the wide, meandering river would be a journey filled with thieves, smugglers and peril. Most of the smugglers were above the law. They'd have pursued their operations until the locals took up arms and ran them off.

Antique crates full of perfumed leaves leached their adventures into my now overly active mind. If they could tell their stories, I'd have enough inspiration for a lifetime of writing.

Meanwhile, Vanessa innocently worked the room, smelling the brown paper-wrapped blocks of fine teas and reading the labels. Such labels not only disclosed the contents, but they told a story. Many of the teas were used for witchcraft or medicinal purposes. And here I thought that tea was just a coffee replacement for the British. I'd make a lousy herbalist.

I looked up again to see Vanessa. She couldn't have been a day over twenty-four, if I did the math right. That didn't settle the guilt that was fermenting inside me, but it helped me understand. That youthful innocence was adorable. Look away, Johnny.

One of the labels that caught my eye belonged to the Hawkhurst gang of England's Kent district. I started to read it when the shopkeeper, an older lady in her fifties, interrupted. "May I help you, sir?"

The reference bothered me. There was no cause for her to call me 'sir' around the young lady. I sure didn't feel like a 'sir' right now. "The name's Johnny. I was looking for some tea."

She gave me a sarcastic gaze. "Why doesn't that surprise me?"

Oh my, the shopkeeper made a funny. What a shame this riot of a woman's humour couldn't be bottled and sold with the teas. Why would she talk to me in that tone? Was it a shot? Was she reading my thoughts? No doubt she saw the dirty old man that I was becoming and wanted to cast her vote on my virtue. Crap Johnny, get a grip.

"I need some Rooibos tea."

"Orange, Lemon, Regular, or perhaps you'd be interested in a blend?"

"Um…" What a bitch! How hard would it have been to just scoop a few ground-up leaves into a bag? No, she'd rather I look stupid.

My lack of tea savvy was rescued when Vanessa put her hands on my shoulders and softly spoke the word 'cinnamon' in my ear. My thoughts quickly returned to the stitching of her jeans. I had just fallen madly and undeniably in lust with this young woman.

"I'll take the cinnamon?" I was a little uncertain, but I think my words came out like a question.

The lady went to get the large can of tea. "How much would you like?" Her words wafted through the air like the blade of a sword. No doubt, it was her disgust.

I scrambled to read the large white-board and calculate the prices. This stuff wasn't cheap. Vanessa lowered her chin on my shoulder and with a whisper-soft voice, came to my rescue again. "You said this was for your wife?"

I felt a little guilty admitting it. "Yes."

"I'm sure she'll love this one. It's spicy and a lot of fun. Get a couple of pounds, Johnny. It's pricey but you can afford it. Remember, you have money now."

How right she was. I hadn't used that whole being-rich thing to my full advantage. "Two pounds please."

I was finding my game again, feeling strong, feeling confident, when Vanessa abruptly derailed it. "My place is just around the corner. Why don't you come on over and I'll brew a pot? And if you're good, I'm sure I can find you a little something for dessert."

Her asking me to come over seemed innocent enough. Dessert sounded iffy, but she was a work friend and knew I was married. I mean, she'd just talked me into buying eighty dollars worth of tea for my wife. So why was every fibre, every bone, and every molecule in my body screaming for me not to go? Because they knew I wasn't strong enough to spend any more time with this voluptuous young creature without getting into trouble. She was beautiful, sensual, and easily as pleasant as a blossoming flower on a spring day. I knew no good could ever come from a lunch date with this woman. I also knew what I had to tell her.

"Sure, lunch sounds great."

I squinted through the windshield of the plane to see a deeper darkness settling in the sky as the last remnants of shadows disappeared. The contours of the mountains and valleys folded into the abyss of night like one might fold eggs into a dark chocolate-cake batter. My roadmap was dissolving into obscurity.

Chapter five

I'd initially smiled at the thought of that day with Vanessa and I hope you understood why. I was smitten. This girl's appeal was more powerful than a speeding locomotive, more addictive than air, and it was as dangerous as the stupidity of a man thinking he was twenty again. After all, she was trying to blackmail me and the half-witted part of me still clung to the prospect of a second date. This was the derangement of the male ego.

Don't get me wrong, I'm aware of the gravity of my situation. It's just hard to forget how wonderfully young she made me feel. Vanessa had become my Fountain of Youth, making a lifetime of old and frumpy disappear with a wink and a smile. But also lost with the frump and drab was a lifetime of wisdom.

A sudden sheet of lightning crackled over the plane like a flock of electrified birds. It snatched me from those tea-shopping thoughts and firmly shoved me back into the reality of the plane. I looked down at the gauges. Their satanic stare was telling me it was time to pay.

Once again, the fuel gauge read empty, so I tapped it and waited for it to roll over to the halfway or three-quarter marker. It didn't. I tapped it again, but it was determined to stay put. I was reaching across to give it another tap, a harder one, when the engine sputtered and re-fired. I swear the gauge was smirking.

"Concentrate!" I said aloud as I levelled the plane and ran my right hand through my hair. "They're stupid gauges; steel, glass and wire." There wasn't any supernatural karma shit going on here.

If there was, I wasn't entirely to blame for everything. Katie played a part in this too. Was it my fault I had to work in California? I did this to give her and the kids a mortgage-free home, braces for Danny's teeth, and newer furniture. None of that was cheap. I often felt like a financial security blanket and nothing more. Hell, I'd been buried under mountains of deadlines, responsibility, and rewrites. A weak moment wasn't that deplorable, damn it. I know I'm not the first guy to have a slight indiscretion.

But to Vanessa, that indiscretion was anything but a weak moment. I knew that now. It was a calculated opportunity. The old-school term was seduction. She had spun her web and I had strolled into it like a little child walking through the forest to find a house made of gingerbread and gumdrops.

Lightning struck to the left of the plane tossing me like a nerd walking through a hallway full of bullies. The accompanying clap of thunder pounded through my chest. That one was close.

"I think I need to set you down somewhere." My words floated through the cockpit as if someone else had spoken them. The first thing they taught me in flight school was to stay calm and I could do that far better from the ground. If nothing else, it took crashing out of the equation.

I took the plane down to a hundred feet above the ground. It was hazardous, but it allowed me to see where I was going, sort of. Mountain ranges generally ran north and south in this region so trying to follow the valleys made sense. My eyes darted through the downpour and I spotted a large field. The placid valley floor presented a number of possibilities. I could set my plane down and collect my thoughts. The absence of glow from buildings or streetlights convinced me that this wasn't some poor town with houses to crash into…unless the power had gone out.

For a final time, I stared down at the red gloom of the dash panel and reduced my speed. The darkness was overwhelming. I strained to guess my height above the ground. I figured it to be about fifty feet and closing.

"Almost there." I could barely hear myself over the pelting rain. I knew I'd be touching down in seconds.

Suddenly the engine began to purr like a well-fed kitten. It calmed my nerves, allowing me to focus on the landing. My hope was to pick up a signal for my phone once I'd landed. Actually, it wasn't my phone. It was a loaner. I'd lost mine at one of those public relations parties last week. Getting a new phone was still on my to-do list. Vanessa had a loaner for me. She'd programmed her number into it, just in case I needed something. This all happened before the blackmailing began.

The fuel gauge continued to read empty and I tapped it again with the desperation reserved for kids who had dropped their last dollar in the candy-bar machine, only to see their Snickers bar teeter, but not drop.

"That's impossible." I knew I had enough fuel to get home and part way back. That was when the engine gave a final sputter.

The prop, now resembling a cock-eyed hood ornament, had joined the gauges in the coup. "Oh crap."

The plane's coup d'état became a moot point when a bright light flooded the cockpit. The flash of lightning was immediately accompanied by a thunderous booming that darn near shook the plane apart. Heat from the blast warmed my face long after it was gone, muddying my senses.

I blindly drew back on the stick as the plane dodged and jerked from side to side. The flash had plunged me into complete darkness. Even the dim glow of the gauges had melted into the darkness.

My bones rattled inside my skin like wind chimes in a summer storm as my senses continued their meltdown. Treetops tore at the fuselage and my muscles tensed up in hopes of holding everything together, but I had seriously lost control. The snapping of branches as they hammered away at the plane had become an inescapable chaos.

Then it all stopped.

Seized by fear, I anxiously waited for the first sliver of light to return. I'd settle for a sputter of the prop, anything to mask that ghostly silence. Everything suddenly felt a million miles away. Was this what it felt like to die? Had it already happened? If it had, was I getting heaven or hell? I was floating weightless, as if suspended on a wire, eerily calm, placid, and surreal.

It was the horrid stench of wires burning that started to awaken my senses. It was the plane's impact with the ground that deadened them.

Chapter six

I looked up from my hospital bed to see Katie standing beside me. Her subtle beauty swept me away, as it always had. How could I have been so stupid as to crawl into bed with another woman? This wife of mine had eyes you never grew tired at gazing into, and lips you never tired of having pressed against your own. She loved me, and it was the unconditional kind that we all hoped to find. I was a very lucky, very stupid man.

"Are you alright?" she asked.

Her voice reminded me of all those lullabies she sang to the kids over the years, songs sung when bugs and scary dreams had woken them in the middle of the night.

"I'm ... fine, I think." And given the circumstances, I felt better than I should have. There was no ringing in my ears and no burnt smell clogging my sinuses. Even the lump on my noggin had decided to give me a reprieve from the pain. Everything seemed fine, except for the young girl crouched down on her knees at the far corner of the room. She was staring at us.

"I'm so glad you're okay," Katie continued. "It was a miracle you weren't killed."

I felt the same. Even though I was new to the whole flying thing, I'd crashed like I'd been doing this for years. I was a natural.

"What did you want to tell me?" She placed a hand on my arm.

I pulled my eyes away from the girl. "Tell you?"

"It's just that…" Her eyes began to pry. "You were coming home on a Tuesday. It gave me a bad feeling about this flight. Why did you need to come home?"

That question brought a rabble of radioactive butterflies. They swarmed my stomach, making it hard to talk. "I…uh…"

"It's okay. We need to talk about this." Those words loaded me with guilt. She knew.

My shame caused the girl in the corner to smile. I tried to ignore her, but my eyes kept wandering over to her. Why was she there? The hair was a tangled mess, held off her face with a bright blue hair clip. It was a big blue butterfly. Her teeth were crooked, and a grubby torn sundress made her look like the poster-child for trailer-park living. With any luck the orderlies would realise she'd escaped from her room and they'd swing by to scoop her up.

Wondering about my distraction, Katie looked over her shoulder and then back to me. She hadn't seen the girl. "Honey, is everything okay?"

"I'm fine." I swear Katie could read my mind at will. Years of marriage hid very little between two people. "You know why I was coming home, don't you?"

"I had my suspicions, but I couldn't be sure until I heard it from you. It wasn't just the mid-week trip home. I could hear it in your voice when we talked on the phone. It was your tone, the words you chose."

"I'm not sure if it helps, but it was just the one time. It was foolish, and I know it." Something as frivolous as sex could never replace, or even challenge, all the years that we'd had together. And yet for those fleeting moments of sin, I was willing to throw it aside. Men can be such idiots.

Her eyes struggled to hold back the tears. "Do you love her?"

"God no!" I wanted to tell her that for men it didn't work that way, that the act of sex and being in love, were in no way related.

"Is she beautiful?"

I didn't like where this was going. Why did she need to know that? The truth was, she was gorgeous. I had never lied to her before because, like I said earlier, I was lousy at it. For once I listened to my instincts. "She was only as beautiful as too much rye might allow."

"Thanks." Her hand moved to mine. Our fingers locked. "But you still don't lie very well. I can't see this happening unless she was pretty. I bet she's young, and skinny."

"Don't." The pain she was feeling sickened me. Every man should get to see that look in their wife's eyes before they cheat. That image is horrific and would make any man put it back in his pants.

In the corner, the girl was noticeably agitated at Katie's empathy. She twirled and fidgeted with the knots in her hair as she frowned.

I could tell that Katie wanted to talk about the affair but she didn't know where to start. Was it her fault? Was it a mid-life crisis? Had she smothered me…not smothered me enough?

Her next words came out strained. "Did you…"

"Honey, all I can tell you is that I'm sorry." I dropped my head. What did she want, martyrdom? Vanessa was incredible, but after we were done, it was over. Too bad the guilt wasn't. It lingered a lot longer than the thrill ever could.

Anticipation always trumped conquest, and this was no exception. The next day I'd struggle to remember what Vanessa's breasts looked like or how it felt to touch her skin because these images weren't the images that held me close at night. They hadn't bought me all those Father's Day cards or tucked my children into bed when I wasn't there. Nor had they cooked my favourite meals or made sure there was always a cold beer in the fridge when I got home after a hard day's work.

The knot in my stomach was crippling.

"Don't be such a little bitch Johnny!" The soothing voice had turned unrecognisably cold. "And rye-pretty my ass. You didn't need liquid coaxing."

"What?" I looked up to see Vanessa, arms crossed and standing beside my wife.

"All you do is lie. That's why nobody wants you now!" Her words were as dark and satanic as her stare. The young girl's eyes lit up as Vanessa lit into me. It made her sit up on her haunches and inch closer.

This was a side of Vanessa that I'd never seen before. Afterward, as she got dressed, she exuded the innocence of a schoolgirl. We joked around afterward and, even though I was riddled with guilt, she made me feel okay about what we'd done. It wasn't until she tried to blackmail me that I saw anything other than that sweetness. I wouldn't have believed she was capable. When she put a dollar value to my cheating, a part of me hoped that she had no choice, that her grandmother needed the money for a life-saving operation. Soon, I accepted the reality. I wasn't as desirable as I was rich.

Vanessa remained cold and calculating as she approached the bed. Then she pulled the covers away from my body, exposing my naked frame. Her sadistic giggle became ominous.

I looked down at a charred corpse. The unrecognisable torso attached to my head quivered and reacted to my every thought. I raised the disgusting limb, attached to what must have been my left shoulder, and slowly turned it. I was hoping for some resemblance that this badly scorched arm was mine. Flakes of skin broke off and drifted onto the clean white sheets like campfire ashes. My gold wedding band glistened on my finger. I started to shake uncontrollably. The trembling caused my flesh to fall like murky snowflakes.

"Oh my God! What happened to me?"

"You crashed, and your plane lit up like a Roman candle while you were unconscious. Gas will do that, you know." Vanessa's laughter billowed through the room much like the thick black smoke that had billowed through the cockpit "It burnt you to a fucken crisp, Mr Pettinger. Oh, I mean Johnny."

I looked off to the girl in the corner. Her eyes clung to Vanessa in wild anticipation. Why was she here?

"Nobody wants you now, Johnny." Vanessa continued her rage "You're going to die alone."

"No." I looked over to Katie.

"Don't look at her. She can't help you. You should have kept it in your pants." She stepped in front of my wife and started to lead her out of the room. "Come on Katie, you can do better."

A tear escaped Katie's eye as she looked back at me. I continued to hold my arm out for her to take, but as I did it started to break apart, the pieces falling to the clean sheets. My wedding ring landed on top of the pile.

"Honey, don't leave me. Please…"

Katie covered her mouth with her hand as she watched the stub of my arm shorten. She wanted to retch, and quickly turned away. Vanessa smiled before looking over to the girl. "Well, aren't you coming?"

The tattered little girl got up and shuffled her way to the door. For her, this whole experience had ended in absolute delight. Vanessa's harsh words, and my reactions to them, had made up for any disappointment she'd felt from Katie's misguided tenderness.

In the doorway, she stopped and turned back to me. "Se-see you on the other si-si-side, J-J-Johnny. I'll be w-w-waiting."

Chapter seven

It was my own screams that woke me from that nightmare. I grabbed my left arm with my right hand and felt for skin. It was smooth and intact. I could feel my wedding ring. It wasn't lying in the ash-ridden hospital sheets. My heart re-fired as if it was trying to crack ribs. I was alive.

Vanessa and the horrid image of charred flesh had scared me wide-awake and yet, looking around, I was in an absolute blackness. Granted, this was far better than waking up in a bed of orange and red flames, the searing heat lifting the skin from my flesh. Instead, I had the dark and very cool night air blowing through the cockpit.

The impact from the crash had knocked me out, I'm guessing from a blow to the head. It was hard to tell, as my whole body ached. A crust of blood on my left temple was a pretty good indicator, though. Blood had also dried on the back of my left hand.

This early assessment was nothing but positive. There was nothing broken and nothing dripping from me. Any bleeding that I might have done hadn't been that serious. These wounds quickly found the bottom of my priority list.

29

What was starting to tickle my attention was the total lack of light. I'd once heard that, in the woods, night skies with no moonlight went beyond dark. This was ridiculous. I'd never opened my eyes to such an abyss of nothingness. Acrid odours lingered in the cockpit like garlic on a blind date's breath. They weren't as strong as the ones I'd smelt before the crash. No orange flames danced in the darkness and that was good. If there had been a fire, it had burnt itself out.

After several minutes, the ringing in my ears gave way to a choir of bugs and wildlife. Manning the baritone section were two, possibly three, bull frogs complimented by a dazzling ensemble of crickets off in the distance. Lead singers of this nightly serenade were a pack of coyotes, no doubt luring in a late-night snack.

There was one other sound. It was a misplaced whisper that hung in the background. It carried through my senses, but I couldn't place it. Constant and gentle, it sounded a little like a peaceful breeze stirring the leaves on the trees. It was safe.

In my mind I tried to slow things down. I had to. I painted a picture of what the morning might bring. I remembered watching those painters on TV. In just a half-hour they could paint a landscape that had mountains, forests, and lakes. It always amazed me how they could use a handful of brush strokes to paint thousands of trees or millions of leaves. And there was always that happy little bunny.

Since morning was likely a few hours away, and I wasn't dying, I had time to paint this picture with detail. The pines would be ponderosa mixed with a few tamaracks and they'd smell just like those little pine tree air fresheners that get hung from the rear-view mirror of your car. In patches you'd find a dusting of white birch. They'd look out of place.

The mountains would climb to the skies, but not tower like the Rockies. And, like some trick from the heavens, the mountains would vary in colour. The distant ones would be a soft sapphire, while the closer ones turquoise or jade. This image reminded me of all the years I'd gone dirt-biking. We wove our way through endless tight trails, never worried about where we'd end up. It was just great to be out there. Too bad I didn't feel the same about this place.

I remembered seeing a field that I'd wanted to use for a landing strip. I'd overshot it. I'd paint it waist-deep with long wispy grass swaying in the breeze. That must have been the leaf-rustling sound that accompanied the band of crickets. Oh, and let's not forget all the Lupines that edged the tree line or the aromatic wild strawberries that grew in patches fed by long days of sunlight.

Regardless of what the morning brought, it would be a welcome backdrop compared to yesterday's drenching skies. My morning image would also be a lot more welcoming than the nightmare of a barbecued Johnny resting on white linen.

I fumbled the seatbelt off and strained to see out the windshield. My eyes stung a little, likely dust kicked up from the impact or the smoke from the burnt wiring. I looked up. Even the brightest stars were too shy to show themselves. I'd bet the clouds that had carried those hammering rains were still lingering.

"I think I'd prefer the commercial flight, complete with the complimentary lap of puke."

Hearing my voice felt oddly comforting. My ears still had a belfry of church bells chiming in them, but the ringing was beginning to fade. What remained, softly enriched the cricket's chirruping.

The portrait I had painted was nice, but it wasn't what I needed to get out of here. For that I'd need to paint an airport or a busy four-lane highway. And while I was at it, a McDonalds serving all-day breakfast would be nice.

"Okay, where the heck are we?" My words came out muddled as I tried to focus.

I leaned forward and waved my hand below the dashboard. I found a coiled chord and used it to make my way back to the radio. The volume knob was to the right. I cranked it to the left until it clicked. Then I cranked it back to the right. That should be on.

"Mayday. Mayday."

The radio had to be on, so why couldn't I get any noise, static, or that little red light? I cranked the knob left until it clicked again. There was no point in killing the battery. "I'll figure you out in the morning."

I closed my eyes and tried not to think about that horrible dream. It was just a dream, and Vanessa wasn't the villain here. Neither was that little girl. There were no villains, just an idiot that, for a few crazed hours, forgot he was married.

Before I could close my eyes and drift off, I took a deep breath of fresh air and reluctantly reached across my body to feel the skin on my left arm again. It was good. I sat back in my seat and enjoyed the wilderness serenade, knowing I'd soon wake to a new day. And what would that day bring? Would there be lupines, ponderosas, and a field of long wispy grass? For that I'd have to wait. I knew there'd be crickets and frogs.

"Brurrraapppp. Chirrup, chirrup…"

That band was singing to fill the tip-jar.

Chapter eight

When I awoke the second time, it was hours later. I knew this because I felt rested. The night sky was still as black as when I had fallen back asleep. Darkness played with my mobility as I reached for the radio. Just like before, no red light illuminated, and no mayday was sent. I really hoped this was something I could fix, but bad luck had been trending like funny cat-videos.

Something wasn't right. The cool breeze that I'd enjoyed earlier had been replaced by a ridiculous warmth. It carried a mossy wet odour. And then there was the humidity, drawing the sweat out of me by the gallon. Again, I decided to paint an image of what I might see when the sun rose. This time I opted for tropical coconut trees, palm fronds and large hibiscus flowers. My mind needed this game and so I ran with it. It was all I had.

What if the humidity came from a wide, slow, meandering muddy river that ran alongside the plane? I should replace the pine tree air freshener with a wet gym sock. I'd also replace the McDonalds with a boat, loaded down with crates of smuggled tea. It would pass quietly under the cover of night. On one of the boats there'd be a beautiful silhouette, a firm golden body glistening with sweat from the first rays of morning light. She'd look over to the shore. The eyes, the cheekbones; it could only be one person.

"Ugh, stop it already, Johnny." I muttered under my breath. Vanessa was the damn reason I was stranded here.

That woman was a dangerous game, but at the moment she wasn't the problem. I had bigger issues, like shaking off the cobwebs and getting my body working. I wanted to start with standing, but I hurt all over. My legs cried out in agony as I stretched them out and worked the blood through the muscles. The pain of the waking nerves begged me to remain still, but I knew the quicker I got them working, the quicker those buzzing twinges would stop.

There was an aching in my head that throbbed like the remnants of a forty-pounder of Scotch. My body needed a reboot, much like a computer. I took a minute to rub the last few flakes of blood from the goose-egg on my temple. I doubt there'd be any gold star handed out for this landing.

In my defence, it was hard to be overly critical of putting the plane down. Hell, I'd give myself an 'A' for effort... I think. Every part of the crash was a blur. I'd bought a book a while back. No, it wasn't about flying. It was about living in the moment. When I first looked at it, I thought it was a book about enjoying the splendours of being rich, but it turned out to be about self-awareness. The book was a decent enough read while I waited for flights and stood in the line-ups at customs. From what I'd read so far, it was over my head. I wondered what the advice would be for this moment. I also wondered if there was a chapter on radio repair.

With no chance at sending a mayday, a plan 'B' was in order. I playfully wiggled my nose like the lady in Bewitched, hoping that witchcraft might get me home. It did nothing. I'd work on a plan 'C' later.

The needling sensation in my legs had gone from painful to tingly, so I pulled myself out of my seat. It was time to take these aching bones for a walk. Upon my courageous ascent from the driver's seat, the low roof struck me across the hairline.

"Damn it!"

A second goose egg would remind me of the peril of standing up in the dark. I was starting to feel like Wile E. Coyote.

Except Wile E. Coyote must have found the baritone section of frogs, who had earlier found the tenors. It was quiet, and the band had either taken its break, or they were all in Wile E's belly. I was jealous. He got to enjoy a full stomach, while mine remained empty.

I reached for the door and pushed it open, spilling myself onto the ground. The clay earth struck me hard in the face. Although my legs were no longer tingling, they had betrayed me. The fall wasn't more than a couple of feet, so was it safe to assume that I had lost the landing gear.

The air was humid and tasted like a wet wash-cloth. I pushed myself up to my knees. Maybe there were palm trees. I felt the soil in my hands and it was more of a clue than I needed. A slight panic swirled around inside my head as I got to my feet. Blinded by the darkness, I cautiously reached out and let my right hand find the plane. It felt the same as the dirt and I drew my hand away as if it was on fire. Now I knew why the band was gone, and it wasn't because they were in Wile E. Coyote's belly. The tip-jar had netted them enough to call it a night.

The heat, radiating from the soil, and from the surface of the plane, could only mean one thing, that it was morning, perhaps afternoon.

I looked up and felt the warmth of the sun on my face. Blinking twice, I hoped to see that sun. All I found was black obscurity.

Chapter nine

Was this really blindness? It sure as hell felt like it as I took a stab in the dark for the plane. My fingers bent back as they jammed against the fuselage. It hurt like a son-of-a-gun, but I had a dire need to keep it close. What was once an exotic toy had suddenly become my life-jacket. All I needed was the handicapped placard on the rear-view mirror. Shit, for all I knew, one was already hanging there.

"God, what's happened to me?"

Grappling for the door, I made my way back to my seat and collapsed in it. I had to get a handle on my breathing. I couldn't slow it down. Not that I was about to run out of air, I had plenty, but suddenly I needed so much more. I also needed to figure this out. I started with one long deep breath and quickly followed it up with a second. It wasn't helping. I couldn't see.

The loss of my sight changed everything. As a kid I had often pulled my shirt over my head and walked around finding walls, stairs, and the dog's tail. It was a no-brainer that my favourite game was 'pin the tail on the donkey.' That fake blindness was just one way of coping with my apathetic parents. With or without my shirt pulled over my head, I was alone. But here was the thing, in that adolescent world I could always flip my shirt down and see what I'd bumped into or stepped on.

On a positive note, I was alive and given an ice-cold beer, I'd even drink to that. My plane may never fly again, but it would make a damn fine shelter. I was a smart guy and I could learn to live with this. It would only be for a day or two. I'd be found soon enough. With any luck, it might even happen later today. If I was truly living in the moment, my glass was half full. I had to start believing in that shit.

I started stuffing positive thoughts into my head like breadcrumbs up a turkey's ass. Positive thought—I'm alive. Positive thought—the radio works and it's gonna get me out of here. I reached for the spiral cord and reeled in the handset. Then I gently squeezed the button. "Hello, mayday. Is anyone out there?"

Silence.

I gripped it a little tighter. My palm was a little sweaty and it slipped around a bit. "Mayday, mayday, where is everybody?"

More silence.

That was when it occurred to me that the warranty on things like radios was useless if there was no store where you'd crashed. This edged a few crumbs of bread out of the turkey. I'd be firing off a colourful email when I got home. Things like radios should be built with the utmost of precision so that they couldn't fail. A cup holder or cigarette lighter was no big deal, but a damn radio was.

My fisted hand shook as I squeezed the button with all my strength. I talked slowly and clearly. "I said Mayday! Whoever built this radio, consider yourself warned. If I find you, and I will, I'm going to make you eat this damn thing, one burnt transistor at a time."

With a quick tug I yanked the handset free from the radio and launched it out the window. I imagined the wires pulling from the radio like veins from a shoulder in some horrible apocalyptic zombie movie.

Why did I just do that?

Hell, why not?

I lifted my right heel off the floor and let it find its path to the radio. I didn't stop hammering my foot against the damn thing until I could hear the pieces hitting the floor. Lord knows I couldn't see the damn things.

Leaning back in my seat, I turned my wrath to 'mother's cold stare'. My feet didn't stop kicking until I knew her evil gaze was nothing more than a mess of broken glass and dangling wires. Even though I couldn't see the damage, I visualised it with every savage blow and it thrilled me to the point of drooling. I just hoped the fuel gauge got the worst of it.

"You still smiling, ya little prick?"

I started to laugh as I imagined its stupid smirk scattered across the floor.

"Who's laughing now, ya piece of crap."

Several deep breaths put me back in control. I didn't feel good about any of this as the first tear tried to surface. I forced it back. Was I mad at the gauges, at the blindness, or did I blame my mother? A downtown shrink would put all the blame on her. A crisis involving a mother pays off the Porsche with enough left over for a weekend in Vegas.

While the pulsing vein in my temple tried its darndest to pop, I quietly sat there and let the next few hours pass. I figured there had to be one of God's little loopholes to draw from, something that would have a rescue team swooping in from nowhere. I just had to wait for them. They'd show up apologising for this terrible misunderstanding. All this was supposed to happen to a guy named Jack Schmuckerbee, who looks a lot like me. He's an accountant from Boston. This was all a simple case of mistaken identity and they'd be happy to reimburse me for the plane. Just sign here to say you wouldn't sue God and you could be back on your way. There'd be no blindness, no bump on the head and no death in the immediate future. This kind of thing happened in the movies all the time.

As the hours passed, the air cooled. It delivered me from numbed thoughts to reality. Another day had passed without a rescue.

These falling temperatures would be my new clock, telling me that the day was becoming night. I remembered from my fishing trips how the cooler breezes always rolled in shortly after supper. The sweltering midday heat was carried off to who knew where. That was when the beer flowed freely, and the badly-embellished fishing stories began. It also meant the waking of critters. Some were harmless, like the band of crickets and frogs, while others were not.

A longing sadness burrowed its way into my heart and it wasn't from the nostalgia for the fishing trips that I may never take again. No, it was from the fact that no one had bothered to pinch me or wake me from this craziness. Helicopters weren't landing with rescue teams, ready to become heroes. Where were they?

I was coming to the end of my second day, the first being my travel and crash day. Most successful rescues happened in the first forty-eight hours, otherwise it became a recovery mission. I was already well over halfway towards becoming a statistic for beginner-flyers.

I slid my right foot back and forth along the floor and felt the pieces of glass and metal under my shoe. There were no regrets. The radio's demise was actually a result of the lightning and not my rage. There was enough raw electricity in that lightning strike to turn that wiring into a metal-art sculpture. It had been the stench of smouldering wiring harnesses that had filled my nose when I came to.

The fried electronics likely included the rescue beacon and my black box. They can handle one hell of a jarring and you can submerge them in water for weeks, but I doubt they're made to handle such a heavy surge of electrons. Regardless, there'd be no signal sent from this plane and my rescuers would be as blind as I was.

My fears quickly caught a second wind as I sat in my home. The cramped space inside the plane was closing in on my sanity like tomb walls in an Indiana Jones movie.

There weren't a lot of breadcrumbs left in the ass of that turkey. Day two, my forty-eight-hour recovery window, had commenced with hope, but ended with a bitter reality.

I was alone.

Chapter ten

A fresh cool evening rejuvenated me as it rolled through the cockpit of the plane. Here I'd spent the better part of the afternoon dwelling on my situation when I should have been putting a survival plan into place. Wasn't that the first thing a survivor should do? Since I wanted to hold on to the idea of getting out of here, I needed to accept the fact that I was alive, I was blind, I had no idea where I was, and neither did anyone else. I was on my own with this.

That being said, I wasn't entirely alone. I had crickets, frogs, and I had stuff, my stuff. I could only imagine the mess in the back of the plane. My first official course of action for making a plan would be to take an inventory of that mess. I was surprised that I wasn't knocked silly by my golf clubs, guitar, or a flying tackle box.

I turned sideways and squeezed myself between the two front seats. As I did, one of the things that I'd referred to as stuff caught my foot and sent me tumbling face-first. While my right hand caught a snarl of loose golf clubs, my left found the tackle box. It was open.

The damn thing clamped down on my hand like a bear trap. Falling back, I recoiled with no less than four flies burrowed into the skin of my fingers and palm. Any fish I'd ever caught would get a laugh from the sight of this. I might have had a chuckle, had I been able to see it.

After a two-minute regroup, I blindly fumbled through the mess with my good hand. I knew there'd be needle-nose pliers somewhere in the confusion of spilt tackle. When I found them, I carefully extracted the bloodied hooks. It took twenty minutes to get them detached and another thirty to get everything gathered off the floor and put back in the compartments of the box. Since there were no marks for neatness, the flies and lures found homes wherever there was room.

Like the fishing gear, the golf clubs eventually found their way back into their bag. It might have been fun to feel the head of each club and guess the size, but my fingers were sore and a little sticky from the blood.

With the sporting gear cleaned up, curiosity got the better of me. I looked over my shoulder, to the gap between the seats. I saw nothing. Was I really expecting to see anything other than Johnny Cash's favourite colour? As I felt around I found a block, tightly wrapped in paper and about the size of two pounds of tea. I held it to my nose and smelled the cinnamon. It seemed ironic enough to evince a smile. "Oh, touché Mr. Rooibos."

I set it aside and went back to cleaning. The next find kicked my taste buds into overdrive. It was a bottle, plastic, and half full of Pepsi. I'd started it back in Oregon. It flowed over my tongue, bringing applause from every taste bud in my mouth. I reluctantly screwed the cap back on with only a few warm swallows remaining.

There was a suitcase, a box of books, and a laptop. I stacked them off to the left. No WIFI meant there was no Internet. Hell, no eyesight qualified the darn laptop and books as glorified paperweights.

So now I had floor space and if I played my cards right, I'd be able to clear an area large enough for a bed. Anything would be an improvement from last night's front seat. Katie and I had once slept in the back of a mini van. We'd wanted an unforgettable honeymoon and we got it. Our van broke down on the way to Vancouver. It was cold, and we struggled to stay warm by curling up under our coats. We missed our flight to Hawaii and nine months later our daughter, Brook, was born. We had a way of turning bad into memorable.

I could make this memorable, but it would help if I knew where this was. For all I knew I was on the outskirts of some city. There was a chance I'd crashed in a farmer's field and he was on the phone wondering how to get the most from his insurance claim.

And where was my phone?

The loaner phone wasn't in my pocket, nor was it on the floor around the seats. The image of it sitting on the dash, while I savagely kicked at the gauges, surfaced. That was where I'd left it, I think. Had I crushed it in my rage? I made a feeble search, knowing I'd have no luck. My only hope of finding it would be if it wasn't in a million pieces, and someone was calling.

I returned to my bed and sat against the inner wall of the plane only to hear the crunch of potato chips. They were barbecue-flavour. I forgot I'd bought them. It was a small bag, but there was enough for a good taste—let's call it supper.

That was my day-two meal and I washed it down with the last of the pop. Unless I could find my gum, that was it for the groceries.

With food in my belly I could relax. I found my guitar and checked it for tuning. The crash hadn't knocked it out that bad. My fingers still stung a bit, but so did my head, my legs, my back, and my stomach. The guitar sounded good after strumming a few random chords, so I tried a song. Sore fingers and headache be damned. I needed this. I'd always liked *Sweet Home Alabama* and knew I could play it blind-folded. Well, this was just as good, so I tried it.

An accompanying cricket was soon followed by a second, so I stopped and stumbled my way to the doorway. This was my front door, my stoop. I started up again and soon had last night's band back together. The frogs, crickets, and coyotes soon sang to the noise I'd created. It sounded much better than one would have guessed. They were in good form as the darkness settled outside my own darkness.

I broke into the chorus. The band sang along, their chirps and burps were close enough to lyrics for me. It felt good to have them out there.

Perhaps it was the sound of the guitar, or it could have been the masses that came out to sing. Either way I didn't find my predicament as desperate with my friends onboard. There was a good chance these next few days would be my last. There was also a chance I'd wake up in the middle of the night to a helicopter-ride home. Both thoughts stroked and caressed my brain, making me forget the words to the next verse.

I continued to strum and listened to the choir while I played. They kept a rhythm similar to a squeaky wheel on a shopping cart. I'd heard worse. But the happiness soon waned. Don't ask me how, but after a few minutes I sensed there was something bigger going on.

It wasn't an intuition, nor was it any sixth sense. It was a shiver, and it slowly built up a head of steam as it travelled up my spine. That was when it happened. They stopped singing. I had also stopped singing.

We were being watched.

Chapter eleven

s if under the command of a conductor, the band had suddenly gone all calm-before-the-storm quiet. An eerie silence settled the mood, and only then did I realise that I had stopped strumming. One of the crickets, a rebel I'm sure, gave a final chirp. He wasn't about to conform. I could only imagine the apologetic smirk he was giving his buddies right now.

Sure, there was a level of paranoia, but I strongly felt the eyes on us. There was little doubt, but who was our critic?

"Hello?" I tried to keep my voice from breaking. This guy could be the one to save me. "Hello?"

My ears strained for an answer from our uninvited guest, but there was nothing. Suddenly, none of this felt right.

"I uh, said hello," I repeated, as I edged further from the doorway. I wanted to yell out, 'Save me, I'm blind, I'm hurt, I'm starving,' but I didn't. I didn't want him knowing that. Whoever this guy was, he wasn't the running-to-my-aid type.

The silence was deafening, as if everyone, bugs and beasts, was waiting in anticipation for a response. I thought about all those old spaghetti westerns I used to watch. In them, two gunfighters stood in the middle of a dirt street, their steely eyes staring each other down until one of them flinched. Guns were drawn and shots were fired. Meanwhile all the townspeople watched from windows, open doorways and rooftops. A few of the more curious stood dangerously close on the boardwalks in front of shops and saloons. They respectfully stayed behind the hitching posts and everyone, except for a few old-timers who had seen far too much death over their lifetimes, thirsted for their blood.

To the old-timers, a man was about to lose his life. They knew all about the inevitable price of pride. They'd seen this dance a hundred times. And, lurking in the shadows, a man in a faded black suit went over an inventory of pine boxes in his mind. Did he have caskets in both men's sizes? If not, he might be forced to root for one or the other. It would be a shame, but business was business.

I needed to lighten the mood. Thoughts like these could suffocate a man. "Okay, I didn't catch a name, but you're welcome to join us."

My pause was in hopes of a friendly response, but all I got was another chirp from my brave, or perhaps stupid, cricket friend. He seemed to enjoy cutting curves into the same thin sheet of ice that we both stood on. Not to be rude, I got up and took a seat in the cockpit. I flipped the lock on the door as I closed it. Not to offend, but I had to protect myself, not that the broken window would hold anybody back.

As I sat in the plane I started playing the intro to a song that had been weaving its way into my brain these last few seconds. It was a catchy little tune and with any luck, it would ease my nerves.

"We'll be taking it from the top." I strummed a 'G' chord followed by a 'D.'

I started to sing.

My half-witted cricket friend, loyal to the end, joined in and I silently thanked him for doing so—I hated going solo. The rest of them eventually started in, but only a few here and there until they felt more comfortable. As our fears subsided, the night air filled with song.

For the band this had only been a distraction. Like the townspeople in the westerns, they knew how to dodge the stray bullets while they welcomed the reckless entertainment into their day. For my cricket friend and I, it was more. We weren't sure what had just happened, but we knew it wasn't over.

As we sang, a flicker, or woodpecker, hammered a new home into some old abandoned tree. His beat wasn't a 4/4 tempo, but he was consistent. Trying to ignore him, I carried on, except on two occasions he messed me up. There's always one in every crowd.

I continued to sing about the Chevy, the whiskey, and the rye. When I got to the part where I died, I stopped. I didn't want tonight to become that day.

The temperature continued to drop, and I found myself rubbing my eyes and yawning. Blind as I was, this was my only way of keeping my days and nights straight. I leaned my guitar against the back of the passenger seat and headed off to my makeshift bed of strewn clothes.

Another evening meant another reflection on what I'd done. I'd always used the evening to go over my day. Could I have done things differently and had I told Katie I loved her? Normally my thoughts included Katie, finances, the kids, book ideas and how my tomorrow might unfold. Tonight, I still thought of Katie, but added Vanessa, my stomach, and a dangerous curiosity with death.

As a writer, my wandering mind gave me all kinds of crazy ideas and solutions to plots that had hit brick walls. For survival in the bush it was anything but productive. Tonight I missed my wife more than ever and I was beginning to feel like I'd already lost her. Whether it was because I knew she'd eventually find out about Vanessa and leave me, or because I'd die before getting a chance to come clean, I wasn't sure. And yes, I was honestly thinking I might tell her. She didn't deserve secrets. That being said, she didn't deserve the hurt either.

Gently, I nudged my mind down a different and less painful path. I imagined what I'd eat if I ever got out of here. Fish and chips at The George came to mind first. It was a local pub and I wouldn't even wait for Sunday, the day with all the discounts.

"Shit." I even had the chance to have breakfast before I left California, and damn if Eric wasn't offering to pay. I could have ordered flapjacks or a Denver omelette, but no, I was too preoccupied with this trip. I hadn't eaten much since my ill-advised lunch date.

As I pushed these thoughts aside, the voids filled with memories of my mother, my kids, my band of crickets, and an abstract of childhood moments. All these thoughts tortured me and kept me from a deep and badly-needed sleep.

Having travelled full circle, my mind finally rested on the very thought I was trying to avoid... that awkward silence. I had hoped that ship had sailed, but it had only floated around in the harbour of my mind until it found a solid place to drop anchor. There had to be a reason.

Now with the morning sun filling my home, and the hidden embers of light warming my bones, I started what I figured to be my third day in this wilderness. It could have been longer. I wasn't sure how many days I'd missed. My hunger pains were telling me it was closer to a week.

Regardless, last night had brought a kaleidoscope of confusion. I had agonised over it and, instead of sleeping, I'd found my answer. I understood what had happened last night. It was the only answer that fit.

I knew why the music had died.

Chapter twelve

Granted, I was still half-asleep when I reached my epiphany, and yes, I was a little weak in the head from a lack of food and sleep deprivation, but my conclusion made perfect sense. I had used my outside-the-box thinking, the kind that comes from the deeper psyche of a writer. In this part of the brain I wasn't governed by the brainwashing ways of parents, teachers, and social media. Trust me, this world meant well, but it was nothing but generations of programming. We even gave it a name, culture.

My thoughts were purely unbiased and pulled from practicality. And although they made sense, they took a bit to wrap my head around. Last night, it was a 'mountain man' that came down to my camp and stopped our music.

You're scratching your head right now, but that's because you're still using that complying part of your brain. I saw a documentary once on one of those documentary shows. It was all about the history of the Northwest prospectors. Spellbound by the idea of finding deposits of gold, silver, nickel, or copper, most of these men had no contact with the real world except for when they traded their ore for supplies.

Eventually, they'd simply live off the land. They were hermits, not willing to leave until they found what they'd come for. While some became rich and returned to society, others let the world pass them by. Those ones lived out their crazed lives knee deep in frigid creek water.

While most of those old prospectors had died dirt-poor, the odd one was still stuck to his claim. They're like the charred remnants of a long-forgotten forest fire after the new growth had returned. I'd even wager that he'd been out of touch with humanity for so long, he'd forgotten how to speak. The coyotes and crickets would give him an easier conversation to understand. I'd even bet he wanted to say something last night but couldn't remember how. It all made sense.

A growl from my stomach brought my mind back to the subject of food. What was the old prospector having? I couldn't smell bacon, but there was coffee in the air. I could taste it on my tongue.

Feeling good about my deduction, I rewarded myself with the scrap morsels in the chip bag. Breakfast was cautiously torn open, as not to drop any, and I blindly started in on them one wet fingertip at a time. They had been lingering in my sinuses all night. I'd decided to save them for a moment where I could truly savour them. A smile found my face while I chewed. Last night's incident had reassured me that I was not alone.

After eating, I sat back and pretended to let my breakfast digest. I could almost picture the old guy living in his cabin. Again, I found the time to paint that picture of what this place might look like. Sure, we'd keep the wild strawberries, lupines, and towering green mountains, but amongst all that would also be our mountain man's cabin.

Now don't go picturing any resort-style cabin with water-saving flush toilets and a metal roof or it won't make any sense. You'll think I was crazy. No, he's in a rustic old cabin that could have a bit of a lean to it because of years of cold northerly winds. It's no more than a hundred yards from me and, in my mind, I can see a shabby version of a front veranda. The aged wooden roof leaks because of the thick moss that has worked its way between the rotted shingles. That's okay though, because the gaps in the plank floor drain away the puddles. In town, this place would be a fixer-upper, or more likely a tear-down. Out here, it fits this forest like a pair of worn sneakers.

From that front deck he could sit in his weathered rocking chair, a loaded shotgun across his lap, and watch time tick away the moments of his life. He's got to be close to ninety and strong as an ox, all without the aid of modern diet fads or probiotics. He's okay with discarding those seconds and sometimes hours. How many years had he spent sifting through muddy water? Unlike the bustling city folk, he wouldn't have a schedule. His life wouldn't be about staying fashionably on the go or drinking cat-crap coffee. He'd live this way until he found gold, or until he died.

Days ago, during a horrible storm, he was given good reason to sit and waste the hours watching the world from his home. Just like I might receive a last-minute invite to a baseball game, he'd had his entertainment land smack-dab in the middle of his yard. With a thud, I had become his 3D high-definition amusement. And even better, I came with no commercials.

Now like that little boy, hiding behind the watering trough at the gunfight, all he had to do was sit back and enjoy the show. The outcome was almost imminent, but how would the stranger die? How long would he last before his fate snatched him up?

I got up and made my way outside, my neck a little stiff from the lumpy mattress of balled-up shirts and crumpled pants. "Hello?"

Again, I waited for the response that wouldn't come. I didn't expect it to. "Whenever you're ready then, old-timer." I wanted to call him Ben. That sounded like an old prospector name, didn't it? Did he still have a name, or had it faded with the years?

I imagined the gaze on his face becoming uneasy right now. Did his trigger finger have an itch? Identifying his presence would have put him on the spot, making him restless. I had to give the man credit though. There weren't many people who could ignore me like he was doing.

"Not a problem. I'm sure you're just shy. We'll talk later when you're feeling more comfortable." I listened through the silence. "Or not…Ben."

Yes, my conclusion was rock solid. Last night he was curious. He walked down to hear my guitar, something that had knocked the dust off an old memory. No doubt he hadn't heard one in quite some time. In doing so he spooked the boys in the band. When we stopped playing he got all panicked and quietly scampered back to the safety of his veranda.

I totally got his shyness and I could easily see why he was cautious. I was the unknown, a real threat, in a bird from the sky, no doubt. Hopefully he'd realise I'm not after his claim and he might share his food and water. For now, I had to stay friendly and pose no threat. Ben had a few rounds of lead to share, so I best be good.

I smiled as I fought the escape of a happy little tear. It was just so damn nice to know I wasn't alone.

Chapter thirteen

I continued to stand beside the plane as the agony of dehydration tried to put knots in my legs. At least last night's slumber took place in the comforts of the back of the plane and not the driver's seat. The great organising job I'd done, after pulling out the fishing hooks, had paid off. I had made enough room for a small makeshift bed. My clothes, although a little lumpy, formed an adequate mattress and my fleece pullover, wrapped around the two pounds of trip-me-up tea, made a first-rate pillow.

I've always known that hunger isn't much fun. What I didn't know was that it fell a distant second to being thirsty. The part bottle of Pepsi and handful of chips were such a memory now that it was hard to believe I'd ever had them. My stomach and intestines opposed my new diet of daydreams and the memories of past meals.

I took a step away from the plane, dropping my hand from the wing. I stood a defiant three feet away from my sanctuary, trembling at the thought of losing it. But as much as I was afraid to venture too far from the plane, I had to. With any luck I might step in a natural spring, stumble into a field of wild strawberries or even find the front door of a Micky-D—you know they really were everywhere.

I gave my mountain man a courtesy wave. Ben had me by the short and curly ones, but who didn't these days? If he gave me water, I'd easily forgive the silent treatment. If he gave me some of his coffee, I'd pass on guitar lessons.

It was safe to say he was to the north of me and that the nose of my plane pointed directly at his front door. I'm guessing north because that was the direction I was flying before the crash. It was a safe assumption that I was still flying north when I went down. That was where the sensation of being watched was the strongest. He was on his second cup of coffee. I swear I can smell it. And I'm sure my moving around had him smiling. His favourite show was starting.

"Nice day, eh Ben." I smiled and continued to stare in his general direction. Please don't shoot me, please don't shoot me…please don't shoot me.

Well, that was enough bonding for now. He needed entertainment and the only way I could give it to him was by staying alive. I'd start by finding food and water.

"Any clues, old man?" Oops, should I be calling him old? But if I called him young whippersnapper he'd think I was being sarcastic.

His silence scrambled my thoughts, but I knew that he'd picked this spot for a reason. It meant there was water near by, a creek or a river. That was reassuring, but only in the same way a lottery ticket is a winner until you check it. Then the harsh reality sets in and you're out ten or twenty bucks. I used to always carry a few unchecked lottery tickets in my wallet. They gave me hope and were worth more unchecked.

But back to being adventurous, I should be scouting any direction but north. If I got too close to his home he might unload a couple of rounds of buckshot my way and the show would be over…no syndication, no reruns. There'd be no Emmy for the guy in the plane.

Right, left, or behind the plane were my options so, after orienting myself, I chose right. A plan had come to me last night and it included the rope from my emergency kit. I wrapped one end around my waist and tied the other end to the driver's door. I'd have used the passenger door, but I couldn't get it open.

I walked around the front of the plane, not letting my home leave the touch of my hand. Even though the plane sat level, the right wing was badly bent downward, and the tip rested in the dirt. Nevertheless, it had fared better than the left wing. That one was missing.

With the rope, I could venture about thirty feet and when I got scared, I could reel my way home. I thought of using fishing line, but the extra distance might just get me tangled up in the trees. Besides, fishing line can break, leaving me lost without a path home. The way things had been going, my rescuers would find me dead and only yards away from the plane. Nah, the rope would work better.

I inched along with my hands outstretched sweeping at the air for branches, trees, or with a little luck, a discount supermarket. I could sense the old fart giggling at my awkwardness and I'll bet he split a gut when I found the pothole. My ankle folded like a greeting card and I fell hard. I could only hope the old man spit his coffee down the front of his shirt.

I picked myself up and flipped him the bird. "Would it kill you to help me?"

Silence.

"Piss on ya then, Ben."

I continued, protecting my eyes from errant branches. Even though they did nothing for me now, they might in the future. They didn't need any further damage. I had to hold onto the hope that they'd work again, someday.

What was that?

A sudden noise, like a branch breaking, came at me from the left. I wanted to replay the sound as I froze and waited for the next crack. After a minute my legs began to ache. I shook myself free from the trance. It was nothing. Damn it, I can't let Ben get to me like this. I continued to root around, still tethered to the door of the plane. The winds were starting to pick up and within minutes the temperatures had dropped a good five degrees. What did I miss? There was no way it was evening yet, or was it? This blind-man's chow-hunt couldn't have eaten away an entire afternoon. That was impossible.

There was a wildcard sensation eating away at me. It told me it was time to get back to the plane. I slowly started to reel myself in. How did blind people do it? Not the blind people like me, lost and useless, but the ones that lived and functioned in society. Were there watches that helped them? I suddenly envisioned a watch with no hands and no numbers. It would have a single button. If you wanted to know the time you simply pressed the button and it would talk to you. Of course, you'd have voice options and I'd pick some flirtatious girl's voice.

'Hello Mr. Pettinger. The time is Monday 1:45 p.m.'

Then it might add, 'You're looking exceptionally handsome today.' Yes, if they didn't have this, I'd invent it.

Then that sensation happened again. "What the hell..."

The odd feeling killed my creative moment. It started in my feet and rippled through my body in a wave. Familiar, I couldn't place it at first. My brain sorted through past experiences to find a similarity. The closest I could find was rubbing a balloon against my head.

The answer came to me just as the following clap of thunder reverberated through my body like a Hulk Hogan body-slam. Rapidly followed by a second, and a third, each strike rumbled through my chest. The dirt kicked up all around me as I scrambled back to the plane.

I jigged left and jogged right, arms fumbling at the rope, as I tried to save myself.

Chapter fourteen

With a firm grip on the rope, I pulled myself back to the plane. I swear I pulled hard enough to bring the plane partway to me. With every thunderous clap I felt my bladder release. Was it luck that I didn't have enough liquid in me to produce anything more than a nickel-sized pee stain? At the moment, I'd have to go with yes.

The plane was my sanctuary and I'd need my rough and ready bed to watch over me as I stumbled my way into it. Being metal, the plane was a great conductor. I never made the connection. My legs had turned to cement, dropping me to the floor. When I tried to roll over, I couldn't. Then I felt the tether. It was still attached.

I untied my umbilical chord and quietly rolled onto my other side. Every skull-shattering boom brought a very powerful fear of dying. Even muscles I never knew I had clenched, bringing an unwavering pain to my chest.

And with the thunder came rain. At first the occasional plink, plink soothed my trepidation, but before long the heavens opened, and the skies unleashed a fury I hadn't experienced since the crash.

I cowered under my suitcase as the plane weathered the deafening barrage. Water poured in from broken windows and cracks in the fuselage. It flowed though the plane and through my bed. The cold and the dampness bit at my body, forcing my teeth to clatter. I sounded like an engine without oil.

When the first tear escaped my eye, I knew my nerves were shattered. It came out of my right eye and took a journey down my cheek landing on my Rooibos pillow. Once the path was carved, it was easier for the next one to follow. The third took its turn and, you get my point. I can't remember the last time I cried, and I mean cried with no hope of stopping. This wasn't who I was. My parents never would have allowed such nonsense.

To ease my guilt, I made sure there were no embarrassing sobs. Nor was there a quiver in my lip. I doubt there was any expression on my face other than a pale blank state of shock, interrupted only by the occasional clap of thunder. Tear after tear made the trek, spaced close enough to keep the path from being lost. This went on for several minutes when finally, after producing enough tears to fully melt my masculinity, I dried up. Phantom tears continued to prickle my cheek, but there was no satisfaction in them. Soon, they too gave up and the stinging eased. The trembling did not.

As the storm rolled through, the thunder distanced itself, the rains eased, and the pee stain dried. This cell of fear had given me its worst and I had weathered it, albeit like a little girl dealing with her first break-up. Remind me never to tease my daughter, Brook, when that day happens. She cried for two days when her best friend moved across town and I didn't get it. I do now.

After the hell was over, I took a second to chuckle. I was alive. What was that old man doing at this moment? Had he heard me crying? Being an old redneck, he'd shoot me for sure if he'd seen that. Hell, I'd have let him.

Nah, the old fart was probably brewing up a squirrel stew, a racoon sandwich, or whatever old prospectors ate. That being said, I'd knock back a bowl of rodent gumbo if he had corn bread and a tall glass of ...water?

Water. The tether quickly made its way back around my waist and with my pop bottle in hand, I charged out of the plane.

For some reason, mud always felt good when it squished between bare toes. Today was no exception as I slipped and slopped around.

The once horrific rains didn't seem so bad now. Even the pine needles pricking their way into the pads of my feet didn't bother me. There'd be no stopping until I found that big fat ankle-rolling puddle.

Anybody watching would have thought I was a madman. The twinges in my ankle reminded me of how I'd rolled it earlier. I'd chastised that damn crater when it had no value, but now I celebrated its existence…that's if I could find it.

My visualisation skills must have been evolving. They say that happens. Senses heighten to make up for the ones you lose. For that reason, it didn't take long to track down my puddle.

The mud absorbed my hands and knees as I dropped to the ground. I lowered my face into the waiting pool of water and drank until my belly ached. The earthy water never tasted so good. I kicked myself for only having one pop bottle to fill, but who planned for a life-threatening crash? Let this be a lesson to anyone who is dumb enough to get in a plane after angering the Adultery Gods.

Just because you might not believe in Karma didn't mean it couldn't affect you. My life up to now had never taught me the laws of fate, but I was finding that they were fairly simple. Do something wrong and bad fortune would follow. Had I understood the shit I'd stirred, I'd have brought a lot more food, beer, and three-ply toilet paper. Had I realised the Karma Gods would have been this angry with me, I'd have brought welding goggles, a crash helmet, and enough bubble wrap to cover myself from head to toe ten times over.

At least I had a puddle, and a pop bottle.

"See, Ben," I yelled up to the cabin. "I just bought me a couple of days."

It was easy to imagine the old codger's prune face twisted in a scowled frown.

"Relax old man," I muttered under my breath. "The time will go quick."

Chapter fifteen

A nother evening rolled in, and along with it came the end of another twenty-four hours. I ignored the mood that was biting at me like a mosquito on a summer night. It was hard to accept my fate as a cold dampness settled in. I knew that somewhere a meeting was taking place. It was casual, over drinks at a local tavern. Their day had been a long one, and it was over. Rescue workers were being told that their work was appreciated, but starting tomorrow, this would be a recovery mission.

What was I thinking? That meeting should have been yesterday. Depression was pulling hard on the rope, but I pulled back. I still had Ben. I think he snores. It keeps me up at night. I wish he'd come down to the plane again. We could talk.

Another lousy sleep welcomed a morning with the distant aroma of coffee. The relenting drizzle continued. My world was still dark, so I couldn't see the tiny drops as they clung to the jagged shards of windshield, or from the pine needles in the surrounding trees, but I could imagine them. If it sounds like I'm feeling sorry for myself, I am. I should be thankful for my belly full of water, but I'm hungry and except for my crickets and Ben, I feel very much removed from everything.

Thank God for them. While Death's bony fingers tried to tap me on the shoulder, I think they were the only things keeping me sane. I get that everybody gets a turn at death, but I expected to get a hundred years. I definitely thought I'd get more than this.

The allotted forty-eight hours had easily come and gone. I had drifted further off course than anyone expected. It meant that no one was coming, and I was anything but set up for a lengthy survival. Still, I had to try.

After a couple of chilly trips to my puddle, I spent the day hiding inside the plane. Once again, the night had the temperature dropping. I'd be able to see my breath right now, if I could see.

I thought about a roaring campfire, but how would I even start one? Outside, everything was drenched. Any wood I'd need would be wet. Tomorrow, I'll gather a few armfuls and store them on the passenger side floor. I doubt it could hurt. Then again, a blind man tending a fire sounded like a reason for a Smokey the Bear lecture.

Tonight, instead of fire, I'll wear a few more layers. This mattress could afford losing a few lumps. 'Burnt to a crisp.' The words resonated through the disturbed hallways of my mind and reminded me of that damn dream.

'You crashed. Burnt to a fuck'n crisp, Darling.' Vanessa's demented laughter echoed through my mind. It was as if she was in the plane with me. 'Nobody's gonna want you now Johnny. You should have kept it in your pants. Come on Katie, you deserve better.'

And how do I argue that fact? She really did deserve better. I didn't want to face that fact, but it was true. She'd be better off, if I wasn't found. So why am I fighting this?

Despair dissolved the night away as a new day and a new distraction came to greet me. A day ago, I had found a puddle and I drank. I drank until it hurt and then I drank some more. Since then I'd gone out in the rain to fill my bottle twice. Now a newer urgency was taking over. It was a crazed desire to pee. Hopefully it was like falling off a bike and I'd remember how.

To the left of the plane seemed the obvious choice. It only made sense to pull water from the right and recycle it on the left.

This side of the plane had no wing and was foreign to me as I ventured out. The ground was warm on my bare feet. I'd left my shoes hanging to dry. I thought of waving to the north, to my new friend. I didn't. After four steps, I stumbled to one knee. The ground was all torn up.

Had the plane crashed sideways? But the wing struts on the right side had been bent straight back, which was not a sign of a sideways crash. It had to be a straight-in crash. What did this have to do with the dirt?

I crawled a few feet further, my hands and knees probing for the truth. A large area had been disturbed as if a rot-a-tiller or shovel had been busy on it. Large chunks were everywhere as I crawled over them. There were foot-deep holes, exposed tree roots, rocks, and what felt like rich dark soil. The plane didn't cause this.

It confirmed to me that I was close to the old guy's cabin. Squatting down, I scooped up a handful of the soil and squeezed it into a ball. The old guy must have tilled this ground in the hopes of planting a garden.

For a brief moment I waited for the shot. He'd be pissed if I were trampling his garden. Still, I felt around in hopes of finding a carrot, some peas, or a row of leaf lettuce. There was nothing but dirt. I must have crashed before the planting.

I got to my feet, legs slightly apart, and drew my soldier out. I couldn't wait any longer. The push was strong. Too bad the action wasn't. Sure, the cooler air always made it more difficult, but I had drunk a gallon of water and I knew I couldn't hold onto it forever.

With my eyes closed, I imagined all the times I'd watered a tree trunk or small shrub. It seemed to help and although the first few drops felt like I was dribbling a strand of molten barbed wire, the flow that ensued streamed nicely. The initial pain soon gave way to a watering session that was pleasingly long. If there had been snow on the ground I'd have written another best seller, complete with rewrites.

After zipping up my pants, I had to lean against the plane. I was exhausted, and my knees wanted to give out. The old man's laughter rumbled in the distance with the wind. That bastard was agitating the shit out of me. I'll bet the old fart was getting ready to make popcorn.

"You liked that?" I'm sure his grin was a shit-eating one. "That's okay. You want to know why?"

There was silence. There was always silence with this guy, except for that damn distant cackling. He reminded me of my Uncle Bert. That guy never talked either. He just showed up and made everybody feel uncomfortable. Once, I ambushed him with silly string. I was young and wanted to see what would happen— okay, it was stupid, in hindsight. It flew from the can and landed on his tweed jacket, on his black rim glasses, on his bristly face and all over that horrible comb-over. And when the can ran out, my giggling turned into a bladder releasing hush. As the urine made its way down into my sneaker, he calmly peeled the web of string away. His eyes never left mine. I think I was hoping he'd snap, give me a thunderous tongue wagging. He just looked down at the wet stain on front of my pants and smiled. Like Ben, he was a tough nut to crack.

"Okay, I'll tell you. I deserve this. They call it Karma." It wasn't a very common word and I'm sure he didn't care. Karma was my word of the day, so it would be his, if he wanted to learn.

There was no response except for my brave little cricket friend. He'd missed last night because of the rain, but he was back now, and he wanted to sing.

"Not now Jim-bo. I'm not in the mood." He had such positive energy, which made it hard to get mad. "Maybe later."

I directed my voice north, back to the cabin. "Have you ever heard of Karma?" I almost laughed. "Okay, okay. I'm sure you don't get out much."

I waited for the blast from his gun to rip through me. Still, only silence. Either this old guy had a sense of humour, or he didn't have his gun loaded. That or I wasn't worth putting the popcorn down for.

It didn't matter. I almost wished he would shoot me, get this over with. Even a mouse, played with by the cat, longs for the end. Understand this, I didn't want to die, but if the odds were against me, I didn't want to suffer. Why go through days of agony for the same prolonged fate. It just seemed cruel.

"Look old timer, maybe you get what I'm saying and maybe you don't. All I want is a cup of coffee or a chunk of bread."

His continued silence pissed me off. I wish he'd just say something, damn it. Then I understood. He's a prospector. He's only about one thing. I took the watch from my wrist and took a few steps toward his cabin. I held it up. "It's eighteen carats. I know you understand that word. It's all yours."

I crouched down and set it down on the ground. I also detected a tuft of grass at my toes. I grabbed at it and stuck it in my mouth. It didn't taste horrible. "Maybe I'll just have a salad today, unless you'd like to share something with me. I'll take muskrat meat marmalade, your squirrel stew, or your gopher gut gumbo. Believe me, I'm not fussy."

I chewed and swallowed as I backtracked to the plane. My wife would be proud, me eating my greens. I normally wouldn't bring myself to eat anything that looked like the weeds ruining our lawn. Other than potato, salads were boring. Add some bacon or gravy and I was in, but that wasn't Katie's reason for getting me to eat my greens. She wanted me to eat healthier. I'd live longer. The way I saw it, I drank, and I smoked for years before quitting. I had eaten junk food all my life. It was a little late to change now.

"We could start over a cup of coffee."

I half expected him to place his hand on my shoulder and hand me a cup. The watch was worth a few dollars. He'd owe me a cigarette. I'd smoke it slowly, enjoying each breath. I'd been known to have the odd one when I'm out drinking. Soon, I would finish my coffee and take a final drag off my smoke.

I'd prefer a basket of spicy chicken wings, or some curly fries loaded with cheese, a beer, and a bus ticket, but what the hell. I just wanted to see my wife again. I was beginning to think I should tell her, but only if I live. It's a moot point if I die. Oh, but what if Vanessa goes to my funeral? She could tell her. Would she? That would be such a dick thing to do. There was no money in it, so I felt safe.

But what if she did? Suddenly, I wanted to write Katie a quick goodbye note. She would need to know it was nothing, and that I never meant to hurt her. I didn't want to leave her this way. I took a minute to rummage around the cockpit for my pen. I couldn't find it.

I flopped back in the seat. "Damn it."

Through my darkness I looked up to the heavens and prayed for help. I had also prayed for Ben to either feed me or shoot me and look what that got me. "Come on God, I know you have a bigger heart than this. All I'm asking for is a sign."

Then, as if he'd decided to intervene, a bottle clinked under the passenger seat and I remembered the rye.

Chapter sixteen

I sat in the front seat of the plane, my brains barely intact, bottle in hand. I needed a drink. They say if you ask for God's help, you'll always get it. He never says no, and in God's usual mystifying way he gave me a bottle of rye whiskey. Who am I to argue?

When I first bought the plane, part of my preflight check was a swig of ye olde calming potion. Flying solo had scared the hell out of me and a quick sip or two before take-off usually eased my nerves. I wasn't sure what kind of sign God was giving me, but there was still some left in the bottle. I gave it a shake—half full, half empty. I didn't care about the philosophy. I just wanted all the thinking to end and the mind to go numb.

"Thank-you, God. You understand me." I unscrewed the top and took a long drink.

I let it ease to the back of my throat, flooding my tongue and back teeth, before I swallowed. A second mouthful not only warmed my throat, but also lit my brain. My head wasn't swimming in any pool of confusion yet, but there was a healthy enough buzz to swirl my thoughts. The next few swallows nestled me right up against my tipping point. I'd kill for a slice of pizza or a bowl of peanuts.

Normally, I was a proud drinker. I'd always been able to go out and knock back a few with the boys. An empty stomach turned me into a teenager sneaking dad's home-made hooch. A tipping point was a warning, telling you that another drink wasn't needed. At that point, one more drink could only bring dizziness, an upset stomach, or a dance in ones' underwear on a coffee table while singing Freebird. I had raced past my tipping point like a drunk flying through a, what-the-hell-colour-was-that, traffic light. It was okay. I wasn't driving, although in my mind, I was flying.

Jim-bo and that evening breeze seemed extra friendly tonight, so I got my guitar out and took my place on the stoop. My little cricket buddy fetched the band. The storm had come, hung around for a day, and left us feeling cool and refreshed. Now, this rain-soaked world was drying up fast. The parched soil had soaked up the rains leaving me with a part bottle of water. But that wasn't what I wanted right now. I wanted the golden nectar. I took another swig as I fumbled the pick with my fingers. The fresh air felt good in my lungs and it was time to break out the band.

An 'F' chord started me singing a tune called *Yesterday*. The coyotes and bullfrogs were quick to join the crickets and we sounded pretty good. Katie was on my mind, so in her honour I decided on a Beatles night. I knew it was one of her favourite bands and it seemed to be a much-loved one with the bullfrogs. Hey, who doesn't love beetles?

We sang, and I drank well into the night. We sang *The fool on the Hill*. It helped me cope with my inner meltdown because I was that fool and my brains were spinning in circles. When my bottle started to lighten, I got worried. Then I remembered my water, or should I say mix. That should carry the fool through the night.

Every Beetles song I'd ever learned was played, some two or three times. By the time the early warmth of the morning came, we'd made the boys from Liverpool proud. When my head finally hit the cinnamon-flavoured block of Rooibos tea, I couldn't remember being in a plane crash. I couldn't remember cheating on Katie, or the words to the second verse of *When I'm Sixty-four*. I

66

had to apologise to my friends for that one. It was a classic and they deserved to hear it. I did, however, remember to say goodnight to Ben. I'm sure that even he had fun tonight. He didn't call the cops.

As I fell asleep, I thought about the alcohol in my system. My ears were doing laps around my head as the freedom juice coursed through my veins. It was stupid to get this drunk, but I had asked God for a sign and this was what he'd given me. He had a plan and I had to see it through.

It wouldn't take long.

Chapter seventeen

When I factored in the amount I drank and multiplied it by the fact that I'd gone days without eating, I didn't feel all that bad when I awoke. My head wasn't pounding, and my eyes weren't throbbing. It was surprisingly nice that my body didn't feel like it had been tumbled around in a commercial-size clothes dryer. There wasn't even the desperation that had gone with my mood last night.

Life was good.

I pulled my jacket, a stray part of my mattress, off my head and tossed it aside. Slivers of light pierced my eyes like shards of broken glass. My lids slammed shut in protest, but only for a second. I reopened them, slowly. My sight had returned.

Sure, there were sandboxes tucked under my eyelids, but I quickly blinked them away as I adjusted to the colours and shapes. I'm sure the smile on my face was wide enough to tickle both earlobes. I tried to stop shaking. My brain grappled to keep pace with my eyes as they swept across my makeshift bedroom. I saw my guitar, the tackle box, laptop, emergency kit and my golf clubs. They were just as I'd imagined them.

The plane couldn't hold me now. I stopped as my bare feet landed on the earth. My tether was still back in the plane. Then I laughed. Like I needed that anymore. The ground, no longer slippery with mud, was still cool to the touch. Oh, so many trees and such beautiful mountains. I saw the lupines, brown-eyed susans and the wild roses that I'd painted in my mind only days before. Green grass seemed to glow against the rich dark soil. The contrasts and depths of colour started to give me a mild headache, but that was okay; it was so worth it.

A harvest sun sat just off the eastern mountaintops. If I had to guess, it was about mid morning. How amazing was it to know the time.

In front of the plane, and about one hundred and fifty yards away, I saw the cabin. Okay, so I was off by fifty yards, but it was there to the north. It had a rocking chair on the front porch that sat empty. He was missing the best part of the show. It was for the better. I didn't need him out here right now.

From the wing of my home I could see that the old guy's view was unobstructed except for a few willow whips poking up through the grass. It was a darn good vantage point. There was an axe stuck in the chop-block that caught my attention. He had firewood.

As much as I wanted to bug him for a cup of coffee, I had to bet I'd end up looking like Swiss cheese, or a butchered slab of meat. With my eyesight back, I was a threat. If I wanted life to continue, I'd have to blindly wander around and continue to play the game. If he came out, I'd start sweeping my arms back and forth and fall down a couple times. The less he knew, the better off I was. I'd be sneaking out of this forested freak-show soon enough and then we could forget about each other.

The watch was still where I'd left it, so I picked it up. It was closer to eleven o'clock. I put it to my ear before putting it back on my wrist. "It still works, Ben. It could have been yours for a cup of coffee or a squirrel sandwich, too bad, so sad. You missed out."

As usual, there was no reply.

The right side of the plane was just as I'd imagined. The pothole that had rewarded me with water was just where I'd expected it to be. It wouldn't give me water today, but I drew comfort from the cool, firm mud on the pads of my feet.

The left side of the plane still disturbed me. This rectangular section of earth had been torn up in chunks. At each corner, a small red flag sat lifelessly waiting for wind. Sod was turned over, but not by any shovel I'd ever seen. Even if there had been a shovel big enough to do this, the old guy wouldn't have been strong enough to use it. In the back of my mind I knew what had done this. I just couldn't get the answer to float to the surface. Surely it would come to me in time.

The damage to the plane didn't surprise me. The deep trench, cut into the soil by the landing gear and the belly of the plane, did. It was one hell-of-a wallop. At the base of a large pine tree sat the crumpled left wing of the plane. It had scarred the tree and scattered a few limbs.

I cleared a few of the downed branches aside and made my way through the trenched-out soil. With my hands on my hips, I stood at the edge of the field that I'd aimed for. I turned back to look at the plane. I'd overshot my landing by sixty feet. I was so damn close.

A light breeze picked up, causing the acres of blue grass in front of me to sway. It had to be some kind of Flax grain. The grass itself wasn't blue, but the tiny flowers were. A sea of blue stretched out in front of me all the way to the distant tree-line. The waist-high grass was some of the loveliest I'd ever seen. I checked the rocking chair on the deck. It was still vacant except for an old wool blanket, so I ventured further.

I carelessly strolled into the field, my hands dangling by my side. The taller flowers tickled my fingertips. With my eyes closed, I enjoyed the sun's warmth on my face. The sound that had confused me when I had first arrived was the grass. The rustle was gentle, soothing.

A voice broke my trance. "Hello."

Startled into taking a backward step, I looked over to see the tattered girl from the hospital. She was chest-deep in the grass and staring at me.

"What d-do you think you're d-d-doing?" she asked.

70

I looked at her in disbelief. A part of me wanted to reach out and touch her, see if she was real "How…"

"H-h-h-ow am I h-h-here?" She gave a frustrated wince as she stuttered.

"Yes. Who are you?"

"I'm your e-e-enemy, y-y-your friend, the g-girl in your d-d-dreams."

"I don't understand." But I think I did. This was a dream, induced by the alcohol. I tried to pinch myself, but my fingers couldn't co-ordinate the move.

"Are you s-s-sorry yet, J-J-Johnny?"

An odd panic edged me back. Why would she ask that?

The girl waited patiently for a reply. She smiled at me and her playful wink broke my silence. I wasn't sure why, but I spoke the words as if they were willed from me. "I'm Sorry."

"Not g-good enough, Johnny. Y-y-you really should try h-h-harder."

"What the hell am I apologising for?"

"F-f-fuck you then!"

"Excuse me? You don't talk to adults like that." Shit, she was seven, if a day.

She continued to stare. A part of me expected to see a nurse or parent appear from behind a tree to usher her away. "Why d-d-do you h-h-ate me?"

"Hate you, I don't even know you." I had to remind myself this was a dream. I couldn't get upset with the kid. "What are you doing here?"

"I w-w-ant to h-h-help you."

"Help me?" I didn't see that coming. "Why? How?"

"I'm your e-e-enemy, y-y-your friend, the g-girl in your d-d-dreams."

"I got that the first time." I didn't, but I was afraid of coming across as stupid. "Am I dead?"

"Not y-y-y-et, but you w-w-will be if y-you're not c-c-careful."

"So how can you help me?"

"Are you th-th-thirsty?"

"Yes." I wanted a beer. Even in a dream, I'd take it.

"Then dr-dr-drink."

I looked around. "Drink, what? There's no water."

"Th-There is if y-you l-l-look for it."

"What are you talking about? There's nothing."

"There's w-w-water. Wake up and f-f-find it, J-J-Johnny. There's w-water all around y-y-you, if you look f-for it."

"Where?"

"Do y-y-you want me to d-d-drink it f-f-for you, t-t-too?"

"Whatever." I started back to the plane. Not that I minded having my sight back, but I knew I this wasn't real. I'd had enough of this foolishness and needed to find the way back to my world.

"Have a g-g-good d-day, J-J-Johnny, and d-d-don't f-forget the eyes. We all f-f-feel them y-y-y-ou know."

"What, that old guy? He's harmless."

"You d-d-don't understand," she continued. "They w-w-watch you at n-n-night and they aren't w-w-what you think. They're a l-l-lot more d-d-dangerous. You underestimate them. That's a m-m-m-mistake. They have t-teeth and they want to b-b-bite you and b-b-bite you b-b-bad. If you're n-not careful, they w-w-w…" She stopped and swallowed hard. "Will."

"Damn whiskey. I need to sleep this off. It's been, uh, nice talking to ya." I was sure the old guy didn't have writer stew on his menu…well pretty sure. I walked back to the plane. I hoped it was time to wake up. It wasn't.

The plane was right where I'd left it and I climbed back inside. I suddenly didn't feel that safe in the open, although I had no idea as to why. I locked the door. The empty whiskey bottle spun as I brushed it with my foot. Mesmerised, I watched it spin slower and slower until it eventually stopped, pointing at me. "What the hell." I wasn't sure what that meant, but it made me nervous. I picked it up and tossed it outside.

As I bent over I noticed a pen, hiding on the dashboard under a pile of broken glass. I grabbed it and started to write a note to Katie on the inside cover of one of my novels. It wasn't hard to find the words. My love for her had never been stronger and it was clear how she had made my life full and beautiful. Soon I'd be dying, so before I went I needed to tell her how I felt, and that I was sorry. She deserved it.

As I wrote, the pen fought my grip like it was fighting my thoughts. I pulled my hand away and watched as the pen finished the note. It wrote a hardened truth, that the only part I'd regretted was getting caught, that I'd have been back for seconds, otherwise. The pen clicked shut and set itself down in the crease of the book. The words weren't what I would have written. I wanted to make them disappear, rip the book up, crumple the page and eat it, but my body wouldn't let me.

There had to be a reason for this dream. What was it trying to tell me? I tried to nap it off, but 'mother's cold stare' had come back to life. The red glow on the no-longer-broken gauges made me want the blindness back. A whispering, through the walls of the plane, warned me to be careful what I wished for. It was the girl. She said I'd be waking up to my blindness soon enough and when I did, the eyes would be watching, because they're always watching.

'They have t-teeth and they want to b-bite you…b-b-b-bite you b-b-bad.'

Satan, or Death, had obviously decided to come along for the ride and they were taking a personal interest in my pain and suffering. I had asked for a sign and received it. I think God was telling me there was no hope. Death was out there, and he had every intention of punishing me before the inevitable happened.

He'd start by waking me up.

Chapter eighteen

My dark world returned, as the girl had promised, and I found my eyes begging for those painful rays of light. My hopes of seeing eventually gave in to the darkness, because this was home.

The dream continued to wash over me, and I recalled the pen finishing my thoughts. Earlier I had wanted to find that pen, but like my phone, it was lost in the crash. I ran my hand along the dashboard to satisfy a stupid curiosity. My hand stopped partway. Did I really want to find this pen?

I must have been a cat in an earlier lifetime. Curiosity always got the better of me. As expected, my fingers found the pen right where the dream had claimed it would be. It wouldn't have hurt my feelings, had that damn pen remained lost. I tossed the pen back up on the dash. "Damn it."

The supernatural had always intrigued me, but was this supernatural or some damn parlour-trick of the mind? It was only a stupid pen and I had more serious things to worry about. My bladder was back to being fully functional. I remembered to use the left side of the plane.

It was dumb of me to drink that rye. It was more foolish to drink the last of my water, but last night I was in a foolish kinda mood. I thought God had a plan. Now I think he also has a sense of humour. Either way, I won't be laughing if it doesn't rain again soon.

Outside, I could smell the coffee. Why couldn't he get over himself and just help me? All I wanted was a cup, black. I'd have to keep working on him. "Good morning, Ben."

I paused for a second, because I thought he'd replied. There was something. Was that a 'good morning' back at me? Had he just cleared his throat? It was faint, but it was as real as finding the pen. I strained to listen, but any further words were carried off in the breeze. It was a start.

"Nice talking to you this morning, Ben." I gave him a wave, and that was when I noticed it. There was a watch hanging on my wrist. I had taken it off yesterday, hadn't I? I'd offered it to Ben. I was pretty sure I had.

I quickly slipped it off and tossed it back in the plane. "Stupid fucking watch." How? My mind raced through the possibilities. Tonight, I'd have to sleep with the tether around my waist.

And what about that field? It was in my dream for a reason. If the pen could be found, then why not the runway that I'd overshot? It never dawned on me that a field of flax was useless to me, but indulging my curiosity seemed important. Could I handle another parlour-trick? I just hoped I didn't find the girl. In a dream a crazed child was okay, but this wasn't a dream. I pinched my skin—definitely not a dream. I ran my hand along the outside of the plane as I made my way to the tail section.

A trek to the field would take blind courage, but I was up for it. The rope wasn't long enough to allow me the sixty feet I imagined I'd need. I could only pray that my inner vision would kick into high gear as my hand left the security of the plane. Each step had to be visualised with the utmost precision. The second step was solid under my bare foot and the third found a dip in the trench cut by the plane's underbelly. There was no fourth step, just the impact of my body landing face-down in the dirt.

I slowly picked myself up, clapped the dust off my hands and hoped the old man was inside his cabin. Otherwise he might have spit his teeth across the veranda. He'd blame me. There was no clattering of teeth on the planks, so I quickly reached back and recalibrated my direction for a second attempt. See the ground…be the ground, o' grasshopper.

In my dream, the field was sixty feet behind the plane. That meant twenty good paces. I could use the direction of the trench as my compass. The damn hole wasn't more than a foot at its deepest, but it made pacing uniform steps difficult.

On the fifteenth step, the trench ended. A sharp rock dug into the pad of my foot on the seventeenth. This was a bad idea. I stopped for a second to let my blindness paint the pathway in my mind. Something was telling me that I was close. The eighteenth and nineteenth steps soothed my dry, cracked feet. It also put a smile on my face. Funny how standing in an inch of cool water could do that.

God had placed a field of blue in my dream, not one of gold. If I'd thought about it, the water shouldn't have surprised me, yet it did.

I badly wanted to plunge my face into the pool. But was this a lake, a swamp, or an oversized puddle. I'd have to drink it no matter what, but I'd enjoy it more if I knew what I was guzzling. Wouldn't it be ironic if I died of beaver fever? I had to remind myself that God had a sense of humour.

Another thought crossed my mind. Had I been flying over this during the day, I'd have seen the greens and blues of the different depths. I'd have seen the gravel shorelines. I didn't. When I flew over, it was dark. The flatness I saw was a blackened landing strip. I was lucky to have overshot it.

Where a puddle would end my hopes of survival, a lake would put the ball back in my court. Reaching down, my fingers picked through the soil and I gathered up a rock. I hoped it was the one that had hurt my foot, but this was a rocky shoreline. There was a good chance I'd find that same rock with my other foot on the way back to the plane. I tossed the rock as hard as I could and waited. On hearing the distant splash, I dropped to my knees and drank.

First the pen, then the water, I was two for two, yet I shuddered at the other part of that dream. In it, the young girl with the tangled hair and the tattered dress had warned me of the eyes. She had told me they were dangerous. Was Ben going to be a problem?

I could feel him staring at me as I drank.

Chapter nineteen

I was barely aware that I'd mumbled the words 'two for two' as I made my way back to the plane. The pen and the blue field were exactly where they were supposed to be. More importantly, there was the girl's mention of 'the eyes that bite'.

'D-d-don't f-forget the eyes. We all f-f-feel them y-y-y-ou know,' which meant the old prospector could hurt me if he wanted to. But this was Ben, and his only problem was that he was stingy with his food. If he wanted to harm me, he'd have done it by now. I climbed into the plane, grabbed the tackle box, and headed for my stoop.

Shrug it off, Johnny. Any thoughts of that young girl had to be put on hold. This runaway stagecoach of emotions needed to be steered back to the path of dealing with something way more important… my hunger.

I flipped the green tackle box open and blindly took out one of the flies. "Which one are you?"

Each compartment had once been meticulously organised and reorganised until everything was right where it needed to be. Hell, I could have found shit blind-folded back then.

That was before the crash, and before I'd found my tackle box with the palm of my hand. Now spinners and extra line sat at the bottom of the box while the fun stuff, like flies and colourful lures, found their homes in the hodgepodge of compartments that hinged open on either side. There was no categorisation, only a pointy, barbed scatterisation.

Three-pronged lures were tricky when it came to the choice of which one to use. Where some dazzled the fish with bright blues and greens, others stood out with florescent yellows. To me they were all black and a little dangerous to the touch. Fish have preferences and I had learned what those preferences were. That wouldn't help me now unless the fish had become colour blind.

The flies would have been the food of choice. I could have flipped them around in my fingertips to get a better idea as to what they were. The smaller mosquitoes always seemed a popular appetiser for any lake fish, but I didn't relish the idea of using a casting rod for fly-fishing. Blind as I was, I'd hook an ear, a nose, or a tree. No, I'd need to use a small spinner for casting. That was when I found it.

Still in its package was the shiny new spinner that I'd bought months ago. Only a couple of inches long, it would be easy to cast and exactly what the trout wanted. Would there be trout? Whatever I caught would taste good. My stomach gave a growl in agreement.

Getting the line ready was important. Losing tackle was never fun, and losing tackle with a fish attached, when you hadn't eaten in days, went beyond unfortunate.

With the knots tight and the hook in place, it was time to think fish food. So, what were the fish hungry for? I had packets of synthetic grubs and eggs. These things had tempted me on occasion over the last couple days, but I knew they'd have no nutritional value. Thankfully the fish hadn't figured that out yet. They just caught the taste in the water from the oily coating.

Opening a pack of grubs with my teeth, the first smell made me heave, but not hurl. With nothing to bring up, there was little point. I squeezed the packet to squirt out a grub and I heaved again.

"Hey little grubby, you better catch me a fish?" I smiled as I imagined it nodding back at me. After slipping the grub into position, I made sure the tackle box was closed. I could see myself knocking it over and falling amongst the hooks again.

My orientation skills were really starting to shine. I could sense the way to go to the water and the way back to the plane. The trench helped. My mind was mapping out the site with incredible detail.

Twelve steps from the plane's tail was a small exposed root to step over, and a handful more steps would take me out of the hole. Since shoes held a blanket over my mapping senses, I enjoyed the feel of bare-footing it. From the end of the trench, the ground started to firm up. After stepping on a few more rocks, I found the water's edge. I threw a handful of small rocks into the water for orientation.

I held the rod close to my chest and decided to say a prayer. God had given me this lake in a dream and hopefully it was for the fishing. The prayer finished with a light kiss on the fishing rod. "Please catch me some lunch." I let out a nervous laugh. "…or supper. I've got all day."

The afternoon heat was getting intense, not that the heat was a telltale of the time. Without heavy cloud-cover, the mornings had also been blistering. I could sure tell when the odd cloud swept by. There'd be such a difference in temperature.

Whirrrrr.

The spinner pulled the line through the air with ease before plunking through the surface of the water. The whisper-like sploosh let me know it was time to start reeling the line back in. Over and over I cast the line, only to bring it back empty.

Dismayed by my bad luck, I concluded that it wasn't me. This spot sucked. One good thing about fishing was the belief in a better spot around the corner. Hunger would push me to find that spot.

It would also push me further from my home.

Chapter twenty

Catching a fish, winning a lottery; they were similar if you thought about it. You started off with hope and you were a winner, providing you could ignore the more likely outcome. As it stood, I had winning lottery tickets in my wallet and I had a delicious meal, inches from my hook. I just had to hold on to that hope.

To find a better spot meant venturing further from the plane. Before I wandered off, I needed to mark this section of shoreline. Losing the plane would be like washing a wallet full of lottery tickets. Worse, it would guarantee my death. I set my rod down and felt my way back to the plane to retrieve the tether rope.

I returned to the lake and worked a branch into the ground about five feet off the shore. I worked a second stick into the dirt of the plane's trench. The ends of the rope connected the two branches. It was by-no-means a fence, but if I kept to the shore, I couldn't miss this marker. Heck, by setting an obstruction up, I could follow the shoreline all the way around this lake if I wanted. I didn't want to, but at least I had a reference point back to the plane.

I took one packet of grubs and the rod. The tackle box was too heavy to drag along. I'd leave it by my makeshift fence as an added marker for the plane's location. My world, now complete with acres and acres of undisturbed nature, a cosy plane, and a lake full of fish was starting to look a lot better.

Casting along the water's edge, I worked my way up the shoreline. Sadly, the fisherman's mojo that I'd hoped for wasn't happening. The waters remained barren to my lure. I kept moving. The shore was easy enough to manoeuvre. Still, without warning, it would knock me over at will. Chunks of driftwood tripped me up on more than one occasion. One particular piece of wood felt like it might be good for clubbing my supper, so I brought it along. Drool formed on my lip at the prospect of catching something. Hell, I'd eat a boot or a snag of weeds.

When the shoreline ended, I had to quickly toss a few rocks to sketch the new landscape in my mind. This part of the shore took an abrupt left-hand turn and the spot sparked my curiosity. I had to try it.

I cast my spinner and it was grabbed as soon as it hit the water. I gave a squeal that sounded like my little girl, Brook, on Christmas morning. My embarrassment was instant and I hoped that Prospector Ben didn't hear me. Bang, bang.

Eating would be a game changer, if I could get this supper onto the shore. The Fish Lottery numbers were being called out and I had the first three numbers. I needed all six to be a winner.

Fumbling with the rod, I almost dropped it into the lake. Yes, I was there to catch a fish and yes, I was determined, but to be honest, I hadn't really expected to catch anything other than weeds and tin cans, at least not today. There had been many times, back home, when I'd gone out only to get skunked. The fish called the shots.

I could feel my line dance and hated not being able to see that part of the catch. It's a guy thing to want to experience it. The bending of the rod and the tug on the line usually got the adrenaline flowing and today was no exception.

Co-ordination took a few seconds, bending the rod, cranking the reel, bending the rod, and cranking the reel. There was a quick splash. It told me that the fish was close and jumping. Without a net, I decided to meet the fish halfway.

The water was cool and the melon-sized rocks, coated with years of algae, were slippery. I staggered from rock to rock and managed to get waist-deep without hurting myself. I'm sure I looked a bit like Andy Capp strolling home after a night of football and drinks.

My heart sunk as I reeled in supper. Suddenly, there was no resistance in the line and the rod lost its bend. Taste buds that had once foamed with saliva were rapidly drying up. The idea of going back to the plane without food had me thinking of a one-way swim. That thought ended when the rod leapt out of my hand and the reel started to whirr again.

"You were playing dead!" I gave out a loud cackle as I scrambled to find the rod in the water. Sometimes the little darlings needed to rest. In all the excitement, I'd forgotten that.

I had five out of the six lottery numbers. So close now.

With most of the line reeled in, I started to work my hands to the end of the rod. The fish tried everything to avert my grip. For a few tense seconds it darted left and then swept right.

I started working my way back to dry land. If I had to, I'd just yank the fish up on shore and fight with him there. That was more my element. I was brimming with confidence as I blindly lunged for the fish. I caught his head. The stick was beside me, jabbing me in the leg, so I grabbed it and swung.

After a second strike, the fish lay still. I could feel the blood flowing freely. It was my blood. I had hammered the hook into my thumb. That didn't matter. They had called out the sixth number. I had a winner.

Now to piss off Smokey the Bear. It was time for that fire.

Chapter twenty-one

The thought of sushi had crossed my mind as I carried the limp fish down the shoreline, but it was short-lived. Lots of people love the stuff. I'm not one of them. My wife had tried to convert me. She took me to a place called the Sushi Boat when we were dating. I promised her I'd give it a chance. How bad could it be?

We got to the restaurant and I was impressed with the decor. A small waterfall dropped a few feet into a pond with some of the biggest goldfish I'd ever seen. She called them something else, but I wasn't listening. The waiter sat us down at a counter that looked like a big boat. Little boats drifted past us in a moat of water. Each one carried assorted dishes of raw fish. I braved the mental image and tried a few, but none of them tasted as good as the Big Mac I'd wolf down on the way home. Still, she loved the fact that I had tried it for her.

I set the dead fish on the front seat of the plane, and quickly squeezed between the seats. I littered the back of the plane as I tipped the suitcase over. This officially ended any struggle at keeping my darkened world in order. Tough wouldn't even begin to describe how hard it would be if I ever needed to find anything.

And you never know when family or friends might show up unannounced. The thought put a smile on my face. I'd be thrilled to have anyone visit if it meant a big fat pizza and a ride back to my house.

"Stay put," I said to the fish as I exited the plane. "I'll be back in a bit. If I'm not back in five, start supper without me."

My steps were careless and childlike as I stumbled back to the lake. There was no counting steps or strategically outstretching hands to protect my eyes. Crazy, I know, but I needed to gather up some of that dried out driftwood. That lone rock, the one that had dug into the bottom of my foot earlier, caught me again as I reached the shore. It didn't hurt as much this time as I almost expected it to be there. I hopped twice and carried on. I was on a mission.

Feeling around and grabbing one handful of wood at a time was futile, but a suitcase full would burn long enough to grill my supper and dry me off. Smokey would never approve of the fire, but I didn't give a shit. Bears love sushi.

I broke the bigger branches into suitcase-sized ones and feverishly acquired a load. One of the longer branches fought me when I tried to snap it. I'm not sure what happened, nor did I see it coming. It cracked me upside the head making the sound of a bat hitting a coconut. In the distance I heard a faint laughter. The old guy must have been back in his chair.

That made sense. I could feel the eyes on me now. They were stronger. I sensed that the old fart had moved from his rocking chair to a more comfortable lawn chair somewhere along the lake. The sadistic bastard was jockeying for a better view. At least he still found me amusing. No doubt he wanted to watch my fire, since I couldn't.

"Get your jollies while you can, old timer. Did you see what I did? I got a fish. You know the old saying, 'the show must go on.' You might get a second season."

He remained close-mouthed, and here I was trying so hard. I really should learn to deal with his silent treatment. We might be putting up with each other for a while. Besides, I knew there was no reason to be an ass. "Well if it means anything to you, you have me and I have you. I think you're the only thing keeping me sane these days, well, you and Jim-bo. I just want to thank you for that."

I dragged the firewood down the beach and marvelled at the idea of eating. The fish could have been consumed raw and I was hungry enough, but with so much driftwood at my disposal, I'd be a fool not to enjoy a cooked meal. I just wished I could boil water. Some Rooibos tea might go with the meal nicely. It wasn't a Budweiser or a Colombian Dark Roast, but it would do.

"Okay, where's my lighter." I patted my shirt pockets and checked my pants, as expected, without any luck.

The cobwebs of my memory eventually divulged that there was a shirt at the foot of my mattress. In the front pocket of that poorly folded shirt was a lighter. It was a never-fail Bic lighter. I snapped it up while I pondered a fuel source for starting the fire. There was tree moss, dried grass, wood shavings, or…how about a best-selling novel? Again, my smile widened as I found the box.

I grabbed a book from the stack. It seemed a little ironic that the one item that had given me so much fame, and got me into so much trouble, was now going to help me cook my way out of starving to death. Yes, irony worth a laugh.

"Sorry, Uncle Jacob," I mumbled. Now I'd be a book short and he'd have to buy his own. He was lucky to even get one after his shenanigans at the last family Christmas party. "Maybe next time you won't stick your face in the chocolate fountain."

Back at the shoreline the pages were pulled freely from the book and systematically crumpled into a pile. The deeper section of the trench would keep the fire from reaching the forest. The lighter clicked, and the warmth started to warm my knuckles.

I think the smaller pieces of driftwood were starting to take the flames because, before long, I had the heat of a real fire. The flames singed my hands twice as I checked its progress. Wood crackled, and the smell of the fire filled my lungs with each breath. White rabbit, white rabbit. It worked as the breeze carried the smoke in a different direction. If only I had a marshmallow or two.

"Hey, Mr. Fish," I giggled, "I'm going to need you for this next part!"

Chapter twenty-two

When I exited the plane, the eyes were on me like dog crap stuck to the sole of my favourite pair of sneakers. I didn't care. Instead I took a deep breath and shook my head. Why was I worried? He was an old man. I couldn't let him ruin this for me. Things were good. I had found water and caught food.

No, these were just the eyes of gremlins, the anomaly that often accompanied hope. They're pessimists and crawl into the mind only to stir up trouble.

"Hey Mr. Cabin-man." I found my voice trembling. "Supper will be ready in a bit. You're welcome to join me. Uh, you can bring coffee if you have any made."

Waving blindly in his direction, I hoped he'd take me up on my offer. It wasn't an offer as much as it was a polite gesture. He's so shy. Who knows, he might come around and cook breakfast tomorrow. We could hang out if we didn't abuse each other's space. If he tired of me, he could walk me out of the woods and drop me on a doorstep, like an unwanted basket of puppies.

Back home I had this neighbour. Every time I was at the barbecue he'd poke his head over the fence and ask, 'So what are we having for supper?' I'd always bite and tell him what I was cooking. I thought he was joking, but a minute later he'd be standing there with a lawn chair and a six-pack. In time I learned to play deaf. He'd repeat himself two or three times before going back in his house. I hoped it didn't make me a bad person. It definitely cut back on the grocery bills.

Other than the paranoia and starvation, I was quite comfortable in my new home. And for now, I still needed to call it home. The lake had eased my concerns about death. Within the hour I'd be eating, and with fresh water only a few feet away, I could survive until they found me.

I was certain that the eyes that belonged to Ben were harmless. That girl in the dream was messing with me. Sure, they could belong to death, waiting for me to slip up—I don't always pay attention. But here's the thing, I'd crashed a plane and lightning had blinded me. If death wanted me, what was it waiting for?

But I was wasting time thinking when I should have been eating.

With my hunting knife I carefully scaled the fish, removed the head, and gutted it. A poor job, I'd do better with the next one. The unwanted parts found the fire while the meat got skewered on a stick and held out over the flame. I lost a few hairs looking for the fire and testing hot spots. The hardest part of this was keeping my saliva from dousing the flames. How cool was this? I even chuckled, inside. This was going to taste amazing.

I've cooked many fish this way, so I knew it wouldn't take long. Five minutes a side should be more than enough to firm the meat. Again, I stopped to acknowledge the eyes. Ben was watching. Was he hungry? Would he come down with a pot of coffee? Would he shoot me for my fish?

Happy thoughts, I needed to think happy thoughts, so I thought of Katie. That brought a smile back to my face. Going home was a reality now. Except this meant telling her about my affair… maybe. Was I really that hell-bent on hurting her? When did I become so sadistic? I could easily make it up to her in other ways. She was a special woman and I couldn't lose her, not over something as meaningless as Vanessa.

My eyes started to well up. And how were these happy thoughts? I blinked the dampness away and took a deep breath. The fish was close enough to being cooked for me.

The first bite was hot and had me fanning my mouth with my hand. I started to chew it as it cooled, and it was everything I thought it would be. Cooked fish filled my senses and had my tongue floating in a mouth full of saliva. I swallowed and took a second bite. Again, I had to fan the hot morsel. I managed to chew it as I sucked in air over the steaming meat.

Now this was my happy place, a five-star campfire and the catch of the day. I'm thinking a glass of chilled white wine might have been the perfect way to cap off the meal. I'd love a nice Riesling from the Okanagan Valley or a Siegerrebe from that winery in Enderby. Hell, if I was going to fantasise, then a twist of lemon or a few shots of butter wouldn't hurt either.

Nah, this meal was perfect and most importantly, it gave me a new lease on life. Never had I felt a meal's importance like I did this one.

The savoury fish, and the fact that I'd go home someday, swirled my thoughts. In that moment I'd forgotten about everything else. I wasn't thinking about Vanessa, Katie, and my blindness. I'd even forgotten about the eyes.

Eyes like the ones I'd been warned about were patient. They were calculating and relied on opportunities. If you dropped your guard, for even a second, they would bite you and bite you bad.

I had been warned, and I had dropped my guard.

Chapter twenty-three

I landed face-first on the ground beside the trench, my arms outstretched. I hadn't heard the footsteps on the gravel. There was no old guy clearing his throat to let me know he was there, just a single solid blow to the back of my head.

I tried to pick myself up. Why had he hit me and what had he used? Whether it had been a shovel or the stock of his rifle, he had finally had enough of me. I had taken a fish out of his lake and that was a punishable offence.

"Wait," I shouted as I scrambled to my knees. I grabbed at the back of my head expecting blood. "You can have the fish. I can explain."

My legs wobbled as I got to my feet, but I managed to hold myself up as I cowered. Should I run? Could I run? I hesitated and that was wrong. He struck me again.

This time it had to be a shovel. It landed across the side of my leg, knocking me sideways and crumpling me back onto the ground. I landed with both knees and a hip in the fire. Embers stuck to me as I rolled through it and to the safety of the dirt on the other side.

"Fuck you, ya son of a bitch!" I slapped at the heat on my thigh.

He wasn't shooting. Did that mean he didn't have bullets? Was I wrong about a gun? I spun to my knees and raised my hands in self-defence as I readied myself for the next blow. I needed to run. He could have been anywhere in the darkness, so I turned to flee. But what if I ran straight into the plane or the blade of that shovel? I stopped.

"No, I need help." I took a defensive stance, keeping my hands in front of me. Was I even facing him? "I'm blind. I'm not a threat."

He didn't say a word. Instead I heard chewing. That bastard had found my damn fish. I kept my mouth shut and backed away. At least he wasn't hitting me. I shook my head. His first blow still had me scraping my thoughts off the ground with a spatula. I gave him a second to eat my supper before I broke our silence.

"I understand you're hungry, but I need food too. Can't we share?"

The old fart gave me a damn grunt, the fucking caveman. Was that a no? He had eaten my fish. If this happened with every fish, I'd not only wind up black and blue, I'd starve.

"Look, there are plenty of fish. We need to share. Say you get first, I get second?" Again, I held my hands up in front of me, but slowly dropped them. I needed this guy to trust me. I needed him on my side.

He let out a sigh, one that had me believing he was thinking about what I said. I moved my hands to my side, palms out. "We're good?"

There were no words. Instead, he charged me, knocking the air out of my lungs. Water hit me in the back as we both landed in the lake. Damn, this guy was strong. He pinned me and held me under. The weight of him on my chest kept me from sucking in a breath. It also kept me from sucking in any water. I grabbed for his arms, face, or shirt. He held me back. Damn it if he wasn't three hundred pounds, or more. I couldn't budge him.

I finally caught his arm. It was huge. He was wearing a thick coat. I swung wildly, striking him in the arm, in the shoulder and I think I caught him in the jaw. That one hurt him. He recoiled, and I rolled out from underneath him and bolted. Water sloshed from my pants and shirt as I tried to find the shore, tried to get away. I didn't get far.

Searing pain shot from my shoulder, down my arm as he clamped down on it. My chest filled with fire and hot coals rattled around in my skull. What was he doing?

This beast forced me to the ground with a flattening thud. He wasn't human. The power of him was raw and explosive. There was another grunt.

Teeth burrowed deeply into my shoulder, causing my right arm to throb. The eyes had caught me, and they were biting me and biting me bad, and they weren't from Satan. They never belonged to some loner mountain man in a cabin either. How could I have missed this?

These eyes had belonged to a bear, watching me while I fished. The aroma must have made him brave enough to come down and crash my dinner-party.

My mind grappled to create the image of the bear. I didn't want this, but my mind needed to calculate a response. It saw the blood smeared on the gravel, the soot from campfire logs ground into my hip, and the bruising to my leg. I didn't want the image of the bright red blood flowing from the torn flesh in my shoulder, or how it turned a frothy pink as it mixed with the bear's slobber, but my mind did. I couldn't shut it out.

Noises, like a dog chewing on an old soup bone, echoed through my ears as the snotty bear growled and tugged at my flesh. There had been no time for fight or flight. This brute's stealth had caught me off guard.

More powerful than any old prospector with a shovel, I placed him at five or six hundred pounds. My left fist fired off a few shots at what I hoped was the bear's head. They glanced off him with insignificant damage. If anything, his face only hurt my hand. I had to switch gears.

"Let go!" It was a scream meant to scare this animal, but it barely distracted him.

With my shoulder torn open, the blood was starting to flow like morning coffee through the filter. I could feel it dribbling down my biceps. It was blood, wasn't it? Could this bear be a slobberer?

92

I hoped for drool but knew better. Sweat trickled down my temple as I squeezed my eyes shut. A quick snort from my dance partner blew it away.

I awkwardly spun around and got to my knees. It didn't help a whole lot, but how could I concede? My left hook used to be a lot more effective back in high school, so I swung again for all I was worth. The bones in my hand jumbled like scrabble pieces being dropped back in the bag.

This time the bear felt the blow, which gave me a glimmer of hope. I recoiled for a second swing. He slammed me back to the ground and pushed me along the soil. Rocks dug into my back and tore at my clothes. Dust filled my nostrils and choked me as the bear swept the earth with my weakened body.

Sticks and roots gashed at my skin. One exposed root caught me in the ribs and the cracking noise had me gasping for breath. It might have been the root breaking, but a betting man might have put his money on bones.

With a sudden shift, I found my chest pressed against the ground. The bear's breath was now stirring the dirt around my face, as his jaw remained firmly gripped on my shoulder. He shoved me dangerously close to the remnants of my fire. I could feel the heat.

"Please God," I begged as I coughed up a muddy mouthful of blood. "Make it quick."

Chapter twenty-four

Praying for the bear to finish me off quickly was an honest request. The blood pouring from me ended any chance of survival. Even if the bear dropped me right now and walked away, I'd still bleed to death. It would be a slow, crippled demise. I had no desire for a death that was long or drawn out. Nor did I want to live while being eaten in stages.

One of the ligaments in my shoulder had come apart, causing my biceps muscle to cramp up in a lump. Small shots of electricity briefly ran in pulses from my shoulder to my fingertips and they were cold. The damage to my socket and rotator cuff would never heal out here. No, a quick death would be best.

Again, while the bear pinned me to the ground, I pleaded for God's intervention. "I'm begging for mercy. I was wrong and I accept this fate. Just fucking end it already."

Rearing up with my shoulder still tightly gripped in its mouth, the bear lifted me to my feet. Like a rag doll, my legs flailed as I tried to co-ordinate my weight.

He slammed me back to the ground, forcing the air from my lungs. A bed of grass didn't stop the breath from being forced out of my lungs. My brain became lost and struggled to catch up. Even with death looming, I wanted, no needed, to keep track of the plane and this grass was nowhere near the plane. This grass was foreign soil. I was losing my world.

I'd be finding peace soon, just like the fish had found his. Somehow, being just a link in the food-chain made all this easier to accept. God, don't you dare let him walk away without finishing me off.

The pain was fading as my body began shutting down. I didn't get a bright light guiding me to greener pastures, or if there was, I couldn't see it. Could we have it wrong, and there is no bright light. I couldn't imagine blind people getting cheated of such a thing.

As I held onto my last ounce of consciousness, something caught my ear. It wasn't a grunt, a snort or even a growl, but it was somehow familiar. I just needed a second to process the sound. My brain was far too eager to shut things down. Like a computer unable to run seamlessly, it froze, started up, and froze again.

My life also froze and restarted. Would I be able to find the rope that led back to the plane? I had life insurance. Katie wouldn't be able to cash it in if they didn't find a body. Would the bear leave enough of me? Why am I still trying to hold my bladder? No, stop and think. What was that noise?

My jumble of thoughts detoured back to the fish and what it might have been doing before I took its life. Did it hope for death too? What would its life have shown if it were passing before its eyes? The noise, damn it! What was the noise?

My brain danced and faded, started, and froze in an eclectic haze. Why was the bear loosening its grip? Don't let him leave me like this.

Then the noise registered.

If you'd heard that noise in the streets of New York, you'd duck under a car or simply run in the other direction. In the woods though, a noise like this meant a hunter. Yogi, Smokey, or whatever this beast's name was, had just been shot.

Suddenly my mind danced with optimism and my life came racing back to me. Once again, my tether rope, the pain of the stinging gashes in my back, my fish, and the idea of seeing Katie and the kids were important.

The old prospector had come through and the grip on my shoulder had weakened.

Thank you, Ben.

Chapter twenty-five

My thoughts were twisted as I tried to regain my senses. I had been dreaming of bears, fish, broken ribs, and a homeless little girl. Had I been attacked in that dream? My bones ached as I sat. I was outside. The torrents of sanity and insanity roamed around for answers like a child's curious imagination. While some thoughts, like the bear chewing on my shoulder, brought comprehension, others like the grass and the gunshot came at me in shorter, curious blasts.

The answers took their time to surface. A little girl, who'd been hiding at the back of my dreams, had warned me about the eyes. I thought the old prospector belonged to the eyes. There was always an off-chance that he'd kill me, but today he was a saviour.

The gunshot replayed as if on a loop. The eyes had belonged to a bear, and by the way he stood and held my shoulder tight in his jaw, he was a grizzly. Stalking me for days, the smell of cooked fish was as good as any formal invitation—it was time for us to meet.

The first time I'd ventured out to pee I noticed the dirt. Churned and torn apart, there was something about it that seemed familiar. It should have dusted off an old memory. Once, Katie and

I had gone on a hike in the Kananaskis area in Canada. The trail, the Ptarmigan Cirque, was a gruelling short climb with breathtaking views.

There were three things I'd never forget about that hike. There were the elevation changes that left me gasping for air all the way up the mountainside. There was how radiant my wife looked, because spontaneous outings always lit up her smile. The third thing was this odd patch of ground.

We'd stumbled across a section of torn and churned dirt. I thought someone had driven a tractor up there. A passing game warden explained that a grizzly had dug it up. He was foraging for roots, flower bulbs, or a gopher, if he was fortunate. Regardless of his motivations, he had done a lot of damage in a very short time.

If I'd had sight, I might have been able to make the comparison between the bear's garden and the patch of soil beside my plane. In my dream, red flags marked the corners of this area. Red flags were a clue I shouldn't have ignored.

And that old prospector, as real as I had made him, was only meant to keep me from being alone. He was an imaginary friend. Sure, I'd smelt his coffee, but he was made up. I feared pissing him off and having to dodge bullets. That was part of my security blanket. Well, that and I wasn't sure that he didn't exist.

At the time, a cabin with a rocking chair helped solve a few mysteries, like the sudden end to our singing that one night. And then there was the smell of stew and coffee that occasionally seemed to linger in the air. And here I thought I was going crazy. But Ben was real and, because of him, I was alive.

I wanted to call out to him, to thank him, but I was still living in a fog somewhere between consciousness and confusion. The best I could handle was a bit of drool escaping from the corner of my mouth. I'm not even sure where it ended up.

With the confirmation of an old prospector, my imagination ran off again, this time with newer images of the cabin. The vision became clearer. I imagined the three nails in the floor of the veranda, the ones that had started to work their way out of the half-rotted wood. The windows were stained with age and a couple of them had cracks from corner to corner. Inside I imagined a small pot-bellied stove. It was the only source of heat and was coated with crusty layers of various stews that had boiled over. That was my lingering smell.

I'm not sure how I suddenly knew all this, or if I knew anything at all, but everything was real enough in my mind. Thoughts became weightless, floating like snowflakes in a fall breeze. They waited to be dissolved by my slow-returning senses.

Touch was the one that came back to me first. I could feel a burning in my shoulder, in my neck and inside my head. It was intense. The waking of this pain told me that my walk through the daisies was over. My reality was returning, and it wouldn't be as kind.

I had prayed to God for a merciful death and he'd said no.

Chapter twenty-six

A boxer, pounding on a slab of beef in a cold meat locker, was the image that came to me. With every punch he threw, the side of beef slowly morphed into a human body. Eventually it became a limp version of me. The aching in my arm and in my back was horrendous. I wanted to open my eyes, see if that bear still had my shoulder in his jaw, but they were already open.

Shit, there'd be grass stains on this shirt. Would Katie be able to get these stains out of my clothes, out of my skin? When I crashed, I was wearing a white motorcycle jersey. Brook and Danny had bought it for me last Father's Day. Now, it sat on my body like a rag. There had been roots and rocks, clawing at my ribs and spine. The kids saved weeks of their allowance money for this shirt.

Again, I had to stop my brain from scrambling. I was not dead. Nor did I feel the blood trickling down my arm anymore. Why? Had I run out of blood or did I no longer have an arm for the blood to trickle down? Neither was good. Then there was that shot, a gunshot that weakened death's grip. That old man had put the popcorn down and saved me.

My breathing wheezed in and whistled out. It was laboured, but my lungs were working. That was a good sign.

And was that stew? The scent drifted across my nostrils, torturing my stomach. It had to be the remnants of gravy stuck to that pot-bellied stove in the cabin. I'd noticed it days ago, but now it smelled stronger than ever. I could smell the carrots, the potatoes, some celery, and a mystery meat. I just hoped it wasn't squirrel.

Was that Ben humming? What was that song? It was the kind of song that gets stuck in the farthest reaches of the brain. It wasn't the kind of song you heard every day. I couldn't place it. It didn't help that songs sounded different when they were hummed.

No, wait, the song *was* coming to me. It was 'My Darling Clementine.' Well, if that wasn't a typical old prospector's song. It dropped a lot of puzzle-pieces into place. One bear, plus one prospector with a gun, equals one heck of a lot of bear stew.

We all have our agendas and this old fart was no exception. He didn't save me because this show was about to end, or because he thought I'd been through enough. He saw a big old pot of bear meat. It made me wonder if he was using me for bait, knowing I'd eventually attract one?

I'd be smart to sit tight. I needed to get a better handle on him. Saying hello could mean the end of me, a bullet ripping through my temple. That being said, the man had saved me, and I was starving.

Chapter twenty-seven

T he words wheezed out of me in an ill-timed cough. "Hey Old Timer." They got caught in the dryness of my throat, so I tried again. This time, I gentled the words out. "Hello? Are you there?"

Saliva from my mouth-watering hunger began coating my throat while I waited for a response. The old man had to be loading gear or chopping up his food. He didn't hear me. I continued to listen to his humming for a few moments before mustering the strength to try again.

"Hello? Do you have a…" I needed to reload a breath. "A bowl for me?"

That was when all the clattering started. A bowl hit the ground and there were footsteps, lots of footsteps. My mind grappled for images of what the old fart was up to, but his movements were jumbled. Clothes were shuffled, something heavy thudded onto the ground and I thought he slipped at one point. I didn't think he was plucking chickens or carving a pumpkin, so what the hell was he up to? After a few seconds the footsteps stopped and he sat back down. He was across from me.

"You're back," he said. "I wasn't sure if you'd make it or not."

"What were you doing?" I was still trying to figure this out.

"Don't you worry 'bout it."

Interestingly enough, I had no problem letting it go. The smell of stew had cornered my curiosity.

"Are you hungry?" he asked.

"Yes." I tried not to sound too desperate.

The crotchety old voice I'd expected was a lot younger and clearer. His English was a little rough, but I had no problems understanding it. Squirrel and bear stew must have anti-ageing qualities.

"You look a little thin," he added.

"Thin, yes." It was my new diet program. I didn't see any point in marketing it though. It was a tough one to stomach.

Like a little bird, I opened my mouth and waited for my first mouthful. Oh, it smelled good. Did it have carrots, potatoes, or peas in it? It smelled like it had peas. Oh man, I love peas.

"What the fuck are you doing? I'm not feeding you!"

I felt the bowl land in my lap, not upside down, but right-side up. The fork bounced off my knee and I heard it hit the ground. I had offended the cook. "Pardon me?"

"You got one good hand and I'm not your mother."

Clearly, he hadn't met my mother. She wouldn't have fed me either. I grabbed for the bowl and accidentally stuck my thumb in the stew. It was warm, like baby bear's porridge. I shovelled a handful into my mouth and promptly swallowed it.

"Fanks. Ifs goob." And I meant every full-mouthed word.

"Use your fork or I'll take it back."

Please, don't do that. I awkwardly put the bowl down and pawed at the soil to find my fork. The damn thing couldn't have fallen too far. The bowl of stew teetered gingerly in the cradle of my lap as I searched.

"What the hell are you doing now?"

He was getting agitated. My words came out like an apology. "I can't see very well...or not at all, actually."

"What are you talking about?"

"I'm blind."

"Idiot, that's just a blindfold. Still, it shouldn't be that hard to feel around for a dang fork. Shit, it's right in front of you." He sounded disappointed at my lack of blindness skills. He should try it sometime.

I reached up to touch the cloth. It felt good around my head, like how socks feel, warm and protective. "I'm really blind, with or without the blindfold."

"Bullshit!" I could feel him studying me. "How could a blind man fly a plane?"

I gave him the wrong answer. "Not very well, as you can plainly see."

"Don't be a smart ass."

"Sorry. I meant no disrespect." I had to remember to keep the old guy happy. "I wasn't blind when I was flying. The crash made me blind."

"No kidding?"

I pulled the blindfold up onto my forehead.

"Hey, don't take that off!"

"It really doesn't matter. I honestly can't see."

There was a pause. I think he was in shock.

I looked in the direction of his voice, so he could see them. "They must look pretty awful."

"Damn straight," he answered.

I didn't need a mirror. His words shook me. I'd hoped for 'they don't look that bad.' "Really? What do you see?"

"They're pretty raw."

I felt him place the fork in my hand.

I took it. "Thanks."

"That must have been rough."

"Painful at first, not too bad now. They sting all the time and they're itchy, attacked-by-mosquitoes itchy. I've learned to live with that." I started to shovel the stew into my mouth.

Like I'd hoped, there were carrots, peas, potatoes, onions, and, of course, bear meat. The meat tasted the best. I can't explain the feeling of eating the very beast that only hours ago, was eating me.

The gravy wasn't the best I'd ever tasted, but it coated everything with an oily film that allowed it to slide down my throat without much chewing. It all quickly made its way down to my empty stomach.

"Slow down or you'll choke."

I could only nod. I'd slow down, but I wasn't about to chew my food thirty-two times per bite. Even as a kid I knew that was a waste of time. He remained silent while I gorged myself. Was he busy doing his thing or was he studying me? I didn't care.

Once the bowl was empty, I set it down. "How'd you end up living out here?"

"What?" The question caught him off guard.

Why did it catch him off guard? I stopped licking the fork and set it down with the bowl. My brain wanted more, but my belly was already stretched. A short break was in order. "I bet your cabin is nice. It seems very peaceful out here."

"I don't live here. What cabin are you talking about?"

I wanted to point, but I had no idea where I was sitting or which direction I was facing. "Um, where-ever my plane is, the cabin is about a hundred yards in front of it." Suddenly I needed to correct myself. The girl had said one hundred and fifty, and I trusted her. "Actually, it's one—."

"Not sure what you're smoking, but there's no cabin around here."

"No cabin?" My mind took a dip back into the fog. No cabin? Then who the hell was this guy?

Chapter twenty-eight

I tried not to panic. "But if you don't live in the cabin, where'd you come from?"

There was no answer as the man got up and grabbed my bowl. He took it to the lake and I followed his footsteps with my ears. I listened to his boots trudge through the trenched soil with ease. Sure, it was easy for him.

"Hello? I asked you a question?"

He returned only silence. There were bowls to wash.

I figured the plane was behind me. It felt good to have my shoulders resting against the fuselage. It felt safe knowing where it was. By the direction of the dish clatter, I'd say I was sitting at the tail section. I was propped up like a large stuffed animal facing the lake.

The old prospector remained by the shore and this time there was no 'Darling Clementine' hummed or whistled. I'd made him angry. I used the silence to reflect and mustered the strength to lift my left hand high enough to check out my right shoulder. There was no disappointment to feel an arm, complete and attached. It had been bandaged and placed in a triangle sling. The gauze was tight and held my flesh securely. It still hurt like hell.

"Hey, thanks for the first aid. You did a fantastic job."

He took a second before responding. "Don't worry about the guy seeing you. He's blind." His words tapered past me as he returned from the lake. The warning wasn't for me.

His next words were. "I didn't wrap you. I ain't no Florence Nightingale."

"Then who—"

The other person's voice came from behind me. It hurt when I flinched.

"What's wrong with your eyes?"

I gently tilted my head back, seeing only darkness. My neck, tugging on my shoulder muscles, pulled at the tape. Why I expected to see anybody, was beyond me. If this guy was as good at fixing eyes as he was bandaging shoulders, then I'd be reading the fine print on soup cans in no time.

He pulled the blindfold up higher onto my forehead. "Oh, shit man. That is nasty. I don't doubt you can't see?"

"I see black."

"Are they sore?"

"Kind of sore, kind of itchy." I didn't know the technical term.

A zipper opened on what must have been a bag and he pushed back on my forehead. "Open 'em and keep 'em open."

I heard and obeyed. "Gotcha, Doc."

The first drop hit my right eye and took me by surprise. My eye soaked the cool wetness instantaneously. After a couple of euphoric seconds, my eye opened wider to receive the second drop. It welcomed that drop like a drunk welcoming the pizza guy at three in the morning. The second eye waited impatiently. This was an extra cold beer on a hot summer day. "Man, that feels good. I don't know how to thank you."

"No worries." He slipped the eye drops into my front shirt pocket and gave them a pat. "I see someone's a real Johnny Pettinger fan."

"Not so much lately." I was still busy blinking the chilled moisture back into my eyes. "You see, I'm that Johnny."

"You don't say, mate," the man who had washed the bowls replied. He handed me a tin cup with water in it. "Did you write all those books?"

I felt a need to correct him and tell him that I'd only written the one and that a magical device called a printing press had made the others. They were all the same book, but you know what, these guys were fans, and the one was a hell of a good medic. "Yes, I did."

"I've got a friend reading that book. He says it's great. I keep meaning to pick up a copy."

I wasn't sure if that was a hint, but I bit. "Take one. It's the least I can do for that delicious stew and these drops."

"Thanks, I will." He paused. "You were lucky we came by when we did."

"Yes, I can't thank you enough."

"You didn't put up much of a fight. I guess it's not a surprise with such a big bear. It took two shots to drop the damn thing."

I only remembered the one shot, but if he said it took two, then I'd just have to believe him. I tend to nod off at the damnedest times.

"I'm going to get the last of this stuff to the truck." The one who was the medic seemed anxious to get going.

"Sounds good. I've already got a tarp on the meat. We're almost ready to go."

Almost ready to go, did I hear that right? I flinched trying to get up, but the phantom teeth clamped down on my shoulder and pulled me back down. Happy thoughts danced through me like the tiny bubbles in champagne. I anticipated civilisation, a warm bed, and a hug from my wife. I was going home.

These men were my saviours and I'd never forget them. "Name's Johnny, but you already know that. What are your names?"

Again, there was no answer from either of them. I mean, it wasn't like I needed an answer, but it would be nice to know who my new best friends were. Instead they changed the subject.

"So how long does it take to write one of those things?"

I was okay with small talk. "I can't speak for all writers, but this one took me just over two years."

"You don't say." My medic friend was impressed.

I was five minutes into telling my story when, off in the distance, a truck started. Then the horn sounded. My spidey-senses quickly ran a few calculations. The truck sounded like it was one hundred yards away. That was the length of a football field and, for me, a problem. I couldn't even stand, let alone hike that far. Even if it had been a well-groomed garden path that led to the truck, I would never have made it. What was the plan? "Hey um, you think I—"

"You just sit tight. Whatever you do, stay with the plane. There's another good helping of stew in the pot, so don't be shy."

"Pardon me!" I didn't mean to be an ungracious host, but there was something about his offer that frightened me. "What are you saying? Talk to me, please. Hello? Hello!"

Rolling onto my good side, I tried to push myself up. I could barely breathe as I fell back into the blanket. "Hello, when are we leaving?"

I stopped calling when I heard the revving engine. My heart sank back into my chest as the truck faded out of earshot. Had I been left behind? I needed a minute.

To be honest, I didn't need the whole minute. The truck was out of earshot in seconds. My new best friends were assholes and I'd never forget them. They had packed up their things and left me behind. Here I was, stranded and injured. They'd saved my life, bandaged me up, and fed me. So why'd they leave me here to die? It made no sense. Even worse, they left me here without a cabin and without a prospector. Once again, I was alone.

"Chirrup."

"Sorry, Jimbo. It's not the same."

Chapter twenty-nine

After an arduous day of throbbing pain and numbed thoughts, I managed to get to my feet. The buggers had left me. They got in their damn truck and drove off. It was like they were leaving trash behind. Assholes! I raised my middle finger on my good hand and stretched it out as far as I could.

"Fuck you guys."

Taking three steps toward the spot where the truck once sat, I dropped to my knees and lost my lunch. A part of me wanted to get back to my feet and run, chase these idiots down and kick the crap out of them. The fact that I couldn't take more than a couple of steps before puking held me back. "Screw you! I don't need you."

But I did.

What I needed more than anything was my Ben. I couldn't do this on my own. I tried to imagine the cabin again, the cracked panes of the glass, the loose nails. I couldn't. It was like they had packed it up with the gear and the bear meat. Why couldn't I form that picture anymore? It was so easy before.

I tried to slow my breathing.

I stepped back toward the plane and the dizziness dropped me on my ass. I shifted myself back against the plane and sat. As the evening rolled along, the temperatures cooled. Jim-bo returned on evening's cue, but I was in no mood to sing. The sound of that motor fading was all I heard. Even the blindness would have to take a number to this.

There was no doubt that the distance and direction of the truck would haunt me through the night. Was there a road? That thought, and the fact that they weren't coming back, kept me awake. Hours passed before I could accept the fact that they weren't coming back.

In the chilliest hours of the morning, I finally swallowed the truth. Like a fist to the gut, it hit me harder than the bear had. I'd get over it. It was harder to accept the fact that my grey-haired old friend wasn't real. Those two idiots might as well have ruined Christmas or shot the head off the Easter Bunny. They'd likely make stew out of him too. Sadly, I'd likely eat it.

I always knew that there was an off-chance that the cabin didn't exist, but it was my lottery ticket.

"Chirrup."

I laughed at God's humour. Of course, I still had a friend in Jim-bo. His happy-go-lucky attitude had me wanting to play my guitar. If only I could, I might have picked it up and did a morning sing-along. My arm, gnawed on by a ghost of a bear, was done for the duration. My biceps muscle was knotted, and my shoulder ached. Ribs felt jumbled, like a three-year-old had rearranged them. I was sure the one tendon in my arm was completely severed. That would make getting the rest of the stew a challenge, not that a challenge would stop me. "Sorry Jim-bo. Just gonna sit here and feel sorry for myself."

At least my eyes felt better. I pulled the blindfold back down over my eyes and let the pressure soothe them. The drops had chased away the itching, but it would return. I'd put more in them later, if I could.

As the sun began to warm my face, I entered a fresh new day. I managed a bowl of breakfast and let the stew ease my hunger. It was good, but they're still assholes. Resting through the night had energised me and even though I hadn't slept deeply for more than a dozen winks, I felt rested. I'd also stiffened up. A walk around the plane was a must.

Badly bruised, I walked with a heavy limp. Even my lungs twinged with each breath. That being said, there was a bigger issue brewing. I'd be willing to hang around and make the best of a bad situation, if I still had the hope of an old prospector saving me. I could also wait for a rescue team, but I had to accept the fact that they weren't coming. They had no idea where I was, which meant I had no reason to stay here. Finally, I'd dreamt of picking up my watch and it was on my wrist when I awoke. I think I may have been sleepwalking. What if I did it again? What if I woke up and I'd strayed from the plane?

Two men driving a truck meant there was a road. Sure, this was just some dirt road that saw next to no traffic, but it had to hook up with a busier road, a paved one. Like rivers, these arteries all lead somewhere and that somewhere was my way out.

It might take days, or weeks, but soon I'd stumble across that town or city at the other end of this road and I'd find people. I'd sat around too long waiting for the what-ifs.

Today I'd continue to rest my shoulder and ribs. Tomorrow, I'd take this freak-show on the road, provided that I could find it.

Chapter thirty

When the morning came I removed my sleepwalking tether. I sat in the doorway of the plane and did a quick assessment. Today was a lot better than yesterday. Still, my blind gaze wandered off to what had to be a road. My mind, always searching outside the box, had grown unmistakably curious over the last twenty-four hours. The truck had driven off with ease. There was no engine over-revving to free the wheels from holes, rocks, or muck. There was a road and it wasn't a bad one.

But here's the deal, that road could span for miles before hooking up anywhere. I might not make it a mile without getting lost, injured, or eaten. My odds might be better if I stayed, but I hate sleeping with a tether.

Taking chances had been the one thing that had eluded me most of my life. It had kept me in my hometown, kept me at a blue-collar job. It prevented me from doing the crazier things, like skydiving. But recently I'd thrown caution to the wind and had written a novel. That bravery had rewarded me. It pulled me from my factory job and out of my hometown, albeit only on a part-time basis. That same courage had me buy a plane and got me back into flying. This defiant nature had also put me in a stranger's bed, and on the wrong end of a bear-attack. Courage is a double-edged sword. Which one should I trust?

After breakfast, I brought the leftover pot of stew into the plane and covered it with a book. No reason to let the critters get it. Then I sucked in a deep breath, stepped outside, and took that first step. As I walked, I counted out loud. "One, two, three, four…" Let's hope bravery has a place in its heart for me.

"Five, six, seven, eight…" I walked straight, keeping my steps pointed toward the memory of the truck's noise. My steps were uniform, in case I had to count my way back.

'Curiosity killed the cat, Johnny.' I could hear my grade three teacher in the back of my mind. But I wasn't a cat, Mrs. Crick.

Why did that woman want to rain on my parade? Why am I letting her? In life's tug-o-war, she and my mother had always held the other end of the rope. This was my way out of this forest and I needed to muster the courage to take these steps, yet there they were, tug, tug. I pushed the negative thoughts back. I couldn't let them win. "31, 32, 33, 34…"

I continued to walk and count. Too bad negative thoughts were like boomerangs. What if it took days to walk out of here, there could be a cliff, and what about another bear? I might start bleeding again or pass out. Push, push.

"69, 70, 71…"

In my mind I saw the things that waited for me, like cougars, coyotes, moose, and killer rabbits like the ones in the Monty Python comedies. It was crazy to think I had a chance.

"98, 99, 100!" I stopped. On a positive note, I hadn't stepped off a cliff. On a sober note, I hadn't found the road.

'I don't see a road, Johnny,' Mrs Crick whispered.

"I know."

My mother joined her. 'Shhh. Be quiet, Johnny, or they'll hear you. And you best stay upwind, or they'll smell you. My, what big teeth they have, but you already know that, don't you?'

"Thanks Mom, that's exactly what I need." I casually turned back toward the plane…or did I? What did I just do? It was far too casual a turn. It had to be an exact 180 or else I'd be wandering anywhere. Was it exact? It didn't feel like a true 180, but it was too late, no re-do's. A rush of negative thoughts flooded through the gates of calm. "Damn it!"

God, there should be do-overs on shit like this. Now I had to cross my fingers, accept this direction, and count 100 steps back. I'd walked the length of the field and I'd done it without my tether. There was no road, so it was time to head back and make another plan. "100, 99, 98..."

I needed to end up at the plane. If not, I'd be lost and only feet from my home. How did people without sight function in the real world? Sure, they had white canes, but how do you know if you're on Fourth Avenue or Ninth Street? North and East become irrelevant. Could they sense it? "83, 82, 81..."

I'd have to get a dog and a smart one. I'd be wise to get one that bites me in the ass when some pretty girl offers to take me to one of those hard-to-find teashops. And he'd gnaw off a leg before letting me go for dessert.

"49, 48, 47..." My heart was dancing the mamba. I'd give anything to bang my head on a wing or fuselage.

Would there be a plane at step zero, more open field or a tree? Please don't be a tree. This reminded me of my very first trip to Vancouver. I had heard stories of the big city from my friends and could hardly wait to see it for myself. They had everything a small town didn't. There was a roller coaster, parks with miniature trains that you could ride, mega malls to shop and eat in and an ocean. The last eighty kilometres of highway, Abbotsford to Vancouver was as straight as the roads you'd find in the prairies only there were mild hills.

"29, 28, 27..." No plane yet.

Like any child, I'd have to ask, 'Are we there yet?' It was a reasonable question. Mom would always answer 'Just over the rise.' She did that while Dad sat quietly behind the wheel. He knew better than to interfere. Well, just over the rise was more highway with another rise in the distance. Disappointed, I'd ask again. Again I'd get the 'Just over the rise.' I asked about twenty times before the appearance of the Port Mann Bridge ended the game. The anticipation drove me crazy.

"15, 14, 13..." So close now.

The trip to Vancouver was everything I'd hoped it would be. I bought my first skateboard and ate at one of the coolest restaurants. Dad called it McDonalds. The food was ready in seconds. At times I thought I was on another planet. I could only hope the next few steps would bring me that same feeling.

"3, 2, 1 and zero." My last step was more an authoritative stomp. I reached blindly in front of me. There was no plane. There was no skateboard.

"Thanks, Mom!"

As usual, mother knew best.

Chapter thirty-one

The absence of the plane knocked me to one knee. Was it the pain, or my sheer stupidity? What was I thinking? Running off to find the road now seemed like a real dough-head idea. This was where my smart dog would come in handy. Go find the plane boy, go find the plane. Right about now I'd settle on that churned dirt or that ankle-twisting pothole.

Standing in the middle of nowhere, I let a fierce argument brew inside me. On one hand, I might be able to do a 180 and backtrack. Hell, I could keep going until I either found the damn road or fell off a cliff. Or, I could guess another direction. That couldn't screw things up any worse.

My heart thumped, dangerously irritating the vein in my right temple. I couldn't stand here forever. Since there were no options to my madness, I inched forward with arms outstretched. With any luck the plane was close. My steps back to the plane must have been shorter ones, no big. Each swat at the air only produced a sickening void. There was no plane, no home, and no sanctuary. At least the old man wasn't laughing at me. I could feel my eyes moisten. I missed Ben.

I thought of the stew and my stomach growled. There was food just a few feet away. If I were a shark or a bloodhound, I'd have no worries. I could track that aroma from miles away. But I was neither and I'd covered the damn pot with a book.

That didn't stop me from taking a sniff at the air. The smell of bear stew was definitely apparent. The irony of me looking for the bear after it had been stalking me for days, made me smile. There was a good chance this would end with neither of us winning. That kind of shit happens.

The stew began its mild attack on my senses from all angles. My nose, unable to pinpoint a direction, let me know I was no bloodhound. The right side smelled a bit stronger, but did I want to bet my life on it? Why the hell not. I inched to the right and heard a clink. My foot had brushed against something. I reached down and picked up an empty bottle.

The shape was familiar and when I put the opening to my nose, I caught the lingering aroma of the whiskey. I'd succeeded in polishing it off only a day ago, or was it two?

So much had happened since that drink. The girl had warned me of the eyes that would bite me and bite me bad, but she said nothing about a bear. I had a pair of hunters bandage me up, although they weren't all that keen on saving me. Yes, I had been busy. At one point I'd thrown the bottle out the cockpit window, so I was sure the plane was close.

A let a mental image flood my mind and I started to take steps to my right. My second step was less careful and more on a mission. Home was just a few short steps to my right and I wanted to touch it, hug it and crawl inside it. The third step was much bolder and the fourth caught a lump of churned dirt and sent me tumbling headlong. I found my home.

My head met the fuselage with a wallop. Good thing I was wearing my headband. Lying on the ground, I crawled forward until the door was within my reach. I took it all in as I sat on my stoop and rubbed my newest lump.

This daring misadventure wasn't the smartest thing I'd ever done, but I'd cheated death. Being back in the safety of the plane, I should have pushed away any more stupid thoughts of the road.

I couldn't.

118

Chapter thirty-two

Stupid, stupid, stupid, was the word of the day, but that lesson quickly faded. Being lost had shaken me, but it wasn't the only thing going on here. I reached for my watch and slipped it off my wrist. I had left the damn thing for the prospector. I had picked it up in my dream. It was on my wrist when I awoke and that scared the shit out of me.

I had to push the thought aside, so, switching gears, I decided to get back to my routines. I'd try some one-armed fishing. It consisted of left-handed casting and very slow reeling as I grimaced in pain. There was no worrying about the eyes anymore. Today I could fish without the distraction of being shot or attacked.

Two fish ended up biting and they slowly found their way to a campfire. It took the better part of the day and I didn't eat them. Instead I finished off the last of the stew. The cooked fish found homes wrapped in the pages of one of my books. It was no different than fish and chips wrapped in newspapers, a very British thing.

With the day's temperatures winding down, I relaxed and let my wife back into my thoughts. I wondered what she was doing. If I had to guess, she'd be lying to the kids, telling them that Daddy couldn't leave work. Kids don't need the truth. They're better off with fun and carefree. Daddy would see them over the weekend, and, if he didn't see them, then it was only because he was still busy. How long could I stay busy?

I had promised a treehouse to my kids last year and I let that shove a little guilt to the surface. I'd been putting it off for a long time. Not to make excuses, but the promise was made before the success of my book, before all the California craziness had taken over my life. Kids didn't care about that. They wanted a house in a tree and they wanted their Daddy to make it. If it looked like a bombed-out doghouse that leaked when it rained, they wouldn't care. Daddy had done his best.

I imagined Katie pulling weeds in the garden. It was the kind of thing she did when she needed to find calm. How long had it been since the crash? Did I wake up hours after the crash or days? Any clocks that had governed my body had given up. Should I be tired, was it day or night? When in doubt, I slept. It passed the time and it wasn't like I had a list of chores to catch up on.

I had often wondered what it would feel like to toss the to-do list; going to work, cutting lawns, garbage day, painting the fence, book signings, meetings with lawyers and agents, the readings, parties and, of course, all that travelling between California and British Columbia. I'd take those chores right about now.

Had the police been swinging by to keep Katie up to date? I bet she'd get them to stop by when the kids were in school. The kids' teachers would be warned to keep quiet. I imagined both sets of our parents would call her in the evenings, just to see that she was okay. They'd offer their support, assuring her that things would turn out fine and that I'd be home soon. What else could they say? He was a definite goner, to suck it up and get those insurance papers out? Buy blue chip and RRSP's, you can't go wrong with a sure thing.

The tears began to roll off my cheeks and I couldn't stop them. I thought of her as she tried to sleep. Katie and I didn't have the perfect relationship, but it was damn good. We'd cuddle every night as we talked about our days. She was so beautiful and what we had went far beyond being best friends.

I sat in the doorway and looked over what I imagined the surroundings to be like. There'd be mountains in the distance and a large field in the foreground. Some of that field had been dug up by a bear, fucking bear. Damn, my shoulder hurt.

I climbed back into the plane and took my place in the driver's seat. It was time for another nap. Like a cat, I didn't sleep for long. My life had lost order. It was nothing more than a series of naps, poorly chosen outings, and bear attacks. Again, I aimed my blind gaze out the side window as I prayed for that truck to return. I wanted to promise myself no more erratic behaviour, but how could I stay here when my family was out there, while I...?

I struggled to tie the tether around my leg, something I'd have to do when I slept. My kids lingered in my mind until I nodded off. How would I pound nails with one arm?

My kids where still in my head when I awoke. I was dreaming about my son, Danny. He was trying out for the Kelowna Colts football team last weekend. Did he make it? We had talked about it, but I hadn't heard the results. That thought brought me back to the road.

The gears in my head were beginning to mesh.

Chapter thirty-three

They say God hates a coward. I'm not sure who *they* are, but I kept that thought front and centre while I toggled my thoughts between the road and the lake. It was a large utopia for fishermen and I'd proven it had fish. But I couldn't ignore the fact that I'd been here for days and not one boat had motored by. So how long could I live on fish and water, especially with my injuries? Thing is, would I fare better on pine needles and dirt? That was what I'd have if I couldn't find the road. Still, getting out of here was quite the tease.

I carefully picked each item I might need and slipped them into a pocket. I took only the things I'd truly needed; a few hooks, some fishing line, the two cooked fish, my putter (to double as a cane), and a book to start fires. I dropped my lighter into my shirt pocket and searched the foot of my bed to find my laptop.

There's always the chance I might not find a road. As tragic as that would be, not finding my way back to the plane would be worse, so I had two forms of insurance—I'm not full-on crazy yet.

If I could start my laptop, and somehow access my music, then I could use it as a beacon to find my way back to the plane.

I'm blind, not deaf. I opened it up and willed it to start playing. It wasn't going to be that easy.

"Okay, so you wanna do this the hard way."

I felt for, and pushed, the button at the far right—power. With a couple of hard drive clicks, the fans started up and it came to life. It would take a minute to boot up and I'd have to wait for the little start-up chime. Thankfully I was lazy by nature and never put a password on my account.

The laptop fired up and a knee-jerk reaction had me reaching for the touch pad mouse. Since I couldn't see the desktop, the mousepad was useless. I hit the start button and tried to bring up my music, but that didn't work either. I tried to find the control key. By hitting control 'w' my music application should be activated. I typed away, but I wasn't getting what I wanted. After a couple of wasted minutes, I had to hit the control, alt, and delete buttons twice to reboot my computer. That would give me a fresh canvas.

As I sat, I tapped my fingers on my temple. There had to be a way to do this. I needed this laptop. My adventure wouldn't be the same without a beacon. The songs would calm me and bring me home when things went bad. I meant to say *if*. In the back of my mind, I expected things to go bad.

At least there were the keystrokes. For all those people who learned about computers through DOS, you know what I'm talking about. The young kids would have no idea. They'd never know how hard it was to make a file or save it to a certain folder. Long-winded paths were needed. These days everything was done with icons that looked like cartoon characters. Nobody missed the old 286 computers or that DOS program that started it all. For us older folk, it was an effective way to learn how computers worked.

I quickly oriented my pointing fingers on the 'F.' That key had a raised marker for those gifted enough to know how to type. I was one of those people. The 'J' also had a raised marker, but my right arm agonised at the thought of typing, or anything for that matter.

There were two ways to pull up the start menu: the control and escape keys, or the Windows Logo key. Hopefully the second one worked, and the menu opened—I had to trust that it had. By striking the 'Shift' along with the 'R' key the 'Run' application should start. Again, I couldn't see it, but the remarkable thing about computers was that they had to do what you typed. With the 'Run' application opened, I quickly thought about my playlist. It was in the 'My Documents' folder and that was on the 'C' drive.

My next set of instructions had to be right or it wouldn't work. That was the other thing about computers. They didn't do close-enough instructions. I started to type, c:/documents and settings/Johnny/my documents/myplaylist.

I hit the 'enter' key and waited for my music. Thankfully I always had a good mix of songs which meant I'd never have to listen to the same stuff. After a few seconds of silence, I knew that I'd done something wrong. I typed the command again and this time remembered that the playlist needed an extension.

"Awe, what do you call those damn things?" Like anyone would give me an answer out here other than Jim-bo. "Nah, the only extension that Jim-bo would know was .chrp. It's a three thingy; MP3, MP4, PSP, M3U…that's it!"

I added M3U to the command and hit 'enter' again. Led Zeppelin's intro to *Whole Lotta Love* started with its infamous riff. It played softly so I hit 'control v' for volume and used the right side of the touchpad scroll to bring the volume up. Yes, computers were wonderful things. I set it down, facing the road, and quickly grabbed my fishing pole.

The music was a good beacon, but it wouldn't be my only insurance. The tether rope was far too short to lead me to the road, so I'd use the fishing line. With the hook end attached to my belt loop and the rod wedged into the door of the plane, I could venture a couple hundred yards. The reel would let me go with ratchet clicks.

I grabbed the two bottles of water, my fish, my book, and decided to face my fate with confidence and a smile.

Like I had said earlier, God hates a coward.

Chapter thirty-four

I had to expect that by the end of the day, anything could happen. I could be rescued. I could also be dead, and I was willing to accept either fate. Because of the latter, I decided to leave a note. With book in hand, I reached for the pen. It was up on the dashboard like my dream had shown me, except it wasn't. I had grabbed that pen after that dream, hadn't I? I was sure of it. My fingers gingerly brushed away the broken glass as I searched. It should have been there, but it wasn't. I closed the book and set it on the passenger seat.

With my gear stuffed neatly into my pockets, it was time. I slid my hand over the plane and let the emptiness fill my heart as my fingers dropped from its touch. No longer would I consider this home. This was good-bye.

I basked in the mental image of my home for a minute, the busted wing and shattered windshield. I could as good as see the badly bent prop and the ground scars running the length of the underside. The landing gear folded under the fuselage as if made from of plastic drinking straws. That bothered me. I loved this plane, with the exception of those eerie gauges. Maybe I could salvage this plane and turn it into the kid's treehouse. I could see the kids and I hanging out in it, me strumming my guitar.

I'm procrastinating.

The laptop continued to wail the tune. That was my cue to move. Not knowing how much battery life I had, I had to act fast. Batteries lasted about two hours when fully charged. Were they? Before I had left Los Angeles, I'd been on it a couple times to check emails. That, and the fact that the battery was a year old, didn't sit well with me. My stomach growled.

"I know, I know." I oriented myself with the plane's door while I patted my belly. "We've got to do this. It's our only hope."

Brimming with confidence, or perhaps stupidity, I took a bold step forward. Mentally, that was what I needed to do to sever myself from all that was holding me back. My foot caught one of those bear-torn ruts and I tumbled to the ground. I landed softly on my good arm and sat there for a second. I'm thinking this is stupidity.

Picking up the book and my whiskey bottle of water, I stood up, unscrambled my thoughts, and started over. Hopefully this wasn't a sign, merely a misstep.

A sense of pride came at every tenth step. Each grouping was a milestone. Each grouping also took me further from the plane which, I had to remind myself, was a good thing. There should be no second-guessing. The fiftieth step was cause for a party. I could have done cake and ice-cream.

The one-hundredth step stopped me in my tracks. I had been here before, recently in fact. I took three more steps and found a downed tree sprawled across my path. After a quick assessment I realised I was better off crawling underneath versus climbing over. I must have just missed it on my first outing. Behind me Led Zeppelin was going to California with an aching in their hearts. Been there.

I crouched under the tree and worked my way through the opening. The rough bark clawed at my back, grabbing my shirt, and holding me back. Getting any lower with this shoulder was a tough sell. The pain was already bad enough without aggravating it further and yet aggravate it I did. It was the only way to continue.

"Damn tree," I wheezed in agony as I straightened up. With my fingers and palm, I grabbed my shoulder. The pressure calmed the throbbing. How many of these damn trees would I have to deal with?

Seven more steps produced another one. These were windfalls, trees blown over by strong winter winds. Strong enough winds often snapped trees at the base. Trees downed like this were difficult to get past. Although a lot of fun when you were out dirtbiking, they were not so fun when trying to make your way home.

This one was barely off the ground, which made it was easier to climb over. One thing was quickly becoming clear, the open field was behind me, and my future involved trees, lots of trees. I doubted they hauled the bear out this way.

I took a drink to wet my throat. Generally, a fairly fit person, I'd spent the last few months eating fast foods, drinking, and sitting at a computer. There'd been no time for exercise. The only thing I'd done for my health was drinking my Crown Royal with water instead of pop. We all had to make sacrifices. It wasn't much, but it helped me justify the neglect.

The lake water was refreshing, and I took a second swig as Led Zeppelin handed over the laptop's stage over to Aerosmith. They were singing F.I.N.E. fine, but as the song continued the man in it didn't sound like he was any better off than I was.

I tucked the bottle away and fanned at the air with my good arm as I shuffled my way to what I hoped would be my rescue. I took turns leading my shambling steps with my left foot and then my right. The trees were thickening and, on occasion, grazed my headband. I wasn't keeping my hand up high enough. I also had to hurry. With that thought, my sweeping missed a branch and I walked into it solidly, knocking me flat on my ass.

"Where is this stupid road already? Damn it! It's not like I'm asking much. I'm willing to do all the work." It was true. I was the one suffering and taking chances. So where were my rewards? I wasn't asking for a subway platform or a bus stop, just a dirt fucking road. This obviously wasn't the direction, so it was safe to say I had drifted.

127

I felt my hairline. The branch had opened a gash on my head that bled with the commitment of a child saving money. My ears rang, and I waited to see the stars, tweety birds or musical notes. Those were the usual things that went with a good knock to the head. The darkness didn't allow them. I shook it off.

Pushing myself up, my hand sank into the soil. The ground was hard except for that one spot. In that spot it was soft and overly mushy. Shaking what seemed like mud off my hand, I brought my nose into the 'what-the-hell-was-that' game. After taking that sniff, I quickly solved the mystery. I had placed my hand in a puddle of deer piss. It was fresh. I had to let out a weak chuckle. Old Mother Nature wasn't done messing with me.

Muddy deer urine wasn't the kind of thing I needed to smell like right now. I'd be a beacon for cougars, wolves, and quite possibly other bears. Carefully, I wiped it on the ground instead of my pants and moved on.

I quickly found that the only thing worse than stepping over downed trees was tripping over the damned things. I was getting experience at both, and each time I instinctively put both hands out to break my fall. It's not something a person gets a chance to do differently—you fall, and you try to protect yourself.

On my last fall, the pain exploded through my shoulder and pulsed throughout my whole body. I cradled my arm, curled up and rocked. It helped me catch my breath.

As I lay there quivering, one finer detail of the fall kept tugging at me. It was a sound, much like the snapping of a fishing line.

Chapter thirty-five

I've heard fishing lines break in the past—snap, twang. Colourful words often followed the sound. Meanwhile one happy little fish got to swim back to his buddies and show them his new piercing.

By staying very still I accomplished two things. It gave my shoulder a chance to stop throbbing, and it gave the fishing line a chance to make things right. By that I meant reattach itself to the hook. I checked to find about three feet of line still attached to me. I waited close to five minutes and checked again. Nothing had changed.

I got to my knees and started sweeping at the ground. The other end of the line couldn't be far. I found the tree that had tripped me up, but not my tether. Stumbling over the tree, I checked the grass for the line. It's amazing how much a blade of grass feels like a fishing line.

"Shit."

To ease my confusion, I started to pull the blades from the ground. I didn't need to go through them twice. This worked until I had piles of what felt like fishing lines all around me. Panicked, I started to tuck the grass into my sling. That way they were out of the way. Where could the other end have gone?

Like a farmer's combine, I harvested the grass and loaded it away. At first it was a neat and orderly process, but that soon turned ugly. I was tearing handfuls of grass, pine needles and dirt from the earth and stuffing them wildly into the sling. As the sling filled, I turned and dumped it over to the other side of the downed tree. I got rid of anything that felt like fishing line. That made sense, didn't it? Soon, I was breathing like I'd climbed forty flights of stairs. I wanted the plane back. I wanted to sit in that lumpy bed and lock the door.

My crazed high, brought on by the panic of losing the plane, only subsided when I started to black out. I had to stop and catch my breath. My arm was dripping, my chest was tightening, and my brain was pressing against the inside of my skull. Covered in dirt, sweat, and blades of grass, my mind had blocked out the music. For those incomprehensible minutes, the music didn't matter.

Except the music *did* matter. It mattered a lot. I had until the music stopped to either find the road or find my way back to the security of the plane. In between the two outcomes was an unforgiving wilderness.

I did a quick calculation on the time that I had wasted. Boston was playing, which meant there had been seven songs since Aerosmith. At roughly four minutes per song, I'd wasted...

"Oh crap, I'd lost twenty-eight minutes."

Chapter thirty-six

At times like this, I'm told one must stay positive. But, since my book hit the shelves, a part of me had been waiting for the other shoe to drop. I think it just fell. I'm still here, and that must mean I'm not meant to die.

I got to my feet. I could only give this foolishness another ten songs. Then, if I couldn't find the road, I'd let the music bring me back.

Sweeping my hand at the air, I forged on. I took a few cleansing breaths to clear away all the negative thoughts. The mountain air felt good in my lungs as I gave this life-is-good crap a chance.

Katie was a spiritualist, in her own way. She studied all those Tibetan meditation books and even had a Wednesday meditation session with her friends. I usually called her when her session was over. Call it greedy, but she absolutely radiated with positive energy and I loved how it made me feel after talking to her.

Since I already had my eyes closed, I tried to imagine myself standing on the road, no, walking down the road. There'd be a beer with an extra-large pizza waiting for me at the other end. If thoughts become things, then why not imagine that beer to be an icy cold one.

You wouldn't think that walking with your eyes closed when you're blind would be a big deal, right? You'd be wrong. Being caught up in the moment had been fun, exhilarating. I could almost taste the beer. I had also dropped my concentration. My next step found nothing but air. I'd been so busy strolling down that imaginary road that I never noticed the embankment.

The first somersault slammed me headlong into a shrub. Had I not been on such a steep incline, I might have been able to grab hold of it and end the journey. Instead, I bounced like a tumbleweed crossing a busy highway on a windy day. I tumbled and rolled down the entire hill. Each impact, be it a head, leg, arm, butt, or shoulder, sent a shockwave through my body. I counted no less than three times when my head and shoulder hit the earth. At the bottom I found sand, which offered little forgiveness.

Judging from my decent, the hill was about four or five somersaults tall. A foggy conversion to standard measure made it about twenty to thirty feet. It all happened too fast for any real accuracy.

I tried to get up but couldn't. Although I'd survived the fall, the landing dazed the hell out of me. The ground at the top of the hill was flat. The ground at the bottom was flat and it had halted me from a fast tumble with a heavy thud. My face had bounced off the sand like a quarter on a poorly made bed.

The haze that accompanied the impact thickened my brain like fast-setting Jell-O. I tried to fight it—so tired though. I closed my eyes. No, I had to fight it. I opened them.

When I did, she was staring at me. "Get up, J-J-Johnny. We h-h-have to g-g-go."

Chapter thirty-seven

S hit! I reared back when I saw her. I had to be dreaming again. She was dusty, like she'd rolled down the hill with me.

"Awe, d-don't be shy, J-J-Johnny. I'm h-h-here to h-help you."

"Again?" I'm sure I rolled my eyes. "How nice."

"You w-want to be f-f-found." Her eyes drew closer and I could see the wild in them. They reminded me of those feral cats that used to tear apart the bags of garbage behind the house. "I need to w-warn you. Be c-careful what you wish f-f-for."

"Why?" A better question, 'why was I asking?'

She turned to run away so I grabbed her arm. Her head snapped back at me like something out of a horror movie. Again, I asked. "Why?"

"W-Why ask m-me? This is your d-d-dream. I'm j-j-just trying to g-give you a ch-chance."

"If you're in my mind, I should know what you're talking about, right?"

The girl started to laugh. It started out quirky, but soon became annoying.

"Knock it off." I squeezed her tighter and she stopped. "You're acting crazy."

"B-B-Bingo!"

"What?"

"Th-think about it. You've g-g-g-gone over a w-week without f-food and you're a b-b-big chicken sh-shit when it comes to b-b-being alone. Why d-do you think I'm h-h-here?"

I opened my hand. "You think I'm going crazy?"

"No one c-c-can blame y-you. You've g-gone through a l-lot." She slowly backed away from me, inching toward a hole in the roots of a large tree that grew down by the bank of a creek. "Come w-with m-m-me. I will t-take c-c-are of y-you."

"I don't get it." I looked past her to the creek. It led to a bridge. "Is that the road? I want the road."

"No." She grabbed at my hand and tried to tug me toward the hole. "You don't want the r-road. You have to be c-careful what you w-wish f-f-for, J-Johnny."

"What?" I pulled my hand free. "Are you saying I shouldn't want to be rescued?"

"The road is a b-b-bad idea. Y-You'd be b-b-better off with m-me. Come." She started down the hole and disappeared in the shadows. Her eyes reappeared through the blackness. A smile quickly followed. "You owe m-me."

"How do I owe you?"

"Don't s-s-say I d-didn't warn y-you." Her smile vanished as she slipped deeper into the hole.

I tucked my head into the hole. I was more curious than anything. It was black, much like my blindness. But in my dream, I wasn't blind. When I pulled my head out of the hole, the darkness came with it. I was back to being awake and back in my reality.

I slowly sat up. I wanted to forget about the brat, but she'd been right about the eyes. How would finding the road be a terrible thing?

Chapter thirty-eight

I eventually shook the dream and let reality return. It brought questions. Why was it so dark, and what had happened to my plane? My thoughts were a little muddy, but they were clearing. There was a plane crash and a bear attack. I remembered the broken fishing line, the pawing at the grass and the tumble down the hill. There were memories of a shrub, somersaults and an ungainly landing.

There was a water bottle pressed against my thigh, so I pulled it free and took a drink. It was warm, but quenched my thirst just the same. I still had the two fish stuffed in my pants and a book beside me. It was all coming back to me. I held my breath as I listened for the music. Aerosmith was no longer singing. Neither was Led Zeppelin, Boston or Kansas. Instead a symphony of crickets had taken over the show.

"No!" I couldn't hear anything other than crickets. "Jim-bo, shhh! I can't hear my music."

Jim-bo and his merry band continued.

"Damn it." I scrambled to my knees. "Shut the hell up, Jimbo!"

I couldn't hear the music. Without my music there was no way of knowing where the plane was or how long I'd been out. But I'd been unconscious long enough for the laptop's battery to die. The day had cooled down and the fact that it was night put a noose around my heart. I'd screwed up and the price was my winged oasis. Without the guiding music, Death had finally managed to get his hands around my throat.

I was beaten. Maybe a signal fire was in order, and by signal fire, I was thinking one big enough to be seen in New York. I'd light the nearest tree and let it spread. With hectares ablaze, it would bring hundreds of fire fighters and do-gooders with shovels. And if it didn't kill me, they'd find my ass and get me out of here.

The odds of finding me alive would be slim. My charred remains would burn and smoulder for days. They'd want to charge me for the careless use of fire—Smokey's friends don't play with matches. But dead is dead, and that son-of-a-bitch started it. He chewed my fucking shoulder.

I fumbled through my pockets for the lighter. I'd set something on fire, start with a bush and let it find its way to the trees. I refused to lose. Logic had been overpowered in a coup d'état by a much hungrier insanity. It was time to give madness a turn and I was banking on the fact that there weren't enough intelligent brain cells left to put up a fight. Even the disturbed brain cells *deserve* their chance. At the very least they should be given the opportunity to fail.

"Where's my fucking lighter?" I slapped at the front of my shirt. It was right here, in my pocket.

I frantically patted at the ground where I had fallen before remembering the fall at the plane. The first step had been a stumble. My heart sunk. It must have fallen out. I had left it behind.

I sat back on my heels. There would be no meltdown today. With the coup d'état foiled, the few remaining cells of sanity regained control.

My best-selling novel could have been the fuel to start my next fire. Without the lighter, the book was nothing more than an empty plate to a homeless man. It sailed through the air and I could hear it rattle through the branches of a nearby tree.

I was scared to think about what might happen next, but I couldn't help myself. Back at the plane, the girl had given me a lake. The blue flax had been water and the fish had been delicious. Granted, one could go further into the story to say that the fish had also attracted a man-mauling bear that had almost killed me, but was that really the point? There had to be something to the girl's story.

In my dream there was a creek, so I decided to take a minute and really listen. I could hear the water tumbling over the rocks. I got up and made my way toward it. Stumbling to my knees twice, I decided to crawl as the sound of water became clearer. It wasn't long before the hand of my good arm found it. It was cold, wet, and I giggled as I splashed it on my face.

Upstream and to my left I could hear the water getting louder. That falling water was also in my dream, the details slow to surface. If the dream was right, it should belong to a ten-foot waterfall. The creek would lead me there. I had to believe this.

I got to my feet and waded into the water. The gravel-sized rocks on the bottom were small and not all that slippery. Only a couple of feet deep at its worst, it was flowing fast. That made it a challenge to trudge through.

At the base of the falls, the water pooled to my waist. If the dream was accurate, I could climb the bank on the right side of the creek. I refilled my pop bottle and carefully made my way to the top, grabbing at the well-rooted weeds.

Climbing this hill would bring me ten feet closer to home. It didn't seem like much, but I had to remind myself that every bit helped. The top was flat, and I had no choice but to rest. The pain in my shoulder had my stomach doing back-flips. It was safe in the sling and I gave it a squeeze to soothe the pain. That helped, but this time the bandage felt like a wet towel. It smelled sweet.

How could being found be bad? To that girl, winning the lottery was probably a bad thing. They say money ruins people. I say stupidity ruins people.

I let my body rest for several more minutes before mustering the strength to stand. It was dizzying and for a second, I thought I'd pass out. A part of me wished I were back in the plane sleeping this off like a bad hangover. But, mistake or not, I was committed to going home. I pulled the bottle from my waistband and let a couple swallows of creek water slide down my throat. The fish that I'd tucked into my pants remained. I'd need them for later. Food rationing was still a big part of getting out of here.

With rubber legs, I shuffled a handful of steps along the top of the embankment before stopping. The last two steps were hollow sounding. It threw me. I shifted to my left and bumped into an old weathered handrail. That brought a smile. I followed with my hand for a few more steps. I'd found a bridge, and a bridge could only mean one thing.

I had found the road.

Chapter thirty-nine

I knew that someday I'd get to know what it felt like to take one of those crumpled lottery tickets out of my wallet and scan it to find a winner. My heart would race as I flattened out the wrinkles, and my eyes would widen as the red laser light swept the bar code. Then I'd await the results. It always took a few seconds and who, other than those who had won millions, knew what happened next? Usually a winning ticket had an accompanying wha-hoo! Did a million-dollar ticket have that, or did it ask you to see the lottery guy behind the counter? Did balloons fall from the sky like on television game shows?

Ninety-five percent of the time I got the 'sorry, please try again' while the other five percent of the time I got the wha-hoo! I'd won a free play, ten dollars, and once, eighteen hundred dollars. That was a heart stopper. I bought tires for my truck and a set of golf clubs that I'd had my eye on. Katie got a nice dinner at the Gasthaus Lounge and a new espresso machine.

Finding the road was in no way like winning the millions, but it was good for a heart full of hope. Having an ambulance pass by would be more like that million-dollar ticket. I can't say that the positive thinking did this, although Katie would strongly argue that it did. I just remembered catching the fish and how all that turned out.

I gently kissed the bridge deck and could taste the dust of a thousand tires. I'm sure most of these tires were from years past, each tire track belonging to someone who enjoyed the great outdoors, people who loved fishing. I quickly took my soggy shoes off, tied the laces together and slung them over my good shoulder like a pair of ice skates. Going barefoot on these old dirt roads seemed as natural as drinking from the creek.

The bottoms of my feet eagerly slapped at the cool dusty soil. So, this was the road that the poachers had used to abandon me. A narrow bed of weeds divided the two hard-packed paths of dirt. Those weeds would lead me all the way to pavement and that pavement would take me home. The humped centre of the road, not as determined to keep the vegetation out, let me know that the road still saw the occasional traveller. I had heard one vehicle this week. I just needed one more.

The waistline of my pants hung on my hips like a hula-hoop. I pulled out one of the fish and took a bite. My steps were shaky but deliberate as I left the bridge behind. I thought of the bear as I chewed.

Bare feet made it easy to keep my way. The smooth polished soil guided me along like a little lamb. A stick, that I'd originally tripped over and cursed, quickly became my cane. I'd use it to sweep my route for other tripping hazards. My golf club, more a distant memory, was somewhere near a broken fishing line.

I might have been a few hundred miles from home, but I had purpose. And what would I eat first? There was McDonalds and they'd get me my food in seconds, just like they'd done when I was a kid. There was always the choice of a big fat pepperoni pizza. Or, how about a steak cooked at home on my own BBQ? I could down a couple of cold ones while the open flames licked at a nice rib-eye. Once again it was all about being positive.

But I was getting ahead of myself. I stopped and I lifted the headband off my left ear. What was that sound?

Don't faint, don't faint, please don't faint. My temple started to throb again and both knees weakened. I had no way of knowing how many steps it was going to take to find a McDonalds, a pizza joint, or my home. But the sound of a baby's rattle gave me a good gauge as to how many steps it would take to step on a poisonous snake.

The answer was two.

Chapter forty

The obstinate rattling unnerved me as I did my best to wait it out. It was like his tail had been hooked up to a speaker or bullhorn. My shoulder continued to drip down my arm, although some of that was perspiration. Sweat flowed down my back like a small creek and my shorts were on the verge of becoming a pond filled with urine. What could I say? I'd been walking for a good ten minutes and I was due for a rest. This wasn't what I'd imagined.

The rattling didn't stop. I knew it wouldn't. Why would it? Again, one of nature's finest was in charge and standing his ground.

For a moment I considered a retreat. I had usually taken that route when life tried to teach me a lesson. Years ago, a cougar almost attacked me. I had walked into a remote part of a lake where blue herons lived. I had just set up the camera and tripod when a noise from behind me startled the bird away.

All I could do was watch as he fled. Then I turned to see what had ruined my shot. Hanging in a tree, one that I had just walked under, was an angry cougar. I snapped a quick picture of him and started to make my way around the lake, through mud, thick brush, and waist-deep water. I'd retreated because I had a choice. I didn't have that option here.

Where would I go, back to the plane? Finding that plane was as likely as building a time machine out of rocks and twigs, going back to that day of my indiscretion and reliving it without making any stupid mistakes. Breathe, Johnny. Don't throw up. The time machine part I could do—not making the same mistake was harder.

The slowing of the snake's rattle eased my nerves. He was either lulling himself to sleep, getting a cramp in his tail, or he wasn't as angry as he was earlier.

The rattling soon stopped as the snake gently slid over the toes of my right foot. His leathery skin was smooth and cold to the touch. It made me wish I'd kept my shoes on. Why wasn't I wearing my shoes?

For the record, I was never, nor would I ever be, the kind of guy that plays with snakes. They were my kryptonite and could get me running and screaming down a path like a small child. Hell, I bet little children could compose themselves better. A lot of this had to do with Jacob Benz. He stuffed one down my shirt back in grade two and that thing bit me eighteen times before I could get it out. It wasn't poisonous, but it still had me wetting the bed for a week.

The snake's tongue tickled my ankle in short little bursts. It was using smell to taste me, seeing if I was worthy of a nibble. On the move again, it rubbed along the outside of my foot. Please God, whatever you do, don't let him go up my leg.

I really wasn't that tasty, and I'd be a bugger to swallow. The snake's body slithered around my heel and its tail followed. Soon the rattles were caressing my toes, scarring the hallways of my mind. Dare I breathe again, or let the lemonade run down my leg? I decided to hold it as the snake moved on.

There was no way of knowing if he'd left, but I couldn't feel him. What was he doing? I imagined him slithering away, his tail disappearing into the weeds at the side of the road. Positive thinking, they say it works.

I remained perfectly still for a couple minutes to make sure he'd left. In that moment, I thought of my wife. In my mind she was forgiving me—I love positive thinking. When I got home, life would be strained, but we'd find normal. It would be better than normal because I'd learned a few things about myself. I'd be a better husband, a better man. I just knew she'd see it that way too. She wanted me home.

But standing here wasn't going to get me there. Was he gone? I had to take a chance. When I did, the rattling came back with a vengeance. I'd broken the peace treaty by advancing and the war was on. His strike was swift and merciless.

I felt a sharp pain drive from the inside of my thigh, down my leg and through my toes. The strike was just below my boys and although I couldn't see or feel the little bastard's teeth, it felt like the chop of a meat cleaver. The pain shot up my back, through my fingers and bounced off every rib before striking me at the base of my skull.

My legs buckled. The damn thing was wrapping itself around my knee.

The blood, pulsing in my ears and behind my eyes, quickly overcame me and I dealt with this attack the only way I knew how.

I fainted.

Chapter forty-one

Are there beds in heaven? I'm hoping not, just like I hoped there weren't any beds in hell either. I say this only because there was a bed beneath me. It seemed like such a long time since I'd been on one. Flannel sheets lightly pinned me to a lumpy yet comfortable mattress that reminded me of the bed at my Aunt Sherry's house. That bed was not only lumpy but had a canyon running down the centre of it. That mattress trapped all that lay on it. I swear there were a few nieces and nephews that were never found. Regardless, it felt great compared to the plane's seat or that pile of strewn clothes.

If I had to guess, I'd say the snake had put me in a hospital. Someone had found me lying there and delivered me to some small-town hospital. But before I could trade my Sunday football games in for church sermons, I'd have to address two odd facts. They were keeping me from getting my hopes up.

First, there was the lack of disinfectant that should have been clogging my sinuses. Even the remotest aid-stations had that stench of soap and antiseptics. What I was picking up was more of a rustic environment.

The other thing that had me wondering about this being a hospital was the fact that I was still wearing my blindfold and my wrists were bound. Thinking about it, that was more of a give-away than the lack of a hospital smell.

The young girl's voice returned, 'be careful what you wish for.' I'm not sure how she did it, but she'd predicted me into quite a pickle.

So, if this pickle wasn't a hospital, what was it? I took a couple deeper breaths, hoping for that bought-by-the-barrel Benzyl-4-Chlorophenol smell. It wasn't there. No, these breaths that filled my lungs were from a dark roasted coffee. Was I tied up in a nurse's station?

The pot had just started brewing. It was the first couple cups that were the strongest until the last few cups caught up. I listened as the pot bubbled and perked. In that moment I could tell it was no commercial Black and Decker thirty-two cup coffee maker. This had to be one of those stovetop jobs that pushed the water up through the tube, splashing it over a basket of grounds. The coffee was incredible with these old coffee pots, if you don't mind a few grounds.

I imagined the pot sitting on some pot-bellied stove, a stove coated with stains of squirrel stew. Except that prospector Ben had been a figment of my imagination.

This was no hospital and I got that, but what about the fact that I'd been half-eaten by a snake? That bite should have killed me. There would have been enough poison to keep me unconscious to the end. I cautiously wiggled both legs, checking them for any sign of a tourniquet. There was none.

I *was* alive, wasn't I? I had to be. Heaven wouldn't give me something this lumpy to sleep on, and in hell, Old Ben would be spitting his teeth out laughing.

Chapter forty-two

Waking from the snakebite had started with the pungent bouquet of a freshly brewed Colombian blend. It was a favourite of mine. It covered up the pine needles, the dirt and the pollen that had been drifting around inside my sinuses with every breeze. It drowned out the once wonderful smell of cooked fish and the musty smell of the plane…my home.

How was I alive? The rattlesnake was small, a young one, and should have produced enough venom to kill three of me. The young ones never know how much to excrete. They panic and give you everything. I bet his bite could have taken down a moose or bear.

The fact that my wrists were tied kept me from getting my hopes up. I wanted to scratch the itch on my nose, but my body preferred I stay still. My shoulder had a fresh bandage and the pulling of the tape against my skin felt reassuring. It also felt warm, like someone had scrubbed it before wrapping it.

Sweeping my toes to the right, and then to the left, I found my feet were untied. The muscles in my right leg seemed a little tighter, but it moved freely. It didn't feel as terrible as I thought it would.

I let the coffee's aroma embrace me while I checked on my surroundings. It was quiet, too quiet to be populated. There would have been the noises you hear, but never hear, like garbage cans clanking, lawnmowers, kids screaming as they played ball in a nearby playground. And shouldn't there be the dreaded ice-cream truck wailing out the theme song from 'The Sting.' Every town, even the small ones, seemed to have an oddball driving a converted clown-van. But in this room, there was only the sound of coffee beans morphing into the start of another day. Then I heard a voice.

"Well, I don't feel good about this."

"I feel the same, but we're in it now." This voice was the one in control, much like a steely-eyed cowboy.

What was the problem? I bet it had something to do with the blindfold and the ropes around my wrists? Whatever it was, it had them worried.

"Check him out while I pour us a cup."

He tugged at the knot. It was a feeble attempt, not that I was expecting him to take my vitals. "He's fine."

Oh, if only I could push a subliminal message to these two, 'pour a third cup.'

I listened as the heavy boots shuffled back across the plank floor. The chair creaked and strained under the weight of the man. There was no clinking of spoons in the cups. They took their coffee black. They were practical, a clue that didn't tell me much.

In a true gumshoe fashion, I tried to fill in the blanks. Had one of them taken cream, I would have deduced there was a fridge, hence electricity, hence power lines and civilisation, but they both drank it black.

"When are they going to get back to us?" The nervous one asked. We could call him Nellie. He wasn't comfortable with whatever this was…go figure.

"I'm not sure. They just said soon."

I watched way too much television because my mind started to race. Could these guys be flesh-eating hillbillies, Zombies, or one of those doctor wanna-be types, like in those nut-job movies? Today, could some tourist get his wish to be a surgeon by carving out one of my lungs? What if they harvested my organs and sold them on the black market? I'd be uncomfortable with that.

A phone rang, and it took me a second to realise what it was. There wasn't the usual jingle tune of a cell phone. It rang like an old-school phone and for a second, I imagined one of those old rotary phones attached to the wall.

"Hello?" There was a brief pause and the chair moaned. The cowboy one had stood up. "Just a sec."

Boots shuffled across the floor and to a door on my right. A screen door creaked as it opened and then slammed shut. The other man, our nervous Nellie, mumbled 'stupid ass' under his breath. Was that a clue?

His words were soft, but had they physically touched me, they'd burn me no less than battery acid. Both the coffee and a heavy tension lingered in the room while we both waited for the other man to return. It only took a minute.

The hinges on the door cried out again, like out-of-tune trumpets announcing his arrival. "They said four hundred, that's two each."

"That'll do." I visualised the smile that had landed on Nellie's face. "What do we do now?"

"Keep him alive and wait for further instructions."

Chapter forty-three

Footsteps shuffling on the plank floor was enough of a hint that this was a cabin. I listened as the two walked around, poured second cups of coffee, and gave each other that awkward silent treatment. I counted steps and listened to echoes. It was a small cabin, no bigger than twenty feet by twenty feet, or the size of my game-room back home.

"Hungry?" Cowboy asked.

I almost answered, 'Starved, my good man. What are we having?'

"Ya, sure." Nellie answered.

Feet shuffled around to my right. A heavy frying pan dropped onto what had to be a wood stove. Was it one of those pot-bellied types? It had to be to fit in the small space. Again, I tried to imagine my surroundings while my ears filled with the sizzling sounds of breakfast. I imagined the furniture to be rustic and plain. There was no need for the fancy stuff out here. My heart sank. It appeared I hadn't escaped that far from the forest after all.

The sizzle came from the first of many strips of bacon hitting the hot frying pan. My ears devoured the sounds as they sent the signals to the brain. Even my frontal lobe started to salivate as my taste buds waited for the wafts of bacon to greet them. The first wave almost stopped my breath. The aroma poured through my sinuses and into my chest. I didn't want to let it go. I wanted to consume it and go for more, but my lungs were at capacity. With a quick exhale, I slowly drew in a second helping. It smelled delicious.

The cooked fish was such a distant utopia now. I sat there with my mind stumbled by the bacon. The two men talked, and they could have been plotting my murder. I didn't care. Memories of IHOP and Denny's had me wondering if I'd ever get to sit down at one of those breakfast-booths again. It was a crime to take pancakes and syrup for granted.

A cracking noise startled me. It wasn't a gunshot, or a bullwhip tearing skin off my back like in an action movie. It was an egg. With the bacon finished and likely shoved off to the side of the pan, it was time to break a few.

"Scrambled?" It wasn't offered as a choice, but more that this was the way it was going to be.

"Sure." Nellie sat while Cowboy did the cooking. They reminded me of an old married couple. One, tired of arguing, often did what had to be done. The other sat on his ass. I'm proud of the fact that Katie and I never did that to each other.

With the smell of bacon hanging heavy in the room, and the eggs popping and spitting in the pan, I went back to work. Their breakfast conversation was all about the money they'd get from the ransom. It was safe to say that, with money in the picture, this was a crime scene. That was okay with me. I had seen horror movies where mountain people ate strangers. I'd even worried about Ben going down that road. Cowboy and Nellie just wanted money for getting me home. I wanted to kiss my wife and hold my kids. We could all walk away happy.

Still, that tattered girl loitered around in my mind, 'be careful what you wish for.' But this wasn't so bad. I was going home. These guys could have all the money they wanted. It had only corrupted me and caused me to act like a horny adolescent.

And these two men were anything but strangers. I had a sneaking suspicion that they had saved me not once, but twice. There was the snakebite, and thanks for that. There were also the two shots they'd put into Yogi. Had they not come around when they did, I would have been eaten alive. Now they had plans for me and those plans included the trade of money for freedom. That worked.

How did I know it was them? Well, there was the delicious food. Not too many men can cook that well in the wild. There was also the first-aid treatment. The bandages were tight. They held me together just like they'd done earlier. You needed training to wrap ribs or a shoulder like that and this guy had it. You also needed a good medical kit and these two were prepared.

Finally, who else knew I was here other than our very own Cowboy and Nervous Nellie? It wasn't like kidnappers drove around in the bush looking to drum up business. Who knows, maybe they did and I was wrong.

Regardless, I knew who they were, but they didn't need to know that I knew. Breakfast was ready, and I didn't want to miss out.

"Excuse me…"

Chapter forty-four

The blindfold made my words sound muffled. It covered not only my eyes, but my ears as well. I wanted to reach up and move it, but my shoulder kept me from doing that. A cup was set down as one of them made his way over to me. I counted four steps.

"He's coming to." It was Cowboy, the one with the phone. "So how are you feeling?"

He had coffee breath. I wished I had coffee breath.

"Well…" Where should I start, the sore shoulder, the bite from the snake, the bacon and eggs, the useless blind-fold, or the fact that I was tied up? "Where am I?"

The other one got up and made his way over. "We can't tell you, boss's orders."

"Well can you tell me whether I'm in the States or Canada?"

"Nope."

I was willing to play twenty questions. "Why does it matter if I know? I'm not going anywhere."

"Boss was very specific about the orders."

"How'd I survive?"

"Pardon me?"

"The snakebite. The damn thing nailed me right in the leg. It was a rattlesnake, then it brought me down by wrapping itself around my leg."

"A rattlesnake wrapped itself around your leg? You mean like one of those pythons?"

"Yeah, like one of those pythons."

His laughing broke the tension. It also played hard against my sanity.

"Rattlers don't wrap themselves around people. They just bite." He gave another chuckle. "And you weren't bit by anything. You just passed out."

Time to regroup. I wasn't bitten?

"Your leg probably cramped up from dehydration."

I thought about it and it made sense. Whatever happened, I was happy that the snake hadn't killed me.

"Is this a kidnapping?" Ugh, did I just ask that? My mind hadn't caught up to my mouth yet. I waited in the silence for an answer that didn't seem to be coming. Why did I blurt that out? I needed to fix this. "I don't care. I have money. I just want to get home."

"I'm glad you feel that way. Keep the healthy attitude and this'll all be over soon enough. Don't do anything stupid and we all get what we want."

"Fair enough. That's cool with me." Lately, stupid had taken residence as my middle name. These two were okay with that. "Could I get a coffee?"

"Water only. Coffee dehydrates." It was a valid point, not that I cared for valid. The coffee would have tasted a lot better than the logic.

"Look, if you want what's best for me then you should talk to your Boss and see if I can eat something." Bear stew and a fish was hardly enough. "I won't last another day this way."

The silence meant they were thinking. The buttons on the phone started to beep and the screen door slammed as the conversation began. I gave a silent prayer for a plate of bacon and eggs. I still held hope for that cup of coffee, too.

"So why wouldn't you want to feed me and keep me alive? Wouldn't I be worth more that way?" I tried not to sound too smart-alecky when I asked.

"It's just the Boss. There'd be hell to pay if we break any of the rules."

This boss had a pretty good grip on these two. They needed permission to sneeze. What was the harm in a cup of coffee or a mouthful of bacon, other than it being a step closer to one of those artery-clogging strokes? I'm betting this boss of theirs didn't trust these two. They were amateurs.

Still, I had to push. You never knew what tidbit of information you might get. "A real hard-ass, eh?"

Nellie remained silent until his buddy with the phone returned.

He worked the knot loose. "It's your lucky day sport. I'll get you some eggs and a coffee."

I used my good hand to slide the blindfold up. It was feeling a little tight and without the threat of trees branches jabbing at me, I didn't need it.

"Whoa buddy, you'll have to keep the blindfold."

"The blindfold doesn't matter." I wanted to add 'but you two already know that.' It wasn't just the sound of their voices, or the food that smelled gourmet, nor was it the first aid treatment. It was the fact that they knew where I was in a world that was pretty damn remote. These poachers had come back for me, and thanks to them for that.

He slipped the blindfold back down. "Boss's orders."

"Of course." I enjoyed my eggs and got most of them in my mouth. The eating utensils still challenged me. After catching the corner of my mouth twice, I put the fork down and reverted to my hands. Utensils were like eating with chopsticks when you were starving. The coffee cup was a lot easier to deal with because it had a handle.

As I sipped the hot brew I debated whether I should try to escape from these two or not. One would normally want to escape a kidnapper, but these two were my only way out. Again, I needed to push.

"So, can I ask you something?"

Chapter forty-five

The food sat in my belly like a well-packed sock drawer. My stomach was bulging. The different sensations, salty, meaty, buttery, and pungent had found every nook and cranny. I wanted to savour this satisfied feeling for a few minutes. I also wanted answers.

"What day is it?"

"Pardon me?" Nellie asked.

"The day. What day is it." To me this was an honest question. "I've been in the bush awhile. Days and nights look the same when you can't see. I mean, I've lost track."

He seemed intrigued. "How could you lose track?"

"I cat nap. I never know how long I've slept when I'm out. It could be minutes, hours, or days. There have been about twenty or thirty naps. I also have no way of knowing how long I was out when I crashed." Disorientation was easy. "I crashed on a Tuesday afternoon. That's as much as I know."

The two sets of whispers broke the silence. How could this knowledge make me dangerous? These two had a paranoia that bothered me. I waited a few seconds before trying again. "I'm guessing it's Friday?"

Cowboy answered. "It's Monday."

"Shit." Katie must be worried sick. "And the time?"

"It's eleven." Nellie quickly piped up. As if a child in a classroom who finally knew the answer and had to blurt it out.

I felt bad asking, like I was dancing on toes, but I needed to know. "Is that day or night?" Inside the cabin I couldn't feel the warmth of a new day, but that could also have been the stove.

Cowboy answered without hesitation. "Shit! It's morning man."

His words were sharp. Like I had wished for this. I swear from now on, whenever I see a blind person I'll take the time to tell them whether it's day or night, sunny or cloudy, or whether their socks match. That is, if I ever get the chance to know myself.

"Sorry. This isn't easy, and I honestly didn't know." It had been nine days. "I need to phone my wife."

"Already done."

"Of course it has." I was sure it wasn't a courtesy call.

The mental picture came to me and I tried to push away, but it swallowed me whole. The phone would ring and she'd grab it hoping for good news. It was a good-news-bad-news kind of call. The last thing she'd expect was a stranger asking for money. She'd agree and hang up with a million questions. Was her Johnny okay, should she call the police, tell the parents, call the bank? Then she'd cry until the kids got home from school—time to pull it together.

"Are you blurry blind or are you, like, seeing nothing?" Nellie asked.

"Imagine the power going out while you're in a basement with no windows." Hell, I was blind enough to have pencils in my cup and a monkey on my shoulder. Speaking of cups, I held mine out with shaking hands. "Can I have a refill?"

"Why not?" He refilled the cup and handed it back to me.

The heat from the coffee worked its way through the cup, into my hands and warmed my entire body. I could feel it all the way to my toes. For the first time since the rain, I wasn't chilled.

"How's it feel, being rich and famous?"

Nellie wanted small talk, I imagined it eased his nerves, but was this guy kidding? Had he missed the first act of this drama? I wanted to scream. I was blind, half-chewed, and had been kidnapped. "Lately, it's had its pitfalls."

"I suppose it has, but what about when things are going good? Like when you're at your mansion or bombing around in a limousine?"

"My mansion, limousine? I'm sorry, but I'm a writer, not a rock star. There's no such life, at least not for me. Maybe if I was one of those big-time writers." I took a sip. I actually had no idea how they lived. "Maybe if I can write a few more books my publisher might spring for a limo. I'm just a one-hit wonder, the flavour of the week."

"Nothing changed?"

"I have a little extra money, but it gets eaten up quick. I sent my wife's parents on a cruise in the Mediterranean a couple months back. It was something that her dad had always wanted to do. He could never afford it on a pension."

"That was really nice. I can't imagine having your kinda money."

"Careful what you wish for. The money gives you friends you never wanted. I mean, I already had enough friends from work before the money, good friends."

"You left your old job?"

"I did. I almost miss punching the time-clock at the truck plant. It was a lot easier."

"You worked at a truck plant?"

"That was my life from 6:00 am to 3:30 pm. Then I'd follow it up with a quick beer before heading home. Katie would have my supper ready and we'd sit and watch TV afterwards. Some nights I'd work on my book and other nights I'd...well let's say Katie kept me busy." I chuckled as I thought of her innocent advances.

"I can't believe you worked at a truck plant."

"Yes. We built thirty-one big rigs a day at that old factory."

"Well that's just like us, mate. We— "

"Shut up!" Cowboy held the phone for a reason. He knew ignorance kept people alive, stupidity got them killed.

It was easy to tell that these two weren't the swiftest currents in the creek. They were blue-collar boys like me. Workers at a lumber mill or a warehouse, these grunts were tired of punching a clock and were looking for a quick way out. Well they could have it.

"I'm guessing you don't do this every day. I mean, one day you're out hunting bear and the next day you have me tied up while you wait for your next orders."

He had called me mate. I'd only been called that once in my life and that was quite recently. That was the guy back at the plane. How else would he have known I was a writer? The two hunters that had patched me up and gave me meat from the very animal that had tried to kill me. Now they had come back with a plan.

There was an eerie silence.

"Look, I had no idea who you were then, and I have no idea who you are now. Nor do I know where we are, or what your situations might be. All I know is that you've saved me twice and that makes you good people. I'm grateful. You're smart not to tell me anything and I'll stop asking. It's better this way. We can all go home if we relax and keep our cool. I just—"

The phone's ringer cut me off.

"I'm sorry. I have to take this." And out the door he shuffled.

"Have you ever talked to this boss?"

His words hovered in the air, like he was watching his buddy outside. "I'm not allowed to talk to her. They're worried I might say too much."

"Makes sense, I guess." He wasn't even aware that he'd already said a mouthful.

Chapter forty-six

The screen door slammed. Cowboy's boots shuffled back inside and across the floor. I waited for the creak of the chair, but instead got a whisper of panicked conversation.

"A what?" The question came from Nellie, the one who had obediently remained in the room, the one who had called me mate. "I never signed up for that!"

"Come on, we need to go for a walk. I'll fill you in."

One chair creaked, two sets of boots stomped across the room and the screen door opened and slammed behind them. The conversation faded into the distance. I caught cold day in hell, boss's orders, and that the boss would be here soon. There was nothing about ordering a pizza for supper.

"Not to worry." I spoke, knowing they were out of earshot. "I'll keep an eye on things here."

I had to laugh—call it giddy to get home. I'd have to write that into a book some day. Blind, blindfolded and left to watch the place while they took off for a walk. Who cares? I was going home, and it was sooner than later. But for them it was an unexpected visit from a boss with not a lot of trust.

Being alone gave me time to think about what they were going through. I really had to be careful because anything they told me could get me killed. They wanted me alive as much as I wanted me alive. Thing was, they were in over their heads. This boss was in charge.

I say it's a good thing that the boss is coming tonight. To me that oozed efficiency. With any luck there'd be a drop, I'd be swapped for a bag of cash, and by tomorrow night I'd be in my own bed. I may not be able to physically see my family, but I could hug them just as hard. I could also put a pond in the back yard. I'll fill it with lily pads so that the frogs and crickets would come. Each night I'll drive my neighbours mad with my guitar and the band.

My thoughts were already picking a spot for the pond when the voices returned. They finished their conversation outside, forgetting that I was blind, not deaf.

"You're sure about this?" Nellie asked.

"Yes. Now shut up, we've got work to do," Cowboy replied.

The screen door didn't creak, nor did it slam shut. I didn't hear them again until they started digging. There had to be a window to my left because I could hear the shovels, and I would know that sound, anywhere. The blades made slice after slice as they cut through the top few inches of good soil. That soon turned to metal screeching through gravel.

Two years ago we had to replace our fence and I, being as cheap as Scrooge, decided that renting an auger would be a waste of hard-earned cash. I'd dig the holes with my bare hands. When I was done, I had blisters the size of quarters on both palms and missed two days of work while I was on the mend. This ended up costing me far more than an auger rental and I'd never forget that digging sound.

A shovel blade cutting through gravel was like the sound of fingernails on a chalkboard. My teeth cringed, especially when the blade glanced off one of the rocks.

I tried to guess what these two were digging up. Perhaps it was a crate of guns or a map to some exotic treasure. Wasn't I the treasure? I tried to find sense in this while they dug. Whatever it was, it had to be big.

161

After some thirty minutes, the digging stopped. They'd been at it too long for guns or buried treasure. This I knew from my childhood digging days. Two minutes later the door creaked open. The two men were dragging their asses as they sat down. I didn't hear the boots shuffle across the floor, nor did I hear the chairs creak. My heart was pounding in my chest and it was deafening.

"Your boss is coming tonight?" I tried to remain as calm as possible.

"Yes," Cowboy answered.

"And was that a grave you just dug?" My words bled with the fear. I didn't want to hear the answer.

"Yes."

Chapter forty-seven

I've lived on this planet for forty-four years, and in that time I've learned that there were certain questions you should never ask; am I being fired, are you breaking up with me, was that the last donut, and, is that grave for me. The answers were usually obvious, and yet you still asked them.

"So, is that grave for me?" See what I mean?

"We're not necessarily going to use it, but if things go bad…"

"If things go bad? What could go bad? You're trading a crippled, blind man for a sack of cash. This is pretty damn foolproof." Hell, little children too young for elementary school could pull this off.

"Just relax."

"Relax?" Scenario after scenario flashed before me, and the ones that worried me were the ones that involved the police. They had a problem with people handing over their money to hardened criminals, or they just hated to see lawbreakers get away. Either way, I was quite okay with using my money to buy my life from these folks. It beat trying out my new grave.

"I don't know if I like this boss of yours. How about I get you guys the cash to let me go. Hell, I'll even let you drop me off back at the plane." Even with that, there was less than a fifty-fifty chance I'd survive. Those were better odds.

I had to think their silence was a good thing. They were giving my offer some thought.

"How does a million sound to you guys? That's five hundred each." I wanted to explain how much better my deal was, but I was sure they could figure out the math. "Take me to any town you choose, and I'll make a call. My wife will wire the money to a Swiss bank account for you guys and you can drive away rich. Leave me in the streets and I'll find my own way home. Drive for minutes, hours, or days, I don't care. Whatever you're comfortable with."

This time the silence didn't feel comforting. It was a failsafe offer and they should have jumped on it. I could feel the hole being filled in on me. The dirt was cold and smelled musty like the plane. Soon I'd be cold and musty.

And what if the police didn't find me. Katie wouldn't get her closure. Her husband was ninety-five percent dead. She'd stay awake at night wondering about the other five percent. I knew I would. She'd eventually hear rumours of her late husband's infidelity. It would be hard to fathom, he was such a devoted husband and father. She would doubt them at first because it was human nature, yet in time they would eat away at her. Was he alive, living with the other woman?

"Not enough? Want more? It'll take a while but I'm sure I can get you more."

I knew I was starting to ramble, but my brain had shifted gears and was travelling in three directions. I was desperate.

"We shouldn't."

Shouldn't wasn't couldn't. These guys had saved me twice. I knew these two from the plane and couldn't imagine them putting a bullet in me. They weren't killers, although the bear might not agree on that one.

I had to find out why. "The boss's coming is not a good thing?"

"It wasn't the initial plan," Cowboy replied. "The Boss was never supposed to be involved on this end. We agreed to keep them out of harm's way. Something's changed that."

"He doesn't trust you guys." I had to plot my next move like a chess game. I calculated the risks and reactions and hoped I wouldn't screw this up. Never any good at chess, I was worried. "We need to get out of here. Shit guys, you just dug a grave. You can't tell me you're okay with that."

Silence.

This recent turn of events had a sobering affect on the room. The Boss was coming, and it bothered them. The grave bothered me. We were all looking at tonight and were unsure of what it would bring. My offer, on the other hand, was solid. That was the reason for the silent treatment. They were tempted.

I let morning become afternoon as I sat up on the bed. As the day rolled along, three troubled minds went over their roles. Would they include murder charges? It was an honest fear, for a potential outcome. Cowboy thought they had the boss's trust. The change in plans had proven he didn't know as much as he thought he did. They were in over their heads.

I let a few hours pass before trying again. "One million dollars and it could all happen on your terms. I know this scares you, but we're the only three involved at the moment. We can keep this simple."

Nellie agreed. "It sounds good to me."

Both men left their chairs and shuffled over to me. Cowboy was to my right. "One million? How would we cash a Swiss bank account?"

"Forget the Swiss banks. Thinking about it, I can give you cash. The authorities won't be upset if I freely give it to you. It's a gift from me to you and there's no crime in accepting a gift. You've done nothing wrong, nothing illegal. I'll stand by that."

"What would the gift be for?" Nellie asked.

"Shit, man. You guys saved my life. A reward is the least I can do. It's easy money for you and great PR for me."

"That's right. We saved you." He was sold. It was up to Cowboy. "I like it, and it's more than double the money."

"It is. Maybe we could..." Cowboy suddenly stopped talking.

His sentence had been cut short when the door creaked open. We weren't alone anymore, and I could feel that first shovel of dirt hitting me in the chest.

Chapter forty-eight

Cowboy got up and met the boss at the door. Nellie stayed behind. This had just turned into a felony—a crime punishable with a life sentence in some states. I doubted that this was one of those states. I was somewhere in the Northwest. Hell, it could have been Canada, in which case they'd be looking at a six-month sentence with time off for good behaviour. All I knew was that with the arrival of the boss, I wouldn't want to be in their shoes. That being said, mine were no better.

Nellie, the one that kept referring to me as mate, was getting a little anxious, pacing between the window and the door. He hadn't thought this through.

He was mumbling out loud. "Why is she here so early?"

"She doesn't trust you," I replied back to him.

It was the only logical answer. Her arrival had bothered, no, pissed them off. Sure, they had no kidnapping experience, but they were damn sure they could handle a blind man.

"Kidnapping isn't that big a deal. Don't let her turn this into a murder. You can't—"

"Quiet. They're coming back."

The door opened. "Come on."

"Is everything okay?" Nellie asked.

"Everything's fine." There was an awkward silence before Cowboy spoke again. "She wants to check out the you-know-what."

I couldn't help but feel a little angered as they left. We were all adults here so let's call it what it is. It's a grave, my fucking grave. It's where I'd be spending an eternity if things went wrong.

The mere fact that she wanted to check out the hole was a bad sign. It meant that it was pretty damn important. If I were the boss, I'd be more concerned with the item in trade for the cash. I was the one that was going to turn an empty suitcase into a three-way retirement.

The voices were outside and to my left. They wormed their way through the walls and into my head. I strained to hear the conversation, but it was like I had pillows stuffed in my ears.

Earlier I had mentioned that I knew the hole outside was too big for a treasure or a gun cache. That's because, as a kid, I used to dig cave forts. Most kids built their forts in trees or above the garage, but I liked the cool comfort of a hole dug with my own hands. I'd spend an hour digging a tidy six-foot wide hole, no less than four feet deep and I'd dig it into the side of a hill. Then I put boards over the top and covered that with four more inches of dirt.

From high up on the hill, the cave was impossible to see. The opening was on the lower side. Because of this, I could stash it with ice tea, cookies and comics. Nobody would find it. I could spend hours hiding from everything that was wrong in the world.

It was cave-life and it was good until Bobby Swanson decided to ride his bike down that hill. His weight, as he went over my cave, collapsed my roof on me. He'd buried me alive. He also grabbed his bike and left me to fend for myself. It took an hour to claw my way out of that filthy fort. My hands were full of splinters from the wood and raw from the rocks. There was dirt in my eyes, in my mouth, up my nose, and in my ears. Tears of joy turned to mud as they made their way down my cheeks.

I never built another fort, nor did I ever talk to Bobby Swanson again.

My last will and testament specifies cremation. Dead or alive, I'm not partial to ever being in the earth again. Just thinking about that day filled my nose with that earthy stench. I beg you God, don't let them put me in the hole.

As I was saying my prayer, the first gunshot echoed through the forest.

Chapter forty-nine

That first shot was followed by a question. "Shit! What the hell are you—"

Okay, it was only half a question. The second shot sliced through the life of that sentence like a freshly forged sword slashing through an ice-cream cone. It sounded like it might have ended with 'mate' had he finished it.

The first shot stopped my heart. The second sent the fight or flight chemicals coursing through my brain. I scrambled to make the right choice. Staying could get me killed, but so would running. And with the blood loss from the last couple of days, how far could I get? Was there a third possibility?

But my tortured body, now energised by a rush of adrenaline, felt stronger than ever and my shoulder was ready for flight. I had to get out of there. The boss was far too trigger-happy.

I found myself on the edge of the bed before I'd even realised that I wanted to run. I stepped on my shoe as my feet found the floor. They were untied so I slipped them on, ignoring the waves of pain. It was nothing compared to the fear of that third shot.

My first attempt at standing failed horribly and I crashed to the floor in a heap. My legs crumpled, and my ass grazed the bed, throwing me forward. I quickly pulled myself back up onto the bed.

A grunt came from the other side of the wall. What sounded like the thud of a body falling into a hole gave me the visual as to what the boss was doing. There wasn't a lot of time.

Having my hands tied tightly together challenged me, but by the time the second body hit the bottom of the hole, I was ready for attempt number two. This time my legs held me. I took one shaky step and followed it up with a second. I headed for the squeaking hinges on the screen door, having heard them several times before. Over the last while, those squeaks had oriented me to the direction of my escape.

Shuffles became steps as I made my way across the room. I had to shed the once-cautious hobble if I wanted to get away. Outside I'd find ruts, tree roots, and rocks to trip over. I had to be ready for anything.

The door was further away than I thought, but I found it. I went to push it open and met with resistance. Was it locked? After a second push, I pulled. It swung open. With one foot cutting through the threshold, a pair of hands met me. Had I expected them I might have resisted. Instead, the hands pushed me back with ease.

Caught off balance, I back-pedalled until one of the chairs caught me. An eruption of pain almost brought my lunch to the surface. I had managed to keep it down with the first and second gunshots. I'd keep it down now.

What a cruel and heartless bitch. Her touch repulsed me. I could only imagine the cold face of a killer. Her hardened stare would be aged beyond her years and her tattooed body would be wrinkled and marred with scars from knife fights in local pubs and pool halls. No doubt drugs, drinking, and a life of crime would have pushed this old gal into a life of misery and despair.

I expected her voice to be a bristly, low-pitched growl, but when she spoke her words were perky. She had a sweet and surprisingly familiar voice.

"How's my tea boy? Long time no see."

Chapter fifty

Vanessa?"

"So, d'ya miss me?" Her voice was playful, as if we'd just met at the mall for a soda and curly fries. "Of course you did. I missed you."

"Where did you come from?" I settled my lunch back down as I tried to make sense of this. Vanessa was here and that was a good thing, right? I mean, she could get me out of here.

Confusion had me wondering if the shooting was as much a hallucination as the rattlesnake's bite. Vanessa was a lot of things, but a killer? I couldn't believe that. Was it possible that the two men had shot each other in a fight over her, and that she was here to save me? That I could believe.

"What just happened?" I was hoping for something a little wittier, but she'd blind-sided me. Why did I want wittier? Because there was something in that voice of hers, because this was the same girl that giggled in the cutest way every time you planted a kiss on her hip. "Vanessa, talk to me. What just happened?"

"I was so worried when I found out that your plane had gone down. We all were."

"What did you just do? Where are those men?" I wanted to buy her sincerity act, but she was in a catty mood and I was the only mouse left.

"You can blame yourself for that one, Mr. Pettinger. Cutting me out wasn't a good move."

She had heard the offer and it had got them killed. "Are they..."

"You look good, better than what they told me."

This couldn't be happening. Damn it, this woman needed a session or two with Dr Labotomy, and if he couldn't help her it was only because she was primed for the circus of afternoon talk shows.

That being said, I felt oddly flattered by her words. I suddenly wanted to run a comb through my hair. Why were men so weak when a pretty girl dished out a compliment? It was like our mid-life crisis started at the age of twelve and it continued until we died. That, and Vanessa had suddenly become my ticket out of here. I had to play nice.

Damn it, she killed two people. "What the hell..."

She cut me off. "This cabin is nicer than I expected."

"Vanessa, please. I need you to focus." Hell, I needed to focus. "There are two dead bodies outside in a grave."

"Stop being so dramatic. I just said you looked good."

"Tell me you didn't just kill those two. Please, Vanessa, talk to me."

"No! Don't you dare put that on me! You did that. I didn't want to shoot them." She grabbed me by the hair and tugged my head back. She brushed the barrel of the gun along my cheek. "Don't you dare blame me."

"Okay. But they were told to dig the grave." She must have been expecting something.

"You surprise me, Johnny. I thought for a writer, you'd have a better grasp of the English language. Those two men are in a hole. They dug a hole. It's not a grave until they're buried. Now get up. I need you to earn your stay."

Outside, she handed me one of the shovels. It was my fault they were dead, so it only made sense that I should be the one converting the hole into a grave. This wasn't what my shoulder wanted. It wasn't what my frail stomach wanted. Again, I thanked

God for my blindness. I didn't know these men all that well, but I knew enough to realise they didn't deserve this.

I imagined the look of horror etched into their eyes when she started shooting. Surprised at her beauty and subdued by her charm, they'd have been easy kills.

We both back-filled the hole slowly. I was weakened by injuries and in a mental state that changed direction with the wind. She likely had to deal with freshly painted nails.

After about thirty shovels of dirt I stopped and broke the silence. "These two guys, how did you know them?"

"I didn't until they called. They told me they found Johnny Pettinger. Said he was in the bush."

"Why didn't they call 911?"

"They're poachers, Johnny. They'd be far too paranoid to call the police. They felt less threatened throwing me an anonymous call with your phone."

"My phone?"

"The one I lent you. It had my number in it."

Hers had been the only number programmed into it. "I have to ask, what made you think of kidnapping?"

"For the record, I was glad you were alive."

"Then why kidnap me?"

"You make it sound worse than it is."

I imagined her smile, proud to the point of feeling all warm and fuzzy.

She continued. "It seemed like an iffy idea when I was flying out, but it's grown on me with time. It's not like I want all your money. I think this works for all concerned. I'm sure you can't wait to go home."

I thought of the hole that I'd been throwing dirt into. At the bottom of it were two men, Cowboy, and Nervous Nellie. Shit, she'd killed our steely-eyed cowboy. I'm sure this didn't work for them.

I started to shovel again. They deserved a proper burial. Minutes ago, I had carried on a conversation with them. They had made me lunch. Now they were the reason why my shoulder was aching, why there was a dull pressure behind my forehead trying to push my eyes out of their sockets.

174

"So, they said you talked to Katie?"

"I'm betting your wife is an intelligent woman. Is she smart, Mr. Pettinger, I mean Johnny?"

Her question made the hair on the back of my neck rise. I wanted to feel my hands around her throat. "She's very intelligent. Why do you ask?"

"When we're done, it'll make the next part a lot easier."

I was afraid to ask. It was another one of those questions where you knew the answer but asked anyway. "What's the next part?"

"You'll see."

And while she tossed another shovel full of dirt into the hole, I turned, dropped to my knees, and lost the fight with my lunch.

Chapter fifty-one

I struggled as I filled the hole, or should I say grave, or maybe it was still a hole full of dirt. At what point did it become full enough to be a grave? Or did we just need the bodies covered. Personally, it became a grave when Cowboy and Nellie were dropped down into it. All I knew for sure was that this damn thing had taken a lot longer to backfill than either of us had expected. I morbidly applauded her foresight in getting these two to dig it.

My shoulder also appreciated it. Even though I hadn't used it much, the activity was more than any doctor would have approved. Vanessa had zero compassion. She was also hurting. This girl wasn't built for labour-intensive chores. She was built for other activities.

I couldn't see her, or where the gun was pointed. Other than that fact, what was stopping me from wrestling her to the ground?

Would I still be strong enough to take her? I'd seen her naked and she couldn't have weighed more than a hundred and twenty pounds. There was a whopping one hundred and ninety-five pounds in my corner, give or take. A bead of nervous sweat dribbled from my forehead and I ignored it. I hadn't done anything brave or stupid in a while, so I was due.

As we walked back to the cabin, I gauged her distance, the length of her stride, and whether she was paying attention. Yes, I had become like one of those movie ninjas. That kung-fu ninja fella had little on me. She was close and distracted by her recent workout. I could do this.

At the cabin door I took a deep breath before lunging for her. I found her right arm. My grip tightened like an anaconda, or was it a rattlesnake? Who knew anymore? I slammed her against the cabin and heard her gasp. We fell to the floor and I used my weight to pin her while I worked my good hand up her arm, toward the gun. There could only be one outcome—I get the gun, I win the battle. Hell, I get to win my way home.

The fight in her was stronger than I'd expected. We tumbled, but I kept a strong grip. I was halfway up her forearm when I angled my body, holding her legs to the floor with my knees. It was the wildest game of twister that I'd ever played.

By the time I reached her wrist, that light-headed feeling was returning. It was her fury against my desperation. I had to make that final surge. With one last reckless move, I rolled off her and smothered her hand. My efforts had just won me a firm grasp of...an empty hand?

The cold steel of her gun was pressed against my forehead and the click of the hammer being cocked forced me to slowly release my grip.

"I'm left-handed, you idiot. Now get off."

I waited for the second click, the one where the hammer hit the detonator part of the shell. It didn't happen, so I moved off of her and let her get to her feet. "You're definitely coughing up a couple extra dollars for these stockings, Mr. Pettinger, I mean Johnny."

At this point I preferred she call me Mr. Pettinger. I didn't want to be on a first name basis. Staying on the floor, I waited for my next instructions.

"Get up." Her voice was unruffled. "I know you can't see it, but it's a 9mm and it can do a lot of damage. It's a shame your buddies weren't around to tell you. You're more than welcome to join them if you want. Just try that again."

"You need me alive." There was no way she'd dig my grave.

"Wrong! I don't need you alive. I could shoot you now and leave you outside for the critters Then I'd go back to work, like nothing had happened. Worst case scenario, I don't get any ransom. I don't need that money as much as you need your life. No one knows you're here, and no one knows I'm here. Someday they might even find remnants of your rotting body, but they'd never think I had anything to do with it."

"You phoned these men. Your phone could be traced back to these guys."

"I used a burner phone." She laughed.

"You stole my phone, didn't you?" And here I thought I'd lost it at a party. "How'd you know you were going to be doing all this?"

"I'm not a damn psychic Johnny, just an opportunist, and opportunists need to be prepared. I wanted to see what you had for contacts. I could use them, if you had any. I also looked for incriminating e-mails. You never know what you'll find until you look."

"And?"

"Nothing but duds, Johnny. You really need to get out more. Now we need to make that call. Let's hope your wife is home."

Chapter fifty-two

Pacing slowly in her heels, the soft clicking of her stilettos echoed through my ears. It was sexy. She was hypnotising me with her step, clawing me deeper into her web. I couldn't let her play that game. "Did you know their names?"

"Don't go getting all sentimental on me."

I could hear her pulling a phone out of her purse. It was probably mine. "Do we really need to call her? Besides, I thought you had everything arranged already? The guys said…"

"Don't be a silly one," she twittered. "I'm surprised I fell for you. I couldn't tell those two idiots the truth. Never put your trust in the hired help? But seriously, they thought what they wanted to, and it got them killed—better them than me. Right now, Katie is your only hope, so don't blow it."

"So…"

"Oh, damn it, Johnny. It's not that hard to figure out." She circled in behind me and whispered in my ear. It wasn't like back at the tea store. "Your pals are gone and you best get over it. You want out of here, your wife wants to know you weren't killed in some disastrous plane crash, and I want some fucking money. Don't complicate it any more than that."

I felt her breath on the back of my neck. It forced me to cringe. I tried to shake my expression as a series of beeps came from my phone. Vanessa must have pulled my home number from the contact list. What would Katie think when she saw my number come up?

I could feel Vanessa's eyes on me while it rang. "One ringy dingy."

"Don't you— "

She pressed the cold steel of the gun against my cheek. "Who's in charge here?"

"You."

"Right. Piss me off and die! Say one word out of turn and you die!" She moved the gun up to my temple. "Do you really want her to hear your brains being rocketed across the room?"

I shook my head and she removed the gun.

"Now why the hell isn't she picking up?" The sparkle in her mood was draining fast. "Oh, hello. Mrs. Pettinger?"

There was silence as Vanessa listened. I was sure Katie would be asking about me, wondering why I wasn't the one on the other end of my phone.

"I know that seems strange, but yes he's okay. I've got him right here."

Again, there was silence. My hearing hadn't improved enough to catch the other end of the conversation.

"Well yes, I may have done him a service or two." She paused. "But if the truth be told, I'm not a nurse. I'm more like his captor."

No doubt Katie was happy to hear I was alive, but also distraught to know I'd become a hostage. What were her expectations? How could she get me back?

Vanessa continued her end of the conversation. "Let's just say, I will trade a shit-load of money for your husband. If you can't, or don't want to help him, he dies."

Vanessa moved closer to me and whispered, "Your kids are in the kitchen arguing over the last piece of pizza and she has to yell at them to go play outside. Her nerves seem a little frazzled. Spoiler alert, I think the girl got the last slice."

I knew there'd be tears wanting to escape Katie's eyes, but she wouldn't allow it. She'd be strong. She'd be asking what she needed to do.

"I want a million dollars and let me make this simple. You cannot call the police. If I see them, he's dead. The million won't come in the form of cash either. Marked bills raise red flags with banks. I want stock certificates."

Again, Vanessa patiently listened. "Take a deep breath, Mrs. Pettinger. I'm making this as simple as I can."

I could hear Vanessa's fingers tapping on the table. She was about to lose it.

"Okay, shut the hell up already! How about I talk, and you listen. Grab a pen and paper, you're going to need to write this down." She sighed loud enough to get her point across. "Buy up a French venture called Phi Mannix and a German equity called Theojax. I want you to buy up three hundred thousand shares of each and make sure you get them in paper certificates. I want the balance of the money in bearer bonds. The 'T's had better be crossed and the 'I's dotted. If anyone asks, just say it's for a mattress fund and that your husband doesn't trust banks. Farmers used to do it all the time. And do this through a broker, not your bank. Oh, and you had better get on it right away. We'll need it for tomorrow and you've got some driving to do."

There were a few quiet seconds, likely Katie writing everything down.

"Okay. Give me a run-through."

Vanessa let her repeat everything back to her. "Oh, and I'll take ten grand in unmarked fifties and twenties, and don't screw this up."

Vanessa remained quiet while Katie bargained a request.

"Just a sec." She handed the phone to me. "You get this right, Johnny, and you both live. Mess it up and you both die. Just remember that."

I brought the phone up to my face. "Katie? Katie?"

"Oh Darling. It is you. Are you okay?"

"I'm fine dear." I needed to hear her voice, let her know I was okay. It iced the nerves that had been dreading this call. Ice was strong. Now I was strong "Whatever you do, don't come here. You can't— "

The 9 mm made solid impact as it struck me in the back of the head. The phone tumbled across the floor, keeping the connection. It screamed my name over and over as it nested just a few feet away from where I'd fallen. A trickle of blood dribbled down my neck.

Vanessa picked up the phone. "Are you quite finished?"

There was a pause. I could hear Katie screaming on the other end now.

"Johnny? He's resting. Now stop it. There's no time for a meltdown. And when you get the financials arranged, call me. You know the number. I'll give you directions as you need them and don't bother trying to track the phone. The GPS is off. And remember, no cops."

The phone connection ended with a beep. She tossed the phone onto the table. "You never did answer my question. Do you think your wife's smart?"

Chapter fifty-three

Who was this girl? For months she was the girl who always had a great cup of coffee ready for me, always had my phone messages arranged in order of importance, and always made me feel like I was a friend. She knew which tea my wife would like.

The woman never struck me as some sadistic monster, yet the mental picture of two ordinary guys heaped in a hole with gunshot wounds told me otherwise. And there was nothing sloppy about it. It was an effective shooting and their deaths were quick. Only the owner of the second shot, whoever that was, had any idea that there was a problem.

She had heard our conversation. She had heard my offering of money to ditch the bitch. I should have kept my mouth shut, but how could I have known?

I could feel her eyes burning holes in me. It wasn't anything like the stare she'd had before we'd committed our sinful act. That one, also intense, made it hard to look away, not that you'd want to. Those eyes undressed you and started the love-making long before the fingers, the lips, or the tongue. She made you feel like you were the only one she wanted, and the only one who mattered. I pushed the mental image away. Those eyes had no place in my heart, or in my mind. They weren't real.

"Sorry about the knock to the head, but you were warned." Her voice, always in control, seemed to be checking in on me. "How are you feeling, a little groggy?"

My body had seen and endured a lot worse. Right now, I was sitting on the floor, trying to find a way to do this exchange without Katie. "I'll cut you the same deal I was going to cut them. You get a million cash to let me go. Just don't bring Katie into this. I'll call you a saviour."

"Do I look like some hick-town hunter?"

"Give it some thought. You get the cash and I get to go home."

"We just called your wife. Sorry Johnny, but now that she knows, there's no going back."

"I can talk to her. She'll listen to me."

"You cheated on her and now you want to give your mistress a million dollars? Think about how that sounds."

"She'd understand."

"Forget it. We're doing it my way. Now lean forward. This should help." She put a wet cloth across the back of my neck. "Hey, this isn't my fault. You need to learn how to play this game. Just do as you're told and there'll be no problems. Does this help?"

"If this is an apology, forget it."

"It's whatever you want it to be."

I blinked twice. No longer scratchy, my eyes had become quite itchy. It wasn't enough that I was as blind as a bat, but I had to put up with eyes packed in kitty litter.

"Are you hungry?" She was back to chipper. It was like flipping a switch. "I brought a few groceries."

I was starving. "No." There wasn't anything I wanted from this woman.

"Well, we're going to spend a day waiting for broker transactions and tomorrow will be her travel day. What do you want to do?"

"How about we play 'jump off a cliff?'" I struggled to remain calm. I had to do better. Sarcastic remarks would only piss her off and dig my hole deeper. "You can go first." Damn, if I didn't suck at remaining calm.

"That's cute, Mr. Pettinger." She gently ran her fingers across my back from shoulder to shoulder, pushing down on the cold cloth. "It helps, doesn't it?"

I didn't speak.

"It'll be interesting to see who walks away, after all this is over. I'd bet a kind and co-operative man might stand a better chance than an asshole."

She was right. This was why I didn't play these games. I was no good at keeping my feelings in check. I preferred to call it as I saw it, but that could get Katie or myself killed. "You win."

"I always do." She sniffed at the top of my head. "I brought shampoo if you're interested."

"No thanks."

"Maybe later then. We were all so devastated when we heard that your plane had disappeared. Everyone at the office felt bad. You should be happy about that. Most writers wouldn't even warrant a shoulder shrug. It made a ton of extra work for Eric. Book sales soared. Then, days later, I got a call from some hunter. Said he'd found some guy by the name of Johnny Pettinger in a wrecked plane. The number on my display was the one from the loaner phone. I had to figure it was a sign. I knew what I had to do."

"Can I get you to lift me up. I need to get off the floor before I cramp up."

"Sure. I meant to do that earlier, but you were all dazed and too heavy for me. Don't try anything. Bang, bang, you know."

"I know."

She grabbed me under my armpit and managed to hoist me awkwardly to my feet. I struggled to keep my legs from folding. As I wobbled, her shoulder rubbed the blindfold down around my neck. I'm sure she thought I was trying another attack, because she let go of me with a shove. I pawed at her and fell against the table as I regained control. Her footsteps put her at a safe distance.

"Nice try Mr. Pettinger."

"Sorry, the muscles in my legs are still napping." I stood there with a hand on the table. The pins and needles were running from my hips to my toes. I'd always hated it when this happened. I took a shaky step toward the chair and then I stopped. It took me that step to realise it, but I was looking at a chair.

Yes, it was very blurry, but it was a chair nonetheless.

Chapter fifty-four

I rubbed at my eyes and reminded myself not to be obvious. The last thing I needed was her knowing that my sight was coming back—advantage Johnny. Was it coming back, or was this some freaky tease? Don't get me wrong, I'd still be considered legally blind and refused any chance at a driver's license, but I could see shapes. I could see the brown lines of the chair.

"Are you okay Johnny?"

"I'm not sure. I think I got some shit in my eyes when you whacked me. They hurt like hell." I looked in her direction, making sure my glance went past her. Reaching for my bottle of drops, I found an empty pocket. The tiny bottle was sitting with my lighter back at the plane, or somewhere on that hill. I sat down on the chair, almost missing it on purpose. "Can you see any dirt or anything?"

"Be careful." I was sure the sight of bloodshot eyes repulsed her. "I don't see anything. They look damn gross. Do you like hamburger hash?"

And just like that she walked away and started cooking. What was I expecting? It wasn't like she could cook either. I'd seen the inside of her fridge. It was all tofu and take-out. I guess she figured she could step it up enough to make it edible. It wasn't like there was a Tony Roma around the corner, was there?

With the hamburger browning in the frying pan she diced and added the vegetables. It sizzled and smelled surprisingly good. Dirt would have tasted good.

An open can of what might have been diced tomatoes or kidney beans was dumped into the pan and Vanessa took a minute to study the can. There had to be a recipe on it. I kept blinking and it distracted her. "What's with your eyes? Are you okay?"

"No. They'd feel a lot better if you let me go."

"Sorry, not going to happen." She put the spatula down and walked toward me. "Are they hurting? There's nothing in them, honest."

"They just so damn scratchy, are you sure?"

"What can I do?" She sounded lost. "I have some burger hash that's almost ready for you if you want."

Because burger hash would be just what any doctor would prescribe. Take two aspirin, a full helping of burger hash, and call me in the morning. There was something she could do. "Do you have any drops? I just need the stinging to stop. It's been non-stop since the crash."

She went to her purse and started rummaging through it. "I have Visine. I never leave home without it."

Why didn't that surprise me? I had to believe that a party girl like her had to have all kinds of goodies to mask the insomnia and drug abuse. I had to believe the purse was a pharmacy, complete with breath-mints, dental floss, and handcuffs. That million-dollar look didn't come without a lot of help. I didn't doubt her car held changes of clothes, bottles of water, toiletries, and extra shoes for when she snapped a heel.

I stared straight ahead until she tilted my chin back. I tried to open them, but couldn't tell if they were open enough. Vanessa took care of that by prying them open with her fingers and dousing each one thoroughly. Blinking most of it out, my eyes had found their happy place. It felt good enough to push waves of guilt through me. I promised myself I wasn't going to take favours from this girl? Right about now, I needed every advantage. I might even have a bowl of her burger muck.

Vanessa didn't seem suspicious. The drops were put away and she hurried back to the stove to stir the meal. My eyes weren't that high up on her list of concerns. She was doing this crazy cooking thing.

The first bowl of food tasted good enough for a second helping. It was tasty and even the worry of poison didn't stop me. Would she poison me? I doubted she'd harm me unless I provoked her. Even then, she'd have to bore me with a lengthy rant before giving me that shot to the head.

As night came, the offer of the bed was given to me. The idea of sleeping on a mattress again thrilled me until she mentioned that I'd be hog-tied. She'd also be on it. I opted for the floor. Sleeping with her wouldn't be as easy to digest as the food. Besides, she had no problem with me sleeping on the floor. She made sure I had a blanket and pillow. I told you she was sweet.

Other than passing out from my imaginary snakebite, I'd been sleeping like a cat the past week. I napped, never really sleeping. As the orange and yellow glows of the setting sun filled the cabin I smiled. I could tell day from night. The colours warmed my heart as they poured in through windows. Then, as the last remnants of the day faded, I slipped the blindfold back into place. It really felt better. I'd let my old world return until morning.

The possibility of getting my sight back was a game-changer. Vanessa was unstable. She wasn't desperation-crazy and that was good, but she had a practical outlook that went beyond scary.

Struggling to stay awake, I ran different scenarios through my mind. I needed a plan. Nothing came. I was still a blind man, crippled, and without a gun. Vanessa was a sighted woman with a gun and a mission. Much of my brainstorming resulted in me carelessly throwing myself at her and wrestling the gun away.

That hadn't worked out so well earlier.

Chapter fifty-five

I knew I was dreaming the moment I woke up, or should I say, didn't wake up. This I could tell because I don't usually wake up in the middle of a moonlit forest surrounded by wolves. Oh, and I seldom strolled the forest completely naked. That being said, my fear was real.

Four wolves circled slowly, giving me a chance to study them. A large one stood out as the Alpha male while the other three served as his dutiful henchmen. This act made me wonder how similar cats were to dogs. These predators had caught their mouse, so what was stopping them from finishing me off? Was it a respect for humans or did they delight in playing with their food?

My cat used to play with mice. She always played with them on the back deck and on more than one occasion she'd get careless and one would get away. Those few brave mice would be my inspiration.

The circle tightened in on me, each one keeping a uniform distance from its predecessor. The once thirty feet had narrowed to twenty. With my odds dwindling, I needed to act fast.

In a dying breeze, I could smell their damp, stagnant odour. The remnants of that breeze felt cold against my bare skin. Steam rose from my body and my breath was expelled in short, quick puffs. Don't panic.

Without warning the circling stopped. Noses suddenly shifted to a scent coming from the east. The breeze had picked up. All eight eyes stared either past me or through me to the same distraction. Their curiosity even had me stealing a brief glimpse before realising my opportunity. I bolted into the woods to the west.

Behind me the Alpha barked hasty commands. Two wolves darted after the lone silhouette, my distraction to the east. The Alpha and the other took chase after me. I had barely seen the silhouette, cloaked in the branches and leaves. From what I saw, it had been a fifth wolf, a shaggy one. It made me wonder if this was a trap. I've read that wolves did that. It's not beneath them to use trickery to lure their prey into ambushes.

Between the overcast skies and the dense canopy above me, the dusk-like setting made it hard for me to see all the branches that were jumping out at me as I ran. Most of them passed by like a parade of spectators, but the odd one lashed out at me, finding my bare skin weak and easily torn.

It had to be an ambush. As I looked ahead, the lone silhouette was waiting to the right of me. I had no idea how the wolf got there so fast, but its presence had me darting left. Over my shoulder I saw the two that had been pursuing me. The one that I thought was the alpha looked as confused as I was.

I was sprinting now, yet twenty yards ahead of me, the wolf appeared again. This was impossible, wasn't it? I darted to the right this time. Slowing to take a longer look, I saw the matte of hair and the ribs pressed against the fur. It was a scruffy mutt, a real loner. It was also hungry and chased out of the pack by the Alpha. This one should have been the threat, yet it wasn't.

I ran wildly through the wilderness. An errant branch tore into my knee, reminding me to pay attention. When I looked forward I saw, and almost ran smack dab into, the loner. I stopped. "What do you want, damn it."

While the other wolves had kept a good pace, Scruffy was running circles around the three of us with ease. I watched as the wolf turned and started down an old deer trail. That, I didn't expect. Was I meant to follow? At least there was a trail. Scruffy led the way and I followed in a full-blown panic. The Alpha and his henchman brought up the rear. Somewhere in the distance, the others were barking. Hells bells grandma, where was Little Red Riding Hood when you needed her?

Who should I trust? The loner was hungry. So was the pack. I'd rather put my trust in the loner for two reasons; he seemed like he wanted to help in 'the littlest hobo' kind of way, and in a worst-case scenario, he needed the meal more than the others. We underdogs had to stick together.

My uncertainty had allowed the Alpha to close the gap. I needed to move. Around the corner my path came in the form of a bridge. Okay, it wasn't exactly a bridge, more of a log spanning a fast-flowing river. Scruffs had already landed on the far bank by the time I reached it. I fed off his urgency and started to hightail it across.

The Alpha stopped, allowing his faithful follower to continue the pursuit. He didn't stop out of fear. At the top of the hierarchy, he wasn't willing to get his hands, or paws, dirty. Oddly, he'd be the first to fill up on the kill.

The half-rotted bridge cracked under our weight causing us both to freeze. I looked back to see the same fear in his eyes that he must have seen in mine. It cracked once more before snapping and plunging us both into the frigid river. As he dog-paddled back to the bank where the Alpha waited, I paddled the further path to Scruffy. Suddenly I was fighting the weight of a shirt, pants, and shoes. What a time to get my soggy clothes back.

I reached the shore where Scruffy patiently waited for me to catch my breath. That was when I noticed Scruffy was no alpha. Missing a few key parts, Scruffy was a bitch. She wasn't into the whole male-domination thing. When she thought I'd rested long enough, she led me down another trail.

The tree-line broke and we both exited into an open field. As we ran through it, a road appeared at the far end. About a quarter mile down the road a car was cruising toward us. I couldn't believe my luck and wasted no time flagging them down. There were four people inside, three men and a woman. They were okay with giving me a ride. How great was this?

"Thanks Scruff." I turned to the wolf and tousled her hair with my fingers. She'd saved my life. "I have to go now, girl."

Confused, she cocked her head.

"Sorry, Scruffs." I wanted to take her with me, but how? "What would I do with you?"

I turn to get in the car. The little girl with the tattered dress was now sitting in the front seat. A bloodied smile spread across her face. The front of her dress was crimson, soiled with blood. The two people in the back were dead. The female driver was also dead. The fourth was holding his intestines in his lap. He'd been savagely torn open.

The girl shrugged. "L-Look what y-y-you d-d-did, J-J-Johnny."

I looked back at Scruffy, but she was gone. A bright blue hair clip, a butterfly, sat in the grass where she'd once stood.

Chapter fifty-six

I slipped the blindfold up to my forehead when I woke from the dream. It was still dark. In the other two dreams, the girl had led me to a lake and she had warned me about being found. There had been a message in each of those dreams, or nightmares. I had to believe that this one also held some hidden meaning. Was it 'don't ride with strangers', 'dogs bite' or that 'the underdog is capable of anything'? I didn't get it and I was paying attention, trust me.

As the hours passed, the oranges and yellows of morning pushed their way through the cabin's windows—my first sunrise in days. Vanessa calmly got up, fluffed her hair, and began making coffee. Even after waking, the wolf had haunted me. There was a moral to that story. I just missed something in the whole Cujo-like ending.

"Coffee?"

I blindly held out my hands for the cup and saw the outline of the white mug. The white cup-sized blob was badly blurred. I stared at it briefly, not wanting to bring attention to myself. Then I took a sip. She always made a good cup of coffee.

"Do you still have those drops?"

Vanessa remained silent, like it was too early for this, but she got up, gently tilted my head back, and applied a few drops of liquid to each eye. "Better?"

Blinking twice I could see her outline. She was barely more than a velvet hourglass, but it was her. I wanted to reach out and grab her. Was she expecting anything and where was the gun? I couldn't take the chance, so I let the moment pass. I continued to look past her. "Thanks. That's a lot better."

She set the drops down and returned to her coffee. I took a moment to pan the room and take in the shapes. There was a rectangle to my right, a door. There was a small square window a few feet to the right of that. Again, the shapes were cloudy, but they were there. Another window, a larger one, was in the wall across from the door. Beyond that window had to be the grave.

The purple shadow grabbed the phone when it rang. She kept the call short, texted some directions and dropped the phone in her pocket. "She's on her way. Let's hope she doesn't do anything stupid."

With that out of the way, Vanessa took her coffee and went out to the car. I heard the car's radio start up. It was distant and crackling. The news would keep her up to date on my disappearance. Besides that, she wasn't a talker until she'd finished her first cup. I was happy to give her that silence. By now, my rescue would be barely newsworthy, more of a blip before heading to sports. The world had to move on.

I took another sip and went back to the dream. Scruffy had shown me that it wasn't necessary to be the strongest to survive. I'd have to outwit Vanessa and get her away from the cabin. If I could do that, I could go from hunted to hunter.

While Vanessa sat in the car getting her update, I was on the move. She'd assume that I was blindly sipping my brew. Instead, my half-empty cup was sitting on the floor by an empty chair. The guy on the radio had just announced three minutes until the top of the hour, and more news.

I shuffled across the room toward the lighted square on the wall. I was barefoot because shoes were noisy. In hindsight, I should have brought them along. With a gentle tug, the window opened. The moss growing between the window and the sill muffled the sound of it opening and I awkwardly climbed through. My feet sank into the loose dirt. Sorry guys. The first part of my plan had worked beautifully. Now where?

All I could think about was getting to the road. Vanessa had the gun, which meant I'd have to get to Katie before she did. I left the window and ran my hand along the side of the cabin. The cars were on the south side, so the road had to be on that side as well. While Vanessa quietly listened to the news, I crept around the building. The woods were calling to me and they'd lead me to the road, a trail or, with any luck, a police station.

I took a deep breath and squirmed my way past the first few trees. If I could hike a hundred yards and make a left, I should end up near the road. Katie was on her way and I had no time to waste.

The music continued after the news and grew fainter until it abruptly stopped. That stopped me in my tracks. I had to be out of sight before she found that I was gone, which would be at any moment. It took a second for my heart to re-fire and I was moving again.

Like clockwork, her scream was right on cue. "Johnny! Where the fuck are you?"

The cabin walls muffled her first scream. Her second scream echoed without restrictions. "I swear I'll kill you both! Where are you?"

I didn't look back as I made my way over logs and through the thick brush. The shadows from the trees thickened, clotting the forest like exposed blood. I crouched down to take a break. How far had I gone? Was it a hundred yards yet?

"Johnny!"

Vanessa's screams were a beacon. They helped me keep a bearing on her. Looking back, the cabin was nothing more than a small brown square. Was she near the cars, or in the driveway? She was right to worry about the road. This would all blow up in her face if she didn't find me.

"Johnny!"

"That's right," I whispered as I continued to look for her. "Keep screaming."

The road was near. I could feel it. The canopy of the forest was clearing as I made my way to the left. The dark greens of ground cover were becoming brighter. Would I find a large field at the treeline? Would there be a car with four people, a wolf, and a small girl? I had to shake the thought.

Soon the long lean shadows of the trees were behind me. I crouched down to feel the edge of a dirt road. I'd found it, but now Vanessa's screams were much clearer. She was also desperate, wielding a gun and she had figured out my plan.

I could hear the branches cracking as she bullied her way through the bush. She was a lot noisier than I had been. Could she see me? Across the road there were no trees. What did that mean? A field, a lake? With nowhere to hide, I followed the treeline along the road. I remained crouched as I ran, which made it slow going. I must have travelled another fifty yards up the ditch when my legs buckled. I thought I'd lost her until I heard the gunshot.

The bullet ripped bark from a nearby tree and the splinters struck me in the face. Echoes of the shot reverberated through the forest. My escape had just deteriorated from desperate to grave. God, how I hated that word.

I scampered back into the safety of the forest, wanting to put some distance between us. My legs had other ideas. And how was diving deeper into the woods going to help Katie? I worked my way along a downed tree, not sure whether I should climb over or under it. The barrel of a gun, being pressed against my back, ended both options. The chase was over. Hell, it was over before it had started.

"That's strike two, Johnny." She spun me back toward the cabin and gave me a shove. "For the life of me, I don't know why I don't just shoot you now."

197

Chapter fifty-seven

Back at the cabin, my hands were tied, a six-inch strip of duct tape was slapped across my mouth, literally, and I was berated. Vanessa read me the riot act and warned against getting any further bright ideas. To be honest, none of my ideas had been all that bright up to now. I should have been scared because, this girl had a gun and knew how to use it. Sadly, I'd been scared so many times this week that the sound of a woman's voice, as crazed and impetuous as this one's was, just didn't carry the same impact as a bear mauling me or the act of turning a hole into a grave.

The purple figure paced back and forth in front of me as I waited for the ranting to end. I kept my stare straight ahead and unfocused, not because acting the part of a blind man required that, but because that had been my last chance to remove my wife from the equation. Now, all I could do was hope for a safe transfer.

When my phone rang, Vanessa kept it short. "Whereabouts are you?" There was a pause. "I'll text you the rest of the directions. You've got everything?"

There was another pause.

"Keep driving and you'll find us. Remember, no police! You may stop me, but your husband will die." Vanessa hung up and typed the last of the directions to Katie in a text.

"Get up, it's go time and we've got a bit of a drive."

"A drive?"

"You don't think she's coming here, do you? That's careless. There's a road that runs parallel to this one. It's about ten miles over."

I got up as instructed and let her usher me to the back seat of the car. My most recent escape would have been futile. I'd never be able to trek the ten miles to save her. Vanessa tied my feet together and fastened my seatbelt. Running the belt around my right arm and over my left she managed to pin my arms to my lap. She had done this before, maybe not during a kidnapping, but on a past date.

"There, your seatbelt is done up. If the light on the dash illuminates, that will mean it's not done up. That's going to be strike three. You don't want a third strike, Johnny."

There was no doubt in my mind that she would squeeze the trigger this time. It was strike three, of course. Besides, I was messing with her 'go time.' The fact that she called it that, told me she was as nervous as I was. We both had a lot to gain, and a lot to lose. I would say I had more to lose, a wife and my existence, but I'm sure in Vanessa's self-centred world, she was the only one with anything serious at stake.

The engine idled for a second before we took off and I could have sworn I saw her check her makeup in the rear-view mirror—seriously? If we were worried about looks for the exchange, then shouldn't we concern ourselves with me? I was bruised, bandaged, half-starved, and couldn't run a comb through my hair to save my life. I smelled of sweat and clotted blood. It was getting to the point where I couldn't even stand the smell of me.

We drove out onto the main road, a barely-used dirt lane. I tried to keep my blood pressure in check. Katie was delivering my freedom and she was a smart girl. Would a smart girl come alone, or had she called the police? A huge part of me was hoping she'd not made the 911 call. As much as I'd like justice, I just wanted this to end.

With only the three of us involved, this day could end 'happily ever after.' A police presence made this all about right and wrong and no good ever came from that.

About fifteen minutes down the one road, and five down another, Vanessa stopped the car. We waited. I watched her take a sip from her bottle of water and I almost asked for a drink. Sandpaper coated my throat. Piss on it. I was back in boycott mode.

"So how is this going to work?" I asked.

"It's easy. I get my money, you get your freedom."

"It sounds easy, but what about Katie?"

"She's got nothing to worry about as long as she does what she's told. There shouldn't be a problem."

I really wanted it to be that easy. "What if she isn't as smart as we both hope she is?"

"That would suck, and we'd need to dig a few more holes. Now sit back and relax. By the time this day is over, you'll be with the one you love. I promise."

She said it with such conviction that I wanted to believe her. It was oddly comforting. Positive thinking—this would go well. Katie would be alone, just her and a bag of stocks and dollars. I could almost feel myself tucked under the covers of our bed with the kids curled up between us like a couple of cats. There'd be a slice or two of a big greasy pizza leftover on the nightstand.

"This is it." She put the cap on her water and set it down.

It took a few seconds, but soon I heard what had caught Vanessa's attention. The distant motor belonged to my freedom. A dust-cloud made its way closer and stopped about twenty feet away. It looked like my truck, in a fuzzy sort of way. Ford, Dodge or Chevy, it was red. I stared as the dust from the road drifted toward the trees.

"Johnny do you own a Dodge Dakota?"

"I most certainly do, 2004, red." We had to be close to Canada if Katie brought the truck. She hated driving it for long distances.

"Good. Now I need you to describe your wife. Quickly!"

"Um, she's blonde, bluish eyes, about five-foot-nine with a birth mark on her left hip."

"Are you for real, Johnny? I can't see birthmarks or how tall she is when she's sitting in a truck. How long is her hair, what's the cut?"

Her impatience rattled me. "It's fairly long I guess. The cut is a sort of a Farrah Fawcetty one. She usually—."

The truck's horn cut me off with two short beeps. She was impatient to get this going. The gesture forced me back in my seat.

"Sounds like your wife wants you back and since we don't need any strike three's, Johnny..." She tore a strip of duct tape from a roll and spread it across my mouth. "I'll do the talking."

I winced as she pressed it into place.

"Just looking out for ya, Tea Boy." She opened the door and slid out. "Stay put. This won't take long."

Chapter fifty-eight

I watched as Vanessa, the purple blur, headed over to my truck, the red rectangular thing. At that point, a blue blur with blonde hair got out and handed her a brown square, leather, no doubt and full of green.

Vanessa took the brown case and that should have been my cue to get out of the car. I almost undid my seatbelt before remembering 'strike three.' Surely it was over with the money exchange. Yes, Vanessa had her money, so I was a free man.

I took my eyes off them while I fumbled for the belt. The latch wasn't even in my hands when a crisp gunshot wrenched my head back to the coloured blurs.

The blue one had doubled over. Vanessa took a step back, raised the gun and took aim. A second shot rang out. It hit the woman in the back of the head. It dropped her to the ground that was painted red with her blood. I pulled my hand from the seatbelt latch as if a jolt of electricity had ripped through me.

I tried to yell out. The tape partially ripped away from my bottom lip. "What the hell did you— "

"Shut up, Johnny," she yelled back at me as she set the gun down on the hood of the truck. "And stay put, or so help me God..."

There was a panic in her voice as she grabbed the women's legs and spun her around. I watched in stunned horror as she dragged the woman's body into the middle of the road. Then she ran back for the gun and the bag. In the distance the sirens were starting to howl.

"Why'd you do that?"

She tossed the bag onto the seat beside her and jammed the gun in the gap between the seat and the console. Gravel flew from the tires and we were off.

A sobering numbness entombed me, pinning me to my seat. It was so senseless, so cold. Vanessa didn't look back as she drove away from the sirens, away from the body. She had dragged the blue blur to the middle of the road for a reason. It was cold and calculated. She knew they'd have to stop to move the body. It was all about buying precious seconds.

We'd travelled a few miles before my trance broke. It was my head being slammed off the side window that brought me back. That was when I puked through the gap between the tape and lower lip. It got all over the seat beside me.

"Damn it, Johnny."

I could hear the front windows going down. The wind howled through the car and I heaved again. At least with Nellie and Cowboy, I'd only heard the shots.

That woman had been killed in cold blood. It was terrible, but not nearly as horrific had it been Katie. I wasn't certain, and I needed to reject that thought completely, but I was ninety-nine percent sure that wasn't my wife.

Katie had always hated car-horns. I think it all stemmed from her father. He loved the darn things. It wasn't that he loved the sound of the car-horn; the man was always in a hurry. The road belonged to him and everyone else was just out there to get in his way. As a kid, Katie watched him stew as he dodged and dove through the traffic. His blood pressure often soared, and she knew he'd die of a heart attack one day. When it happened, she was only twelve.

It wasn't the car-horn she hated as much as the reminder of her father's impatience. It had cost him his life. Vanessa didn't know it, and I wasn't fully sure myself, but she had just shot a cop.

Chapter fifty-nine

S haken not stirred, I felt like one of those famous James Bond martinis. My head had bounced off the car's window no less than three times. For a change I was glad that I was wearing my seatbelt. At times I heard distant sirens and they comforted me. I was not alone.

Days ago, I had sat on the shore of a lake hoping to catch a fish. Now, three people were dead and I was on my way to becoming the fourth. Sirens were closing in on us and this day would eventually end, but how? Would Vanessa be dead, would she be captured, or would I still be living this nightmare when I was ninety. I quickly tossed that last thought aside.

The other thing I had to rid myself of was the image of the blonde police officer. She had no idea what she was walking into. I had no idea what we were walking into. It was as if Vanessa had a death-quota to meet. I tried to catch my breath. Back at the drop-site, a woman was lying in a pool of her own blood and all I could think about was that it wasn't Katie. Did that make me a horrible person? What if it were my wife? Stop it Johnny, you can't go there.

The sirens continued to get louder. They wailed the praises of their talented drivers. These people got years of training for when days like this happened. They'd have to meet stringent standards. This shouldn't take long now.

Except that Vanessa piloted the car with ease. She was also talented. We drifted by trees sideways and I doubt she lifted once. That was a surprise, but what really surprised me was when the rough growl of the gravel road ended with the clean biting of rubber on asphalt. Out of nowhere civilisation found us and we left the forested wilderness behind.

Granted, these were rural roads, but they were roads none the less. They were also better conditions for this vehicle. If I wagered a guess, I'd have to say the car was a BMW. My uncle owned one. It accelerated smoothly, like high-end automobiles often did. Long windy roads swept left and then right as we passed farm after farm. Behind us, the sirens were beginning to fade. They were no competition for this car. With any luck, we'd run out of gas.

As if on my suggestive cue, the engine's high revving stopped and I felt the seatbelt tugging hard at my waist and wrists. The anti-lock brakes had the tires hugging the road with textbook efficiency. My left temple bounced off the window once more as the car slowed and made a hard-right turn. While Vanessa pulled the car into the overgrown pullout, I tried to shake the dizziness from that last blow to my head.

She'd found a hidden clearing. At one point this spot might have been a driveway to a house that never got built, or a spot for our young kids to make out. Regardless of its past purpose, it hadn't been used in years. From here we could see the road while camouflaged by a grove of spindly willows.

We sat and waited as the sirens grew louder. Even though I'd done nothing, except crash a plane and get kidnapped—neither considered a crime—I still felt nervous hearing them. They were the police. Vanessa didn't share my anxiety. Wanted for murder, she sat and calmly went over the papers in the blood-stained bag.

"It's all just useless newspaper." She stuffed a handful back into the bag. "Well, now we know your wife wasn't so smart after all."

It was safe to say this was strike three. With no money she'd have to abandon her kidnapping plan. She couldn't go back and call Katie. As far as she was concerned, Katie had a hole in her abdomen and another in the back of her head. There was no need for a witness, albeit a blind one. So once again I had to ask a stupid question, one that I'd have been better off not asking. "What's next?"

"You sound so deflated. There's still a plan 'B' in the picture."

The joke was on her. Deflated was back at the plane. A part of me wished she would just end it already. I was never going home, and she wasn't getting any money. Do what the bear couldn't, kill me and move on.

The sirens were on top of us now and I had to turn my head away as they sped past.

Chapter sixty

T he car door slammed, and I found myself following Vanessa with my eyes. She was headed for the trunk. On the way she started peeling off the coloured layers of clothing. Purples gave way to shades of beige and well-tanned bronzes. Even badly blurred, her nude body was hard to look away from.

I'd seen her naked before, when my sight was much better. I remembered studying those curves thoroughly and with the lust of an eager teenager. Vanessa was a very attractive woman—she had to be. I mean, here I sat with my eyes fixed on her after she'd killed three people. It was stronger than any kind of voodoo.

Now dressed in jeans and a white top, she opened my door. "How ya holding up sport?" She yanked the tape free.

Having duct tape ripped from one's lip hurts like a son-of-a-bitch, but it's especially painful after not shaving for a week.

My words came out fast. "You'll never get away with this."

She unbuckled me. "How do you figure?"

"They've read your plates." I had seen my share of P.I. movies. "They're going to wonder about you at work."

"Nice try. They never got a plate number, I doubt these rookies even got close enough to see what it was they were chasing."

She was right on that one.

"You hate me, don't you?" She asked.

Was she just figuring this out now? "Yes."

Reaching behind her back, she pulled out the gun. I should have kept my mouth shut. Then she handed it to me. "Here then."

She jammed it into my hand before I could figure out what she was doing. "What the…"

"Go ahead, Johnny. Just don't miss. I'm not one for pain and a glancing shot would hurt like hell. I'll keep talking so you can get a bearing on me. Hold the gun firmly. Get a good feel for the trigger before you pull it."

I did as she told me. I felt the trigger on my finger and gave it a gentle squeeze, not enough for it to fire, just enough to get a feel for what it would take. This was my freedom.

"You have to do it, Johnny. If you don't I'll take that gun back. You and I both know it's the only way this ends."

I had a good bearing on her and she was right. If I squeezed off a shot, it would all be over. I could step over her body and make my way to the road. I could go home.

"Johnny, just pull the damn trigger already. It's not fair to make me wait. That's cruel and it's not who you are."

She was right. I should shoot her quick. Katie could be in my arms in hours. I gripped the gun tighter but didn't fire it. I couldn't fire it. It wasn't who I was. My grip loosened. "Damn it."

Vanessa grabbed the gun back. "You really are one of the good guys. You should be proud, but you'll end up dead with that philosophy. I guess we're back to doing this my way."

"You can't go on like this. Three people are dead."

"I doubt any of them will rat me out and they're the only ones that could. As for work, I'm on a week off as of yesterday. They think I'm in Aspen with friends."

I was scrambling. "What about the car?"

"It's rented, fake ID, Johnny."

I didn't want to implicate anyone else, but I did anyway. "Eric knows about us!"

"He won't be talking."

What did that mean "Did you—"

"Hell no, that would be stupid. I just reminded him of the photos his wife would see if he said anything. Besides, he knows I'm no idiot. I'd never do anything this crazy. And even if I could, who'd want to mess with that? He knows he'd be next."

A seducer, an extortionist, and on occasion a contortionist. It was getting easier to see her as a murderer. And even if Eric did figure everything out, he'd be a fool to go to bat for some one-hit wonder. I was a commission cheque, not a friend. I let out a heavy sigh while the sirens disappeared from earshot.

"So why not kill me now? This way you can go back to work like nothing happened."

"I don't want you dead. My plan 'B' wouldn't work without you."

"I'm your back-up plan?"

"Here's how I see it. I met this writer at a party. We had sex and I fired up a wonderful relationship with this guy. He's smart, wonderful, and good looking. The only catch, he's married. He told me that if he ditched his wife, she'd get everything. We couldn't have that, so he decided to fake a kidnapping."

"What about the hunters?"

"They were in the wrong place at the wrong time. When they stumbled across our cabin, you had to shoot them."

"I shot them?"

She cut me off. "I thought it was a little extreme and at that point, I knew I was with someone dangerous. I became scared for my own safety."

"You little—"

"Oh, it gets better Johnny. After you buried those hunters, you made me call your wife. You also made me tell her to come alone. That way you could pop her, and we'd be free and clear. You might have to hide out and go through some suffering to make it look good, like blindness, but it would be worth it. I mean if you were willing to crash your plane to get rid of your wife, you were capable of anything. I was just along for the ride at that point, terrified and unable to stop your madness."

"You didn't have to kill her."

"We can't have any witnesses. Besides, you wanted to finish her off. She's worth a lot more dead than alive."

"How do you figure?"

"Oh, that's right. You took out an insurance policy on her yesterday, a big one."

I felt my ribs tightening around my chest. "How'd you pull that off?"

"I have a friend that does policies. Your signature is an easy one to copy. I used my autographed copy of your novel for practice. Hey, and thanks for putting your prints on the gun. I couldn't have done this without that."

This was check and mate. I had played right into her trap.

"Was the gun even loaded?" It was a morbid curiosity.

"Sorry Johnny, no do-overs." The giggle was blood-curdling. "It wasn't, but it is now." There was a click as the loaded clip locked into place. "Now get out. We're done with this car."

We weren't keeping the car? Well I was done with walking. She'd have to shoot me. I undid my belt while she pulled the green tarp off what looked like a brand-new Lexus. Of course I ended up in the backseat, fastened to the seatbelt in the same fashion as before. She quickly took her place behind the wheel.

"Where are we going?"

She pulled out onto the blacktop and turned left. It was the direction we'd just came from.

"There's a small town a few miles up the road. I checked into a motel before I came to the cabin. We still have the room for a couple of nights. We'll have to try the chicken take-out down the street. The sign says it's the 'Breast Chicken Anywhere.'"

"And then?"

"And then, Johnny, you and I are going to have a serious talk."

Chapter sixty-one

We rolled into town with me playing the part of the blind man, when in fact I was taking in as much as I could. There wasn't much. Three short blocks down the main drag and we were at the motel, or the other end of town, whichever way you wanted to look at it.

The town reminded me of a place just outside of Cranbrook where Katie grew up. That downtown consisted of four blocks. There was a hardware store, a pizza place, a real estate agency, a handful of small restaurants and two specialty shops that sold the handmade trinkets of local artists.

From the chicken place to the general store, these small towns were all the same. Everyone knew everyone and they all looked out for each other's kids. They also knew everything about everybody, like when old man Brown got home from the pub last night, that little Jack Turner sneaks cigarettes at the cemetery after school, and did you know that Mrs. Reed wears a wig, the poor thing. These townsfolk also saw everything so, what were they thinking when they first laid eyes on Vanessa? Ladies hide your men.

Vanessa had dressed down with the denim. She wanted to fit in and fit in she did. Her faded jeans were very different from the designer duds she was accustomed to. And that sweetness, the one that had won me over, could easily win these locals over as well. They would never consider hiding their men, not from a girl like this.

Vanessa parked in front of the motel, turned off the car and spun around in her seat. "Okay Johnny, here's how it's going to work." She grabbed a hat and sunglasses out of the glove compartment. "Put these on."

I fumbled them into place.

"No talking. Got it?"

I nodded. We'd parked in front of room number five. There were six. The last one belonged to a nosy eighty-seven-year-old great-grandmother. We weren't even settled before she came over. In a conversation at the door, she told Vanessa all about her cat and how it had accidentally turned on the stove and burned their house to the ground. Right Gramma, the cat did it.

She'd lost everything, except for the cat and a few porcelain figurines. Vanessa showed remarkable patience with the old lady. I would have bet on shots being fired after the first story. After a while, the old lady grew tired of standing there and left. She had made a new friend of this stranger and that was good.

"I bet I know what you're thinking." With the curtain pulled back she watched the old lady leave before turning to me. "You're curious about the 'Breast Chicken' in Dinkytown?"

That wasn't what I was thinking. "So why didn't you shoot the old lady?" It seemed like a valid question. I'd only seen or crossed paths with three people in the last week other than Vanessa. They were all dead. "She's seen you."

"She's insignificant, a better ally." She thumbed through a phone book that resembled a flyer. "Besides, I'm hoping for cookies. I bet she's a baker."

I couldn't believe it, Vanessa was hoping for home-baked cookies.

She set the open phone book down on the desk beside the phone when she found the chicken place. "We should get the chicken coop. It is twelve pieces with fries, coleslaw, and home-made biscuits, all in a box that resembles a little hen house. Don't you just love this place?"

As she dialled, I wondered if I'd be able to eat. Sure, my stomach craved food, especially after losing my hamburger hash in the back seat, but my mind was anything but hungry. Within minutes there was a knock on the door. I'm sure they walked our order over. Vanessa pressed her eye against the door's peephole to get a look.

"Okay Johnny, he's a cute one. I bet this kid hasn't seen sixteen yet. That means he's likely a virgin." Then she grabbed the gun. "Say one word and he'll die as one."

I already knew the drill, people died if I didn't behave, people died if I did. I thought back to the police officer as Vanessa paid the boy. That blonde hair wasn't dark enough to be Katie's. I had to keep telling myself that. Then I wondered if she had a husband, kids, or a cat. She must have had some form of a life. Were there friends, or old school mates, a young man named Bobby who was trying to drum up the courage to ask her out on a date? In a couple of days, they'd all get a chance to say kind words about her at her funeral.

When the door closed I smiled. The pimply-faced Archie Andrews would get to see his 16th birthday and someday, Mary-Anne's knockers. And the chicken really was the 'Breast anywhere.' Hunger always trumped sorrow. I had two pieces before mastering the courage to ask a question that had been on my mind since the cabin. "Why'd you lie to me?"

"What?"

"You said by tonight I would be with the one I love." It came out as if a pouting child had been denied dessert. "You promised, or did you just say that to shut me up?"

"Have I lied to you yet?"

How did she want me to answer that? I say yes, and she blows a gasket, I say no and I'm a liar…and she blows a gasket.

She put down her chicken and licked at the tips of her fingers. I made a point of looking past her, like she expected me to.

"I never lied to you about this being a kidnapping. I never lied to you about those men or why I killed them. I've even come clean on my back-up plan. No, I haven't been the one lying."

"So, what about me being with Katie tonight?"

"I said you'd be with the one you *love*." Vanessa smiled as she shrugged. "And you are."

Chapter sixty-two

I pushed the plate away as the chicken in my stomach churned like poison. "Katie's the one I love and she's dead. You shot her."

"First of all, I wasn't born yesterday, Johnny." She swallowed a mouthful of coleslaw and twirled her fork while she talked. "You're eating chicken. I couldn't imagine eating chicken after losing the one I loved. Besides, those cops were too close. They were waiting for us. They'd never put a civilian in harm's way like that."

"You knew it wasn't her?"

"I wasn't totally sure, but then I saw you munching on the chicken. You got a lousy poker face. Also, the woman looked distant, like she was doing recon work. She didn't look over at you once. I would think a wife that thought her husband was dead, and now alive, would've been less interested in the details and more about getting him back."

She looked over to me. Her eyes met mine and I looked away.

"Hey, if it's any consolation, I hoped it was your wife. It would make us easier for you to accept."

216

"There is no us."

"Think what you want." She walked over to the window to check the street, "If she loved you, why was that bag full of newspaper. A loving wife never would have tried a stunt like that. They'd have paid."

The bag of paper had been left back with the BMW. At the time there was no rage and no concern. That was because this was never about the money.

"Sorry, Johnny. The truth always hurts. She put her trust in these cops, but they were in over their heads. It's small town living out here." She picked up a drumstick. "They're more about saving cats from trees, or arresting kids for stealing candy bars."

"I can get you the cash."

"That again, Johnny? I doubt that very much. I'm sure they've frozen your accounts by now. You couldn't muster enough money to buy me a coffee. Face it Johnny, you're more cut off from the real world than you know."

"You have to let me try. There has to be a bank in this town somewhere."

"Not going to happen." She started to pack up the supper. "We'll stay here. Forget about the money. Although it would have given us a nice start, we can always find more."

She'd used the word 'us' like we were a couple. I didn't bite. It was a crazy fantasy contrived from a deranged girl. There was no way she could be in love with me. It was a stupid one-night stand.

"Talk to me, Johnny. What are you thinking?" She batted her eyes.

"You need to forget about me, Vanessa. I don't love you."

"Not yet. I know what you're thinking, that this gal has a few screws loose. We made love and now she's mistaken passion for love, but that's not true."

It was more like she mistook my animal urges of wanting to do some girl half my age for actual emotions. All I wanted was a walk down memory lane, a lane where breasts haven't nursed children and where there were no stretch marks or scars from hysterectomies. I wanted to tell her that by hopping on top of somebody younger, I had become younger. It was nothing more.

"Look, you're damn sexy. I was lonely, high on myself, feeling bigger than life. I never should have gone to your place. But more important than that, I love my wife."

"I won't deny your feelings for her, but you also have feelings for me. Just admit it."

"All I wanted was sex." There I said it. "You're young and attractive. I did something that I enjoyed, but it was a greedy mistake. I see that now."

"No, I don't think so. I saw the way you looked at me when we were at the office, how you loved the hand-holding that day you bought the tea. You couldn't get enough of me."

Her voice was softening like the day of our dreaded lunch date. It was an enchanting form of bait. That day her sorcery had lured me in. She had made me feel desirable. She made me forget about my frumpy, dreary world. Her looks were an aphrodisiac and they had put her in charge. I had no way of knowing the details hiding in the fine print.

"I'm sorry you misunderstood my feelings."

"Okay, you keep telling yourself that. But, if I remember right, you had a gun in hand and could have ended all this with a single shot. You couldn't pull the trigger. If you really thought I was such a bad person, you'd have taken that shot. You'd be home with that wife, the one you love so much. Think about it."

It made me ill. There had to be a shred of truth to what she was saying. "Why are you doing this? Plan 'A' was killing Katie. Plan 'B' involves my agreeing to you and me being an us. If you've got a plan 'C', you might want to bring it out."

"Nothing yet, but when I was a kid I had a friend. This poor girl showed me why you never quit. We're all given the power to control our destinies and we should never abandon our dreams. I want to tell you her story. Do you want to hear it?"

I was still alive, but I was regretting it by the second. "Do I have a choice?"

Chapter sixty-three

I got up from my chair and moved over to sit on the bed. I needed some distance. Vanessa got up and moved over beside me. "It's not like you really have a choice in this, so listen up."

I stared blankly at the wall trying to focus on an electrical outlet. There was no way I'd be reading food labels any time soon. It was like looking through a bottle of water. As for her story, there was a part of me that wanted to hear it and a part of me that wanted to drown myself in that bottle of water.

She was working on a plan 'C' while I had to be up to plan 'M' or 'N' by now. Thank God the alphabet only had twenty-six letters. I'd shoot through a few more before having any success.

"Pay attention, Johnny. This girl's name was Doris. She was such a dork. Now I'm not saying that because she looked like a chess player, or because even the debating team avoided her. Doris always looked like she'd just crawled out of the trash. This girl was poverty central."

"Why are you doing this to me?" I'd always had a tough time keeping my tongue during story time.

"She lived in a small town like this where the town folk knew everybody's dirty little secrets and her family had a lot of them. Her parents were drunks and, when she was six years old, her father left them for a waitress in the next town. I guess he'd had enough of her and the whole parenting thing.

It didn't help that Doris was a runt and didn't speak well. Her teeth were stained, crooked, and when she slouched, she looked like a crotchety old gypsy. And everybody recognised her clothes. They were clothes donated to the local thrift store. A lot of what filled her closet was from the old folk's home, you know after the old cronies died. Sadly, these crappy outfits looked better on the old people."

I couldn't imagine this poor girl having to endure such a life. Worse than that, she had to endure it with Vanessa. Life would have been hard enough without the designer bitch at her side.

Vanessa continued. "In school, the teachers had given up on her. With all that was going on in her home life, she was too distracted to learn. Each year she got uglier and stupider. I'm surprised her mother hung in as long as she did."

"Hung in?" Against my better judgement, I had to ask. See how I have a hard time keeping quiet. "What do you mean?"

"She overdosed on pills one night."

"So how is any of this relevant to us? Did this friend tell you to fall in love with a married man? Did she ask you to kill people?"

Vanessa frowned, but carried on with her story. "I watched her make mistake after mistake; the way she spoke, her posture, the way she was quick to put up with other people's crap. She had no backbone. This pitiful thing had been programmed to put up with crap and to accept the small pittances that came her way, but it was all brainwashing."

"She didn't know any better."

"Exactly!" Her eyes lit up knowing that I understood. "That's because they didn't see the big picture. They didn't see what this world had to offer. It wasn't crackers and water. It was champagne and caviar. Successful people know better because they've been there. They visualise what they want. They see what this world has to offer and they seize it."

"But I'm a person. What about what I want?"

"What you want? You wanted to have sex with me and you seized your opportunity, or have you forgotten. You wanted it and because you believed, you made it happen. Back in the car, that trigger wasn't pulled when you had the chance. Deep down inside, you truly care for me. I'm an upgrade, a newer model. All your life you've been told it's wrong to leave your wife, but by listening to them, you're fighting your true feelings. There isn't a man out there that wouldn't trade his old wife in for a younger one. You're just trying to do what's socially acceptable. You have history with Katie. But nobility isn't practical, Johnny. I'm the new and improved. Follow your heart, Johnny. All you've got is the here and now. Live for today, because there are no do-overs. You owe yourself."

"All we were was a weak moment. I wasn't myself."

"I think you were more yourself than you care to admit."

I wasn't admitting anything. It was ridiculous. "I need to ask, what happened to Doris?"

"She died shortly after her mother's death."

The girl had known Vanessa and she'd ended up dead. Why didn't that surprise me?

Chapter sixty-four

Knuckles rapping on the door woke me from my sleep. Vanessa was already at the window, peeking through a crack in the curtains. "Shhh, not a word."

Oh yes, the drill. The knocking repeated and I realised it was next door. A muffled voice introduced himself as officer something-or-other and there was something about a manhunt, followed by needing to have a look. This wasn't good.

Vanessa dashed past me. I could feel her glare, like this was somehow my fault. When she raced back to the door her head was white. She'd wrapped her hair up in a towel. The old lady was mumbling something about cookies and the officer was giving her a 'no thank you ma'am.' Then it was our turn.

Like the last door, the first knuckle-rapping was polite. The second knock was impatient. Vanessa was willing to wait him out, but through the door you could hear the officer asking the manager if he had a key.

The door quickly popped open, but only as far as the chain would allow. Only Vanessa's head was visible to him. "Forgive me officer. I was in the shower."

"I'm sorry, but we're doing a door-to-door check for a fugitive."

"Why I'm dripping wet."

"Not to worry I'll give you a couple of minutes to get dressed. I have to search the room."

"I can assure you I'm the only one here."

"I have my orders." He pulled the door shut. "Two minutes, ma'am."

"Shit." She sat down on the bed, rubbing her temple with the barrel of the gun. How ironic it would have been if she accidentally blew a quarter of her brain away. I chuckled inside and waited, but it wasn't meant to be.

After a generous five minutes, the officer asked to come in. He was ignored. I had to remind myself not to look at her, but I was curious. The fact that she was rubbing her temple with the gun meant she wasn't sure how to handle this. The fact that I could see this was still amazing me.

"Open the door ma'am or I'll be forced to kick it in."

"You'll be responsible for damages," another voice shouted out.

Vanessa rose and let the towel fall to the floor. Her temple no longer needed the barrel of the gun rubbing it. Squaring her feet to the door she lifted the gun and took aim. It was targeting a spot about four feet up on the door. Within seconds her target would be the officer. He opened the door and the chain caught it. I wondered if he had any idea what he was getting himself into. Did he have his gun drawn?

Before I could yell out, his regulation boot efficiently kicked the door open. The chain snapped. I'm sure he expected to see a half-dressed female, but Vanessa was fully clothed and ready. Her first shot struck him in the gut sending him back into the outside world where he'd come from. In that world, people screamed their disbelief and scattered for safety. In their wildest dreams no one could have imagined anything like this happening in Dinkytown.

She almost ripped my shoulder from its socket as we made our way to the car. "Let's move."

The young officer was in a heap on the ground, moaning as we passed by. His wound wasn't a fatal one. Vanessa raised the gun to his head. Why not, he had seen her. We all knew a badge doesn't buy special privileges. My knee caught her hip as the gun went off sending a slug into the fender of a car.

For a small woman she had strength to compliment her anger. I found the back seat in record time. In a cloud of tire smoke, we howled out of the parking lot and sped down the main street.

A black-and-white cruiser met us halfway through town. I wasn't sure what it was until the red and blue lights started bouncing off the buildings. The back wheels locked up as it spun a one-eighty. I'm guessing Vanessa's lead foot had caught their attention.

There were no cars to weave through and no pedestrians to mow down. Even the stray dogs had left for the safer back alleyways. The scream of the siren didn't relent because in a town this size, speeding made us public enemy number one. They had no idea about their downed brother yet.

About a mile out of town the cruiser slowed, pulled over and turned around. They had just received word about their friend.

Vanessa was seething. Not because she'd dug a deeper hole for herself, or because she'd forgotten the leftover chicken back in the motel fridge. She was mad at me.

"So…how long you been able to see?"

Chapter sixty-five

I had given myself away, not that I had a choice. He had seen her, and she was in some crazed video-game mode. Like some soldier of fortune, she was capping anyone and everyone that could identify her in a line-up. Had I not stopped her, who knew what she would have done? Grandma next door might get popped right between the lookers while the chocolate-chip cookies she was baking for us browned nicely in the oven. Oh, there's a little boy eating ice cream across the street, blammo, not anymore. Nope, I was right to make a stand, stupid, but definitely right.

"I'm waiting for an answer, Johnny." I didn't need to see her nostrils to know they were flared. "You can see again, so you better explain."

All I gave her was silence. It was safer, since I was in the doghouse anyway. All I could hope for now was to wake up and find that this was all some horrible dream. This couldn't have become my life. I installed Freon lines at a truck plant. I went fishing on the weekend, up at Dee Lake. I was your typical average Joe, as boring as they came.

"Damn you." I heard the sole of her shoe slap against the brake pedal and in seconds we went from a screaming one hundred miles an hour, to her rummaging in the trunk. The car was sitting sideways in the middle of the road at the end of four black lines. I prayed nobody came by. She'd start shooting and we'd be off to Walmart for more ammo—again, my fault.

The door opened and, setting the gun on the road, she swung my feet around. As she tied them, I remained perfectly still.

"I can't believe you Johnny Pettinger. This is not how we build trust."

Not how we build trust? That triggered me to remember part of my dream. The wolf had killed three and injured a fourth. Oh my God, Vanessa was my Scruffy, but how, why?

Maybe what she needed was a little bad-boy Johnny. She wanted a Johnny who was strong, confident, and not going to take any shit from any woman. I think most women want that dominant male, secure and masculine. I could do this. Taking a deep breath, I became that guy. Exhaling that breath, I developed second thoughts. Did I really need to stand up to her? Would it make a difference or just get me killed? I needed to go with my gut.

"Look Vanessa I –" My words were cut short by the gun barrel's pressure on my carotid artery. It was cold, like I imagined death's bony finger would be.

"Not now Johnny. I'm too pissed for an apology."

Well, I had tried. What more could a man do? And then there was the seatbelt and the duct tape, ripped from the roll and plastered across my mouth. I'm no shrink, but I doubt these were common trust-building practices.

Another poor trust-building practice was having a scarf draped across my eyes and tied at the side of my head in such a fashion as to bring tears to my eyes. She'd caught hair in the knot and by pulling it tight I swear she yanked the hair from my scalp. When I flinched, she gave it another tug, just because. The pain brought more tears and before the blindfold could absorb them, we were back up to speed.

What was next? I'm not sure if my safety was ever in question, but everyone else's seemed to be. Nobody else needed to die because of what I had done. I still had a hard time accepting the fact that three people were already dead, and that a young cop was on the ground in a parking lot, blood pouring from his belly.

Earlier, she had kept one eye on the seatbelt light. I doubt she was watching that light anymore. I inhaled. I was mustering courage, courage to stop her before she killed again. I'd been selfish to put my safety ahead of everyone else, but how could I have known? I took a deep breath, held it while I imagined my death, then I exhaled. I couldn't fail the next person, or the next people.

Another deep breath was held, bringing calm and courage. Then, with as much force as I could muster, and thank God these cars had good leg room, I drew my legs into my chest and thrust them into the back of her seat.

The car crossed the centreline tearing the steering wheel out of her hand, so far so good. I quickly recoiled as she regained control. I jammed my feet back into her seat. This time her blonde locks snapped forward and her head struck the steering wheel. Through the windshield I could see the left side of the ditch followed by the road and then the right side. It came up fast.

Thankfully, I was wearing my seatbelt.

Chapter sixty-six

We were airborne for a split-second before slamming into the earth. The car skipped through the ditch and into the field like a flat stone on a still pond. Okay, there were a few bone-jarring impacts and one of them popped the hood open. Another crumpled the front fenders.

At this point the hood kept me from seeing through the windshield. I missed seeing the fence posts explode into toothpicks. I missed the clumps of grass and dirt as they rode up and over the grill like waves rolling in on a Mexican coastline. The doors buckled, and the front wheels folded under the car. I missed that too.

When we finally came to a stop, we'd travelled fifty yards from the road. It would've been further if not for that half-buried rock. I think it was called an erratic, a rock dropped by some glacier centuries ago. Whatever it was called, it was solid, and it pulled the seatbelt across my chest so hard I swear I heard ribs crack. Vanessa should have been launched through the windshield, but the previous impacts had jostled her to the floor. This last impact had stuffed her under the dashboard.

The seatbelt had cut into my wrist like a bad rope burn. My ears rang as if a fire alarm was going off in my head, and my blindfold had ended up by the dashboard. I swear my legs were two feet shorter, and as bad as I felt, Vanessa had to be feeling worse. Her crumpled body lay on the passenger floor, twisted and lifeless.

The stench of scorched motor-oil and anti-freeze wafted through the holes in the windshield and into the car. Had the ground torn the oil pan off? Had the splinters of that fence post punched their way through the radiator? When they roped off this crime scene with the yellow tape, people would slow down to look at the skid marks and they'd stare at the gaping wounds to the Earth. They'd look at the car and wonder how it happened. Speculation might include a deer or alcohol. They'd all be buying tomorrow's newspaper to see if their guesses were correct.

At least it was all over. I had survived and she hadn't. In the next hour or two a car would drive by and they'd see us. I'd be going home and Vanessa would be on her way to joining her friends in a hole that, when filled, would be called a grave.

I tried to open my door but couldn't. Waiting in the car wasn't an option. Still, there was a part of me, albeit a small part, that felt a need to check on her. It would be the responsible thing to do. Somehow, I knew that if I did, it would turn out bad. I wasn't sure how I knew this. I just did, yet I looked anyway.

She was breathing. I looked away to the cottony plumes of smoke as they slowly curled up from the front fenders and drifted up into the sky. Shouldn't that have been a sign of closure, a white flag? It wasn't.

Her voice, weak and groggy, called out. "Johnny?"

What the hell? This woman had unstoppable powers. With my legs tucked up against my chest, I started on the knot, that is, right after I illuminated the seatbelt light. I didn't figure I needed to worry about it after what I'd done.

"John…" There was a bewildered impatience.

She'd need a minute or two to collect her thoughts. I had to be gone when she got them gathered. Trembling hands fidgeted at the knot, but my blood was making the rope slippery. It took a minute.

I got my feet free and tried the door again. The body of the car had twisted enough to seal me in. The side windows were too small, so I spun around to kick out the back window. That was when I noticed it was already missing. Missing wasn't exactly accurate. It was in the backseat, the front seat, and all over the floor—thousands of little diamonds. I was wearing a few of them as I rolled off the trunk and landed on the ground with an awkward thump.

My legs were stiff, and my knees felt like tree stumps as I pulled myself up. Curiosity had me looking in through the windows to see if I could find the gun. I swear I would use it this time... maybe... doubtfully.

"Johnny, where are you?" Her arm was folded under the glove compartment.

She was awake, collecting her thoughts. My options were back to the road, where I was a sitting duck, or to the tree-line, which was at least a hundred yards away. Vanessa's arm was free. I looked but couldn't see the gun. I couldn't waste a lot of time worrying about it.

The grass was waist-high as I hobbled through it without looking back. Stumbling twice, I picked myself up and finally reached the trees. I was about to look back when a bullet ripped through a branch only eight feet away. Vanessa was free, and she had found the gun.

And because of me, another tree had been shot.

Chapter sixty-seven

At this point I'd be a fool to believe she hated the trees. Accepting the fact that the bullets were meant for me, forced me deeper into the forest for shelter. Another shot sent several small twigs flying as it whizzed past. There was no looking back. I had to keep moving.

With my hands in front of my face I could count fingers. I could see my wedding band. Trees that were ten to fifteen feet in front of me became brown vertical or horizontal lines. Climbing over or under the horizontal ones, and side-stepping the vertical ones, I established a rhythm.

"Johnny." Her voice made my stomach lurch. It never ends, that is, until it ends. "I forgive you. Just come back."

But the gun had done enough of the talking. I gauged her to be about seventy-five yards away. I was losing ground. I tried to run, but my legs went out from under me. Mud, or something, tripped me up and I fell to the ground with a sickening thump. My shoulder took the brunt of the pain.

But this wasn't mud. This was the 'or something'. The pungent smell told me it was fresh. It was also all the way up my right leg to the hip. The brown lines I could dodge like a linebacker. The brown pile of bear shit took me down like a wet sheet of ice. With scat all over me, even a city girl like Vanessa could track me.

"Johnny, where are you? We've got to get moving before the cops come." Her cries were closing in on me.

"That's right, keep screaming." I muttered to myself. With any luck Old Smokey would find her before finding me. He had just made room for another meal.

I picked up the pace. The fall had cost me thirty yards. Soon I'd be in her site lines.

"Oh, Johnny." Her laugh became hearty. Only she could find humour in anything right now. "Did my man step in bear poop?"

Damn if she wasn't closer than I thought. There was no looking back. Ahead of me I could hear rushing water and I headed for it. I could cross the river and lose the smell at the same time. If the water was cold enough, she might not follow.

The underbrush grew thicker as I trudged toward the river. Branches slapped me in the face and gnarled roots tried to trip me up. And through it all I left a trail of bear scat. The river couldn't come quick enough.

When the density of trees finally thinned, a sudden clearing gave me the most majestic view of the river. Sadly, it wasn't in front of me. From high up on the cliff ledge, I got to see the blurred river below. I also got to see the waterfall that fed it. That was to my right, along with an impassable wall of jagged rock. Had my eyes been working better, I'd have tried climbing it, but they weren't. To the left of me the cliff continued around the corner. The drop was a hundred feet, maybe more.

I was boxed in and this was my final stand. There was no more left in the tank. Above me the clouds were growing darker and moving fast. A storm was coming. When I turned around, I saw Vanessa, standing there with the gun.

The storm had arrived.

Chapter sixty-eight

"Were you really going to leave me to die?"

She stood twenty feet away and I could see that the brows of her eyes were turned down. I blinked twice. Yes, they were definitely angry. My sight was getting better by the second, not that it did me any of good. Her locks of blonde hair were tangled. Blood dripped from her hairline, over her eye, and down her right cheek. Still, the girl found a way to smile as she stood there.

"What about you? This is the second time you've fired shots at me." I tried to match her confidence as I held my end of the stalemate. "You could have killed me."

"Warning shots, you ass."

"Bullshit!"

"If I wanted to h-hit you, I'd have hit you." She lifted her arm and squeezed the trigger, firing a round into my left leg.

"Fuck!" Damn it, I was tired of being wrong. The bullet ripped into my thigh and staggered me, but I refused to let it take me down. As for the pain, a gunshot was surprisingly better than a bear's jaw. It was quick, a burst of heat followed by an instant cramping sensation. "No more, Vanessa."

"See Johnny, I never shot you b-before because I didn't want to. I really do love you."

"Why?" I looked back over my shoulder, sizing up the drop to the river. That was not an option. "We were only together the one time."

"Of all the times I've…you know, it's always been cold, simple, dirty. Two objects bumping in the night. You were different. The way you caressed my cheek when you kissed me, the way you h-held me afterward, it was r-romantic." She shook her head as she briefly rolled her eyes. "I enjoyed you touching me."

"But I…"

"Answer me this." She tried to fight back a tear but couldn't. "Why n-not me? I'm young, perky, and I know you liked what we did."

"Here's a question for you. Why not someone your own age, someone who doesn't have a wife and children."

"Because I found you."

"I'm sure I'm not the first one to touch you or have feelings like that. Other men must have—"

"Other men? You were m-my first man, J-J-Johnny. The others were not men. They were foster fathers, too scared to wake their wives in the middle of the night. They were businessmen that promised love but gave me trinkets and b-black eyes. I was one of their whores."

"None of them loved you?"

"They couldn't. Their damn w-wives w-w-w…fuck! w-wouldn't let them."

I'd never seen her so vulnerable. Her lip quivered, and her tears glistened in the late morning sun. They rolled down her cheeks, morphing her into a human. I could only stare.

"What is it about me Johnny? Am I still that ugly girl?"

"What?" I must have missed something. She had a beauty so powerful it was lethal. It allowed her to take whatever she wanted, including my better judgement.

"Come on. I felt your p-passion. It was raw, animalistic, and yet so tender. You enjoyed me. I did something wrong, didn't I? What was it?"

"You did nothing wrong, Vanessa. I'm a married man. Surely you knew I couldn't go any further with this."

"That's not it. Being m-married didn't stop you, because you don't love her. You wouldn't have t-touched me like that if it were just sex. I know sex."

Her gaze dropped down to my leg. She was worried about the bleeding.

"I do love you, Johnny. Did you know I c-cried after we made love? I'd never been so happy. You made me f-feel special."

"Vanessa, it was wrong." I never realised the feeling on the other end of what we'd done. This girl wasn't as bad a person as she was desperate and alone. I had fed on that for a few hours of pleasure. I was nothing more than a catalyst. "I never meant to hurt you."

"I'm sure you didn't. Just as I'm sure my mother and father never meant to hurt me. Nobody ever means to hurt me. It just happens. I had seven sets of foster parents. Three didn't want a girl, too needy for them. Two didn't like my age and wanted younger and c-cuter. One thought I ate too f-f-fast which was not very lady-like, and the last one's wife caught us late one night on the couch. None of them meant to hurt me.

S-s-seven times I was fostered out and s-seven times I was returned like one might return a cat to the animal shelter. The tail's too short, it stays up too late at night, it sheds, the hair is too short, or the hair is to long. This one climbs curtains. What the f-fuck, Johnny? So now you want to throw me back too? Except I'm not a cat. I'm a human being. I have feelings. Shit, even all those c-cats have feelings. We don't deserve to be cast aside after you find we're not p-perfect."

She raised the gun and started walking toward me. "Have you ever f-felt rejected?" The barrel was trained on my left eye. I could see the darkness hiding in the barrel.

My sight was coming back, almost too well. I tried not to show her the pain. On the verge of buckling, my leg and shoulder throbbed uncontrollably. Blood trickled down my leg.

"Vanessa, please. We have to stop this. I need to see a doctor."

"W-we all have needs, J-Johnny." She continued to aim her gun at my head while she closed in on me. "I'd n-never reject you, and you're n-n-not going to cast me aside or r-return me either. I'm cute, intelligent and I deserve to be happy. I'm not a l-loser anymore."

Here I thought it was just sex, no strings and no guilt. But what we'd done wasn't anywhere close to that, nor was this a kidnapping. She wanted Katie dead because she wanted what Katie had, a loving man, a family. She wanted what had been eluding her all her life…love.

It sickened me, what she'd been through, but what sickened me more was that I was no better than the other men in her life. Now three feet away, the gun was directed at my right eye and the hammer had just been cocked.

Doris was about to kill again.

Chapter sixty-nine

Sirens, once wailing in the distance, grew louder before stopping. Above, a helicopter searched for the two occupants of the abandoned car. Traces of red and blue light were beginning to flash through the trees behind her. I was responsible for all of this. It was something I couldn't take back. Chances are, there'd be more death before it was over. I had to make this right while I still had time.

Vanessa had told me the story about her pathetic friend. She had been abused, neglected, and had never felt the love that every child deserved. This girl had been unwanted, and it showed in how she dressed, how she carried herself, and how she felt about herself. Most people saw her as a loser, if they even saw her at all. Vanessa said that her friend had died shortly after her mother took her own life. I now understood what she meant. The transformation had been incredible, but it had come with a price.

"I'm so sorry for this, Doris."

"Doris is dead." The gun remained between us as her eyes hardened. "And are you sorry you met me, or sorry I had such a pathetic life, because I am not p-pathetic. I learned a lot from being that child."

"I'm sorry that I was one in the long line of assholes that hurt you."

"Do you see what you just did? Because that's what makes you special." She was smiling again. "You're different from the rest." She paused. "We could still get away, b-but we need to go, now."

The barking of the dogs told me that the police were closer than she thought. There'd be no escaping. This was going to end here, and in the next couple of minutes. "I'm sure, if things were different, but they're not."

"No J-Johnny, they're not different and they never are. If only I was a little younger, a little older, if only you weren't m-m-arried. It's the story of my life."

"We're not going to run. I want to help you. I want to be there for you, but you need to get help." I had to make a stand, if not for me, for her. She'd had a lifetime of hurt and confusion and now it was time to start turning it around. She still had the rest of her life. "As a friend, I'll take those first steps with you."

Now she heard the dogs barking. "I can't go to jail."

I held out my arms as a gesture for a hug. "You have to deal with this, get the help you need, and I'll be there to help you. I promise you won't have to go through this alone."

I wasn't sure if I was overwhelmed with guilt, or perhaps it was the blood loss from my leg, but I truly meant it. Deep inside that troubled mind was a sweet girl. She just needed to feel the love of a friend.

"Like your wife would let you."

Would I even have a wife, after she heard about all of this? The one thing Katie found admirable about me, was my need to right the wrongs in my life. Hopefully she'd understand. "She doesn't have a say in this."

I took a shaky step toward her and she met me halfway. Her hands dropped to her side as I drew her close with my good arm. Her quivering body gave in to me and I held her tight as those first tears began to fall.

"Th-Thank you, J-Johnny."

Doris was nothing like Vanessa. Doris was innocent, young, and just wanted to find her place in this world. I had slept with

Vanessa but hurt Doris in the process. It made me sick when I thought back to that day. What it had meant to her would haunt me, but Doris could get help and I'd be there for her. Hopefully in time, helping her would lessen the guilt.

Inside her tangled mind there had been a struggle. Vanessa had given into Doris. Even she wanted change, wanted to know what a normal life might feel like, a life with love. Both were lost and very much alone. As a child, I had known that loneliness.

I let her drop her head on my chest. "It's okay Doris. I'll be there for y—".

"Freeze! Police!" A curt voice shouted the command from the trees. "Drop the gun!"

Given another ten seconds I could have taken the gun from her and this journey would have ended peacefully. Instead, Vanessa pushed Doris aside and scrambled behind me as she squeezed off a shot. It had been as instinctive as a dog's bark when the postman rang.

The next two shots, both fired by young police officers, struck me in the chest. The force of the bullets knocked me backwards. Surreal plumes of smoke hung in the air as I fell.

I landed face-down at the edge of the cliff. "Doris!"

In a far-away world I heard a man yelling. "Hold your fire! Hold your fire!"

Chapter seventy

I clutched the grass at the edge of the cliff as I watched Vanessa, now Doris, falling helplessly over the edge. Those two shots had hit me in the chest and pushed me backward into her. She had run out of real estate.

Her look was calm as she looked back at me, as if preferring this fate over having to deal with Vanessa. I closed my eyes before she hit the edge of the cliff, fifty feet below me. I'm sure she died with that impact. When I opened my eyes, her lifeless body had landed face-down in the river and she was bobbing and rolling with the rapids.

When life bit, it bit hard. Lives were changed; Vanessa, the two hunters, the two police officers and all the families involved. And as life-changing as these events were, outsiders saw it as just another day at the office. I'm sure the paramedics saw it that way. Tonight, they'd go home and turn on the game. Sure, they'd tell their friends that they'd worked on Johnny Pettinger, or they'd call me the late Johnny Pettinger. They'd hope their friends had heard of me. He was an author, or a poet, or something. One or two of them might be curious enough to go out and buy my book. It was the excitement they fed on. There'd be a search for some woman's body. They did this kind of thing all the time.

Soon our story wouldn't compare to the one about the chair-lift accident with the drunken college girls in bikinis. I know I'd rather hear that story. One thing for sure was that no one in Dinkytown would ever forget Vanessa. Her beauty, and her ease at putting fear into all their hearts, would last for generations. Too bad they never got to know Doris. She was one of them.

Since there was no guarantee that I'd make it, I must thank you for listening. My guilt for Katie, for Doris, and for those who were simply in the wrong place at the wrong time festers deeply. I honestly had no way of knowing that a romp with some young girl would change so many lives. If I could take it all back I would, but life doesn't work that way. In real life there are no do-overs, just a whole lot of knowledge acquired from getting it wrong.

To have one's life flash before your eyes is like living a dream. A heightened awareness reveals the truth and the lies. In the end it also provides one with two options. You can continue living the lie, or you can embrace the truth. Me, I'm more partial to the truth. Even if I live, and Katie doesn't take me back, I'd still have a lot to live for.

You're still in my head and now you know my story. Sorry it wasn't a prettier one. My beaten and bloodied body floats weightless on the gurney as I'm carried off to the hospital. This place, with bleached white walls and its stench of disinfectant, will decide how my story ends.

Thank you for listening.

Again, I ask one simple favour. If you see Katie before I do, please say nothing. I need to be the one to tell her.

Chapter seventy-one

My eyes opened slowly and once again I was blind. The shoulder didn't hurt. My mind carried me back to the days on the plane. A lone brain cell bounced around inside my head searching for logic. Had the car-chase and shootings been a dream? Had the bear attack not destroyed my shoulder? Where was Ben? With any luck Vanessa was still just a misguided young woman behind a desk at my publisher's office. There was no abused child named Doris hiding in the corner of my hospital room while her grown-up self laughed at my charred corpse. The two hunters would not have dug the hole beside the cabin, and tonight, a blonde police officer would be watching television with her cat, if she had one.

I had to believe that, when I got up, there'd be a lake behind my plane and the fish in it would taste amazing. I also believed that the whiskey that launched these crazy dreams would leave me with one whopper of a headache.

But the logic, found by that lone brain cell, wouldn't find that. It would find a hand, lightly and lovingly holding mine. With my arms weighted like sandbags, all I could muster in response was a gentle squeeze. I knew right away that this was Katie's hand. Only her hand fit mine this well.

"Johnny?" The voice was as comforting as a warm summer rain, and as gentle as the breeze that often followed it.

"Hi, Darling." My words were no more than a whisper.

"Try not to talk, you've been through a lot."

It was safe to assume that the kidnapping wasn't a dream. Back on the cliffs I remembered Doris falling. I saw it. If that was real, why was I blind? It didn't make sense. "What happened to me? I can't see you."

"Your eyes are bandaged." Her voice was soothing. "I should get the doctor. He wanted to know when—"

"Don't go." I gripped her fingers tighter. "We need to talk."

"You need to see the doctor, John."

"After what I've been through, I think he can wait a few minutes. I need to tell you something."

"About what, the bear attack, the old man in the cabin, the two dead hunters, or… Vanessa?"

How was it possible? The only ones that knew these stories were either dead, or they were crickets.

But Katie was never in the dark about anything. She always knew what was going on, and it wasn't just the kids wondering if this woman had eyes in the back of her head. "But how?"

"You've been mumbling some fairly far-fetched tales since you got out of surgery. For the last twelve hours I've heard bits and pieces of a pretty remarkable story. A lot of it didn't make any sense until I sat down with the sheriff. I also had a talk with Eric. I wish you would've told me."

"That's why I was coming home."

"Sounds like you were debating on saying anything."

"At first." Had I told her about why I'd brought my fishing pole and golf clubs? I never knew when to shut up. She must have been the one in my head. I had confessed everything to her. It wasn't the way I wanted her to find out, but at least my shame was out, and I'd been the one to tell her. "You know I never meant to hurt you."

"I know."

There was a silence that quickly became awkward.

"Where do we go from here?" I mean I wanted to go home, but that was asking a lot. "Let me prove I can be a great husband."

In her silence, I heard a no. If I put myself in her shoes, it wouldn't have been that easy to forgive. Before this, we had an unspoken trust, a love that was unconditional. Our love and that trust were what defined us.

"You know I love you, Katie."

"I know."

The pain in her heart had the tears running down her cheeks. I didn't need to see them to know they were there. The bandages were not only protecting my eyes, they were protecting me from seeing her heartbreak.

Her fingers slipped from my grasp. "I'll go get the doctor."

Chapter seventy-two

Y ou gave us quite a scare Mr. Pettinger. You lost a lot of blood. I'd say you owe our bank a few pints." The chipper doctor carried the air of someone busy and yet, oddly, he was in no hurry. "We operated on your shoulder and leg and they're coming along nicely. The shoulder will need more surgery, in time. Your ribs caught the two slugs without doing any internal damage. All things considered, you're a lucky man."

I didn't feel lucky. My chest felt like there were concrete slabs resting on them. "Are you sure, Doc? My chest hurts like hell."

"I'm sure it does, but I can assure you those rubber bullets did nothing more than bruise your ribs. You're on some strong painkillers, but you'll feel that tightness for a few days. I'll take the tape off your ribs on Friday. That should help loosen you up."

Rubber bullets? They had hit me like bowling balls. "What about my eyes?"

"We had to treat the scarring from the lightning flash. It was very similar to a welder's flash. You were given drops of atropine to relax the eyes and an antibacterial to make sure there was no infection. They'll continue to heal in time. Do you think you're ready to see again?"

"Definitely."

The doctor started to peel back the tape while holding the gauze pads in place. "Nurse, can we turn the lights off and close the blinds halfway."

"Sure doctor." Her obedience darkened the room.

"Okay John, I'm going to remove the gauze, so close your eyes. I'll get you to open them slowly. Take your time."

The returning of my sight was finally going to happen. I couldn't wait. In the woods, all I could think about was seeing Katie. Nothing was going to keep me from that vision except...

"What do you see John?" The doctor asked.

"I see an old man with a gun and a silver star on his chest." It wasn't exactly what I had expected, and it wasn't my wife.

"Hello Mr. Pettinger, I'm Sheriff McCall." He announced the name as if there was importance linked to it. "Two of my rookies did this to you and I just want you to know that I'm terribly sorry."

"I should be glad they weren't better shots." I mumbled.

"If they were, they'd have hit her instead of you. We're working on them."

It was a reassurance that wasn't all that comforting. At least he was smart enough to step aside when Katie tapped him on the shoulder. She moved in next to me and took my hand.

"Hi, Katie." The concrete blocks on my chest became heavier. "I've missed you so much."

She said nothing. What was there to say, she was glad I was alive, but my stuff was sitting on the front lawn? She could share how she felt each night, thinking I was dead, or how she cried when she first found out about Vanessa.

The doctor stepped in and pulled a small penlight out of his pocket. He flashed it into my right eye first, followed by my left. "Let's fill you in on a few basics. You're at Deaconess Hospital in Spokane."

"Did I crash near here?" Spokane was two hours from the Canadian border.

"Your plane was found south west of here, out at Otter Lake," the Sheriff answered. "You got my attention when you rode through Lakeland County, which is in my jurisdiction."

Lakeland County? So, it wasn't called Dinkytown.

Katie squeezed my hand and gave me a smile. "You might want to tell him about the cabin, Sheriff McCall."

"Oh yes, the cabin." He chuckled. "Me and your Mrs. talked about what you told her. We were trying to piece things together. Oh, and before I forget, I'm going to have to get a statement from you, but not until you're feeling better, of course."

"Of course." He was the sheriff and I wasn't going anywhere. I remembered the cabin and how my heart sank after talking to the hunters. I had that old prospector in my life only because I needed him. Then Cowboy and Nellie showed up and just like that, I was alone. "Actually, I feel a little silly about that. I know there was no cabin. I was going a little loco, being alone in the woods and all. It gets pretty big out there when you're by yourself."

"I won't argue that. Most people don't know it, but that cabin is there. It's just a burnt out mess with a rusty old potbelly stove in the corner. A bunch of crickets were living in it the last time I was out there. It was about hundred and fifty yards in front of your plane, hidden by a lot of overgrown grass and weeds. You had mentioning that place and that was how we found your plane."

"Seriously?" I felt a tingling at the base of my neck.

"My grandpa used to hunt in that area and he knew the old guy who lived in it. The old codger spent a lifetime as a guide, dragged thousands into the area to hunt. He died in the winter of fifty-nine and six years later a forest fire burnt his home to a cinder. Grandpa continued to hunt in the area and swore that whenever he got near the cabin, he could smell the old man's raunchy stew." His clumsy smile peeked out from under a bushy grey moustache as he finished the story. "Crazy, huh?"

"Not so much."

"I hate to interrupt a good story, but I have rounds to make. The eyes look good. How are they working?" The blinds were open now. "Does the light bother them?"

"No. They're good. Thanks, Doc."

With a smile and a reassuring nod, he patted my good leg and turned to leave. "I'll check back in an hour. Try not to overdo your visits. You need your rest."

The sheriff also took that as a cue to leave. "I'll come back tomorrow for that statement." At the doorway he turned back to me. "Sorry about the way this all turned out, Mr. Pettinger."

I shrugged. "I'm still here. I wouldn't have put money on that a day ago."

I heard his laugh as he left the room and started down the hallway. The chuckle reminded me of Ben, the old prospector.

With the sheriff gone, I turned to Katie. She still had my hand in hers. "Can you ever forgive me?"

Her smile wilted.

Chapter seventy-three

The last two weeks of recovery had been a blur, but no longer because of my sight. That had become crystal clear. When I left the hospital, both Katie and I agreed I needed my own apartment. We weren't sure what we were doing, and I had to accept the fact that she needed some space. I couldn't blame her for that. As much as I was struggling with my guilt, she was struggling with her heart.

In this time, I had faced a few harsh realities. The first was that, no matter how much two people loved each other, there are certain boundaries you cannot cross. I'd crossed that boundary with Vanessa and hurt Katie in a way that made her realise that no love is unconditional. The innocence of what made us a good team had been tainted.

For the sake of the kids, we'd stay friends and I knew she still had deep feelings for me, but we'd lost a big part of what made us work so well. She wasn't vengeful, nor was she capable of hating me. Because of that I always got to see the kids.

The kids were my second big reality. I knew I'd hurt Katie, but I didn't get the full effect that all this would have on Brook and Danny. They also wanted answers. We wanted to give them answers, sparing the details. They had a harder time with the break-up than either of us thought. Katie took the brunt of their frustration. Again, I was off the hook, not held responsible. I wanted to be. It wasn't fair, but that was life.

I was also off the hook for having to see the pain in the eyes of those who lost loved ones. The female cop turned out to be single. Still, her parents had to be crushed when they received word. I never found out anything about the two hunters and I didn't want to know. They had saved me twice and kept me fed. I'd always think fondly of them.

A few days ago, there was a funeral. I attended it alone. Doris's life had ended and the least I could do was see her off. Three people showed up and they didn't have much to say about her. The pastor was even lost for words, so I went up and said a few. She wasn't just a beautiful girl and a wonderful person. Granted, she tried to kill me, and succeeded in killing others, but that was Vanessa, not Doris. We needed to understand that there were two different people living inside that body. It wasn't any different than having an evil twin. That was what I kept telling myself.

Doris, the world will miss you. You just needed to rid yourself of Vanessa. In some ways she made you strong, made you beautiful, but in the end, she was holding you back. Her bitterness kept you from finding love. It was out there. It was just a matter of trusting your path to bring it to you. We all have a Vanessa in us and that's not a terrible thing. We just needed to know when to stand up to her.

On a good note, my mother hadn't called me since the whole scandalous mess hit the news. I went from loser son, to winner son and finally took my place as the asshole. It all happened so quickly. At least I'm not a boring son. I doubt she'll ever forgive me, but there's not a lot I can do about that. I've learned to be okay with that.

My new home keeps the rain off my head and the flies out of my soup. Modest for a man of my wealth, it humbly serves all my needs. The kids visit on weekends and stay in the spare room. Katie brings them over faithfully and she never speaks poorly of me to them, her family, or anyone else. She even defends me to her friends and I appreciate that.

And from all the bad that had come from this, there were a few silver linings. I had my sight back and I had a whole new perspective of myself. I even got that book, the one about living in the moment. Eric said I had an even bigger lining. Scandals had a way of making celebrities even more popular with their fans. In short, this meant a book deal was already in the works for this misadventure.

I was three chapters into that novel when I decided to take a break. A can of Pepsi sat beside me on the end table and I grabbed for it. There was nothing easy about moulding these horrid events into words or chapters. Without Katie and the kids, there was little inspiration.

When the phone rang it startled me. I picked it up knowing it was Eric. "What did they say?"

"It's a go, my friend." This was money in the bank for him, for us. "Let's not waste any time, John. Remember, time is—"

My thumb ended the call. I was pretty sure I knew how it worked.

Chapter seventy-four

B efore I knew it, a month and a half of writing had passed. The place I had found, when I got out of the hospital, had become home. It was ordinary, but I didn't care to have anything more than that. At least it was in the same neighbourhood as Katie and the kids. As much as I'd tried, I didn't fit into the champagne, caviar, and mansion life. I really did prefer the odd beer with a bag of chips. I always will.

Last week I graduated from a cast and cane to a bad limp. My shoulder had been operated on a second time and I had limited use of it. It will get better in time, if I take it easy. I spent eighty percent of my time in my armchair typing, so resting it wasn't a problem.

Most days I was writing pretty good stuff about what I went through. True stories always sold, and Eric said we had to work fast. I was still in the news and that was publicity gold.

I put the pop down and continued to type.

Perfection in a woman comes in two forms. We have the girl next door. Her beauty is angelic and she radiates charm, loving, patience and respect for everything. A true nurturer, she's the first one there in times of need. She easily wins the hearts of parents, grandparents and kids and, although she may not turn heads quite as fast as a supermodel, everyone notices her and smiles as she passes by. Imperfections in this woman are cute, quirky features and are adored.

The other creature of perfection not only turns heads at the beach, she gives the boys whiplash. She hides her imperfections by bringing her strong points to centre-stage. She knows when to say those trivial things that float your ego high enough into the stratosphere to cloud your judgement. You not only feel good around her, you feel great around her. She takes years off your age and your friends have no choice but to envy you. With her on your arm, you can ride success effortlessly, all the way to the bank...

I had to stop. Where was I going with this crap? I didn't need philosophy. I needed an ending. Who wanted to read a story about some lame-ass who cheats on his wife? A bear eats him, he meets a ghost who makes squirrel stew, and he gets kidnapped by a psycho. He survives all that, only to get dumped by his wife? That was not the best-selling ending that this book needed.

This was crap. How did my protagonist evolve? How did I evolve? What was it about human nature that always had us looking for the upgrade? Is never being satisfied tempered into our soul?

If I parked a new Cadillac in my driveway, I'd be on top of the world? I would be until my neighbour drove up in his new Porsche. Now my Caddy might as well have been a Pinto... hatchback. He'd be on cloud nine until the guy across the street bought a Ferrari. But that Ferrari couldn't be driven when it rained or if the wind picked up. And try finding a safe place to park where it wouldn't get dinged. Only then did you realise that the fancy car was just a royal pain in the ass. Oh, and did I tell you his winter beater was a Pinto... hatchback.

I got up and grabbed a fresh soda from the fridge. I think part of my writer's block stemmed from Eric. He phoned every day, bringing a solid foundation of guilt with each call. I felt for him because he needed this book out as soon as possible. Strike while the iron was hot, make hay while the sun shined, blah, blah, blah...

When this book is finished, it'll start on the bestseller's list. It should sell twice what my first book sold. I didn't need the money though. My old book had returned to a solid place in the top twenty. But the energy over my next book was electric. Everyone liked reading about an asshole that got tortured repeatedly. The masses wanted to hear how I lusted, suffered and survived. It was always more fun when it happened to someone else. It gave them someone to relate to. Yes, we could all relate, because we all wanted more.

Whatever the reason for Eric's impatience, he had a tough job keeping everyone happy. Writers were artists and didn't seem to care how long it took. It had to be perfect. Publishers had quotas and deadlines. They didn't care about perfection for a hot story. They just wanted it good enough to put on a shelf. The story sold itself. Then there were the printers. There was nothing worse than a machine sitting idle on a promise. I was glad it was their responsibility to choreograph this shit and not mine.

This .doc file sat at a hundred and forty-five thousand words. It was typed out in such a way to thrill my readers, but I still needed that last handful of thoughts. I had stalled. In real life the ending kinda sucked. Besides, Katie was due to drop off the kids any minute now.

'*Driving down the highway...*' My phone started to vibrate and dance to the AC/DC tune. '*...going to a show.*' I loved that one.

"Hello?" I answered it like I didn't know who it was, but it could only be one person.

"Hey John, it's Eric."

Too bad there wasn't a prize for knowing.

"John, I had a dream last night. In it I had a manuscript."

"It's just about done."

"You've been saying that for two weeks now. The publisher is killing me on this end. He wants a book."

"Well then, how about you finish it?" I was getting sick of the excuses and so was he. "It's the ending. I don't have one."

"Put down anything. Trust me when I say, the ending isn't that big a deal. The readers want the sex, the adventure, and the murder. John, they want the excitement. Come on now, you're a writer. You say you know how all this works. Prove it. Pump it out so we can all make some money." It was like he'd grown tired of coddling me, tired of playing the game.

"Well it's a big deal to me!"

"I know, and you're right." There was a pause. He was recomposing himself. "What happened to you was bad, but this kind of thing gets cold. You're hot now. Who knows what they'll want next week. We need to act on this while it's still in the press."

"But the ending is the biggest part."

"The reader doesn't care. The publisher doesn't care. Trust me. You bagged a real bimbo in Vanessa. She tried to kill you and now she's gone. Just be glad it's over."

"Her name was Doris."

"Who cares. Because of her, you stand to make millions. You know what you need to do, so get busy. Do it, Johnny!"

"You're absolutely right, Eric." I ended the call before he could get another word in. I knew what I needed to do and Eric, of all people, had been the one to inspire me.

Go figure.

Chapter seventy-five

Eric had hit the switch in my head and the light bulb had finally flickered on. The darkness was gone, and the clarity had arrived. You see, when I got the notion to write the first book, I ran it past Katie. She gave me all her support and we hoped that someday it might make enough to scratch at a few bills and pay down the mortgage. That was all we wanted. It was a much simpler life without the deadlines, the commuting, and the social responsibility. This book wouldn't make me a better person or a better son. Nothing could do that except understanding Doris.

She died trying to do what I was doing now, trying to prove my worth to a world I could never satisfy. How many millions would it take? She never thought she was good enough for anyone and yet, she was. Her life ended as a scared little girl who had missed out, only because others didn't understand.

In my dreams, she was that tattered little girl in the corner of my hospital room feeding off of the pain of others. She was the scruffy wolf I was willing to leave behind, wounded by my rejection. Love is found in different ways and for most of us it lies in the approval of others. Too bad it was so hard to love ourselves.

This book would never express who Doris was and it wouldn't get Katie back or define who I was, but I knew what would.

Unplugging the cord on my laptop, I calmly folded it shut and tossed it ten feet into the wastebasket by the doorway. It felt good to hear it hitting the bottom. I'd be okay with never seeing another keyboard as long as I lived.

I quickly grabbed my phone and dialled Joe Lamborne.

"Joe here." His voice was gruff.

"Hi Joe, its Johnny."

"Pettinger?"

"I'll never get one by you. So how are you keeping these days?"

"Me? I'm good, but I'm not the one crashing planes into mountains. How the heck are you doing?"

"I'm okay. Hey, I was phoning for a favour."

"I'm not sure what I can do for you, but shoot."

"I was wondering how business is doing, like are you hiring?"

"Are you serious? I know you took quite a knock to the head. You're a writer now and a darn good one. Why would you want to come back here?"

"Ah Joe, I'm not a writer. For a little while I dabbled with the dream, but I'm back. So how about it, you guys hiring?"

"Shit Johnny, there's always a place for you here. Come in Monday if you want. Bring a box of donuts and we'll talk about when you're healthy enough to return."

It felt good to hear him say that. "Thanks Joe."

"Hey, and Johnny, I just want to say how sorry I am about you and Katie."

"Thanks, but it was my fault. She's a good woman. Sadly, I needed a stupid reminder." An awkward silence told us both that the call was over, so I said goodbye and hung up.

With my writing career in the garbage and my old job waiting for me at the factory, I sat back and tried to enjoy the moment. This was what living in the moment was all about. It wasn't about self-improvement, nor was it about spending money.

It was about mastering the art of self-satisfaction. Damn, that wasn't so hard.

A knock on the door got me out of my chair because that gentle rapping could only be Katie. The light scent of honeysuckle greeted me as I opened the door.

"Hi, Johnny." Her voice was as polite as a whisper.

She looked as sweet as she always did, and I wanted to drink her up. My heart grabbed at ribs like a kid playing on monkey bars as I gazed hopelessly into her eyes. She welcomed them with a smile.

"Can I come in?"

"Sorry, Dear. Of course you can. Come in."

I noticed the wiggle of her back pockets as she walked by. They were nice. Her hair hung down in a ponytail between her shoulder blades and I had to remind myself to breathe.

"Oh no." The concern in her voice caught me off guard. "I'm guessing your laptop gave up the ghost?"

"More like my writing career." I animated a smile across my face. She wanted to ask but didn't think it was her place, so I offered. "Eric will be waiting a long time for my next book. I'm no writer. I'm a factory worker."

"You mean you…"

"I just got off the phone with Joe and I'm seeing him on Monday."

"Good for you. I know how much you liked hanging out with those guys."

I reached inside the fridge for a bottle of water. "Want one?"

"Sure. But I don't want to stay long." Her hands fidgeted. They only did that when she was nervous.

"Okay." I'd noticed earlier that she was alone, but I'd enjoyed the conversation too much to bring it up, until now. "So where are the kids?"

"About that. Can we go for a walk? We need to talk."

It was like she'd been rehearsing this talk all afternoon. That scared me. Was I going to be regulated with the kids? Was she moving? Was I going to need a good lawyer? I walked her to the door and held it for her as we stepped outside.

"I'm still mad at you Johnny, but I miss you." She took my hand. "The kids miss you."

I was speechless as we started down the sidewalk.

"I don't want you seeing too much into this, but I was wondering if you'd like to go to a movie?"

"A movie?" My eyes welled as I squeezed her hand. "I'd love that."

Her smile was playful yet warming. "You know you're paying, right?"

"I don't know if I can afford a movie on a factory-worker's salary."

"I'm sure you'll find a way."

Outside the sun was shining bright as it burnt off the last traces of a morning shower. The sky was especially blue. There was a Chickadee twittering in a tree and it was like he was singing just for us. I was a teenager again, and this time it was for all the right reasons.

"And don't try any of those fancy moves on me. Remember we've dated before and I know your bag of tricks." She gave me a wink. "Walk with me, just like we did on our first date. Maybe I'll let you buy me some ice-cream."

I nodded. "I can do that."

Kevin Weisbeck

Other Books by Kevin Weisbeck

Madeline's Secret

Madeline suffers from amnesia when she wakes from the car accident that killed her sister. Her parents, husband, and small child are all strangers. As she accepts these people into her new life, she learns that her sister had a secret, one so dangerous that it could ruin her if it ever got out.

The Divine Ledger
Coming in June 2018

Detective Violet Stormm is a woman on a mission. She'll do anything to catch the man responsible for a series of gruesome murders. Victor Wainsworth is the man doing the killing. He's fuelled by a ledger, a book that not only holds the names of his next victims, but clues to the *Eve of Humanity*.
(This is the first of five books in the *Eve of Humanity* Series)
(This book also introduces the *Violet Stormm* Detective Series)

About the Author

Kevin Weisbeck is a Canadian author, born in Kelowna, British Columbia and currently living in Okotoks, Alberta. He's had several short stories published in magazines and newspapers, and currently has one in McGraw-Hill's iLit academic program.

He can usually be found on the couch with his laptop in front of him and his Ragdoll cat, Franklin, on his shoulder. It's not an ideal writing set up, but Franklin doesn't mind. Otherwise Kevin enjoys hiking, kayaking, camping, photography and golf (when the weeds and water don't get in the way).

Made in the USA
Columbia, SC
27 May 2018